Once Upon a Time...

...fantastic things happened to fantastic characters. Unforgettable things. Unforgettable characters.

And then the unforgettable was forgotten.

What happened to these characters? Where did they go? What did they do?

And what's with that curious moving van parked on your street, the one unloading all the odd packages and strange furniture?

Could it be that your new neighbors are a part of old stories?

Could they actually be...

FABLES

CRITICAL BLAST PUBLISHING
APPROVED BY THE READING CODE AUTHORITY
The Fables Next Door
Edited By R.J. Carter

Critical Blast Publishing
624 Sunnyhill Drive
Belleville, IL 62223

Second Edition September 2025

0 9 8 7 6 5 4 3 2 1

ISBN-13: 979-8-90020-007-1

CONTENTS

BILL WILLINGHAM
Who's Afraid of the Big Bad Wolf?
A BLACK TOWER STORY

BILL WILLINGHAM has written stories, and drawn some of them too, for nearly 45 years, mostly in comic books. He writes prose too, and worked on a number of film projects you've never heard about, because the films were never made. He's working on a few new things, some of which will happen.

They say the actual Black Tower of legend still exists somewhere, and perhaps it does. In its heyday more than two hundred immortals belonged to the Black Tower Society. Some worked from there, traveling the known realms on their myriad (mostly) heroic quests. Others worked from satellite offices in various cities, on various worlds.

According to some, a great and strange city grew up around the Black Tower over the centuries, perhaps attracted there by its dark allure. In time Baron's Deep, for such the city was called, became too public a place in which to host a secret society. Or so they say.

Having fallen on hard times over the past century or so, offices closed, one by one, as members died or quit. Today the society's few remaining members, the last hangers on, worked out of a considerably less impressive third floor walkup in Milwaukee, Wisconsin. It was a small office, saved from being called shabby, only because one of its members made an effort to keep it clean and tidy. It had a modest main room, a kitchen nook, and a small bathroom with a working shower. Its one small window looked down on the next-door tar and gravel roof of a popular watering hole called the Safe House. The view included the alleyway off of North Front Street, where one could contrive to be let into the Safe House, provided you knocked on the correct unmarked door and knew the password.

On this particular November morning there were three people in the office, comprising 75% of their remaining membership. Childe Roland, the society's founder and the Dark Tower's original owner, by virtue of discovery and long occupation, sat on a rusty orange colored couch, paying bills with a checkbook, envelopes and physical stamps. He made precise entries into an old-fashioned paper ledger. He'd have preferred to work at the room's only table, but it was occupied by Snow White and Prester John, playing some sort of novelty board game that involved answering complex questions in words of only one syllable. Roland wasn't quite sure of its point, except for being loud and silly.

"Seven different streaming services are costing us a fortune," he said, during a lull in the caveman hilarity.

"We need them though," Snow White said. She had skin as pale as a graveyard angel. Everything else was black; her motorcycle leathers and her even blacker hair. "Otherwise, we'd go crazy from boredom, waiting for the rare job to come along."

"Our fault for cleaning out the villains and monsters from too many worlds," Prester John said. His skin was as dark as hers was light. Except for the odd visible scar or two, he looked to be about sixteen or seventeen at the most. However, he was considerably older, by a factor of nearly two millennia. "Legitimate new jobs have become few and far between. But that's a good thing, remember? It's what we set out to do."

"You could always read."

"True," Snow said, "and had you not sold off most of our formerly vast library, that might be a more attractive option."

"There were expenses."

"TV it is then."

"Point taken, but we still need to trim our monthly nut, which includes dropping three or four streaming channels, at least."

The phone rang. Like most of the other features in the office, it was an antique device, with a curled cord (always tangled) and a rotary dial. As a general rule, streaming services apparently being one of the rare exceptions, immortals are slow to adopt new ways.

Since Snow and John had already returned to their game, Roland reluctantly set aside the paperwork and crossed the room to answer it.

"Hello?" Then a pause to listen. "No, you tell me who you were calling, and I'll tell you if you succeeded." A bit rude for old school phone etiquette, but a secret society is secretive by definition. Roland's side of the conversation was mainly listening. After a few minutes of "interesting" and "you don't say" and "are you certain your information's good?" he hung up.

"Sounded a bit like that may have been a job offer," John said. He wore no whiskers, his impressive beard of the ages having been recently consigned to the ashbin of history. His hair was cut as short as possible while still suggesting a definite hairline.

"It was. At least it might be. Turns out Snow's old boyfriend finally stuck his head up, long enough to do a job in Marrakesh. Made a bloody mess of it, I'm told, but got it done. After all these years he may be on his way back to America."

"My what?" Snow said.

"Lucas. You two were an item for a while, a decade or three back, yes?"

"No, we never were. And I've grown tired of that rumor, almost certainly begun by Lucas to annoy me, though he never admitted as much."

"Whatever the case, about a dozen dormant contracts become reactivated the moment he steps back on North

American soil. Maybe not rich, in the old definition, but we could find ourselves pretty flush, if we were the ones to close the deal on this guy."

"He's an evil one, and deadly," John said. "Too many innocent souls are stacked in the 'payment due' side of his ledger. I've no objection to the three of us – "

"I do," Snow said, surprising the other two.

"Why?"

"The three of us aren't going to bring him in, for three reasons. First, because too many of our friends and colleagues died trying to take him alive. There aren't enough of us on hand to attempt to take him in a fair fight. Second, because he's my business. Alone."

"You sound adamant."

"I suppose I do."

"You said three reasons."

"The third reason is, if he is in fact on his way back into the country, I know where to find him. Maybe I'm the only one who does, which seems a viable reason to insist on dibs."

"How do you imagine you can fight him on your own?"

"I don't intend to fight him. As I said, that's a foolish approach. Suicidal, in fact. Instead, I intend to surprise him. May I have the keys to the gun safe?"

Three weeks later, Snow White, bundled in a long winter coat, moved frictionless through the crowd along South 12th Street, approaching Hennepin Avenue. She didn't have to expend a costly spell to navigate so easily through the awkward clusters of people. Having long passed her thousand-year milestone she'd simply aged her way into preternatural grace, as most immortals did. She had no physical uncertainty left in her.

12th was a one-way street, with traffic coming towards her, leaving little chance anyone might try to follow either of them, neither her nor her prey, by car. On a Friday night, in this, one of the trendy parts of town, decorated in Christmas attire at the moment, the pedestrians were thick on the ground, despite the new snowfall drifting down from a gray sky. It added to the slushy accumulation of previous days, making the evening cold and wet. But miserable conditions in most other parts of the globe are merely another ordinary winter night in Minneapolis. Pedestrians were numerous and undaunted here. That, along with the concealing snowfall, meant she could walk relatively close to her target, without much fear of being spotted.

Coyle Lucas stood four inches over six feet, making him easy to tail. Even in these conditions he stood out. As expected, he did all the things an oft-wanted man should do when walking alone through any city. He checked reflections in passing windows, and stopped abruptly every now and then, all designed to catch someone following, or even paying him too much attention. But such precautions were cursory tonight. He'd been away for more than three years. No one knew he was in town and almost no one knew what he looked like in human form. He was safe enough.

Except that Snow White knew both things. She'd met him once, more than a century ago, when she'd first moved to the New World and to Minneapolis, after finding it prudent to leave the corrupted territories of Europe.

Coyle used a different name back then, but he was still the gravitational center of what was a very small local Weird community at the time. They'd get together, once a month, at a friendly public house, where he was the perpetual guest of honor; handsome, always holding court, and always charming, in a dangerous way that too many in the group found attractive. He was the fierce lone wolf, when all other wolf thropes had long ago joined a formal pack, for mutual protection and guaranteed status.

Some gregarious soul had dragged Snow to the event, to introduce the new arrival to the entrenched Twin Cities supernatural community. The night's central item of discussion was whether or not there'd be a war in Europe (almost inevitably) and if the United States would be dragged into it (still a subject of debate, with self-appointed experts opining on both sides). Having recently arrived from the continent, Snow White's opinion was solicited with off-putting vigor. She wasn't yet used to intrusive American candor.

Some variation of, "I couldn't say," were her standard answers, each time she was pressed for one.

Of course the introductions eventually included Coyle, back when he was using the name Baran (or perhaps he was still going by Faolin).

"Snow White?" he said. "I've heard of you. A heartbreaker of renown."

"If true, it's a notoriety I've never sought. People will so often build their hopes and expectations in the absence of any encouragement, and I can't be responsible for the fragile hearts of quixotic gentlemen."

"And the occasional woman too, or so I heard."

"Are you attempting to be intentionally provocative, sir? Let me assure you I've actual accomplishments for which I'm more properly known." Though she'd never entertain the idea of confessing her association with the Black Tower

Society, even among fellow immortals, Snow had already begun to build her reputation as an accomplished sorceress by then. "And you're hardly the one to make insinuations. You've amassed quite the reputation of your own. The Big Bad Wolf. The terror of, well... so many places."

"Guilty as charged. But you shouldn't be afraid."

"I'm not. I promise. Nor will I be."

He wore no manufactured scent. His natural musk harkened of animal brio and the deep forest. It wasn't entirely off-putting.

"What's that you're drinking?"

"I'm not sure. Someone gave it to me. A gimlet I think." She wasn't actually drinking it, but it served as a convenient prop. Continuing to hold it would prevent additional cocktails being pressed on her.

"Want to get out of here?"

"Excuse me?" she said, surprised at the sudden shift of subject.

"You and me. Alone. We can escape these dull hangers-on and go find a real drink. Tomorrow I can show you around the town."

The implication in his offer, that she'd still be in his company the next day, didn't go unnoticed. There was ice in her voice when she answered him.

"No thank you."

And those were the last words they'd ever spoken together. She left the pub as early as she politely could, but not before he made sure she saw him with his arm around some other easy conquest of the evening, as if to communicate, "She and you are entirely interchangeable and of no real consequence."

In the intervening years she'd spent little time thinking about Coyle, until her profession required otherwise. Spurred on by a growing list of his violations against the community codes, she'd spent the past seven years hunting Coyle, entirely on the down low. She amassed intelligence, marked patterns, in preparation for this evening which she knew would come someday. Connecting elusive bits of scant information, she'd gradually discovered Coyle liked to come home after a significant kill, to privately celebrate a job well done, by having a specific meal in a specific location.

Now he'd reached the corner of 12th and Hennepin, where he paused to glance this way and that, as if he were unsure of his way, before turning right. One last quick check for unwelcome company. That's when Snow thought it expedient to spend the one spell she'd selected for tonight's undertaking. She attached herself to the Fount, drew on her personal library of spells, painstakingly collected over long decades, connected it to her cache of Source to power it, and quietly spoke the trigger word.

"Tassara."

The spell activated. She could feel it crackling out from around her, in a wide radius.

Don't notice me. Don't remember me. Don't describe me, she thought, repeating the temporary mantra over and again in her mind.

She reached the corner and turned to follow Coyle. He was only a few paces ahead of her now. He walked past a small open parking area to a low, one-story restaurant across the street from a tall red brick high rise. Ducking under a small awning, Coyle entered The Butcher and The Boar, an upscale steak and chophouse. The very place Snow expected him to visit. He paused just long enough to slip a folded bill into the red bucket of a Salvation Army bell ringer stationed outside.

"Cold night to have to stand outside, in one place," Coyle said in passing.

"Not so bad," he answered. "Born and raised here. And merry Christmas."

Snow White waited a moment, to make sure she wouldn't run directly into Coyle in the restaurant's foyer, then followed him inside. She didn't put money in the red bucket.

Don't notice me. Don't remember me. Don't describe me.

The spell remained centered on her, following her where she went. If it functioned as promised, it would affect everyone in a wide radius, and last for at least 30 minutes. She had no reason to doubt its quality, having purchased it, at considerable cost, from a reputable wizard's agent she'd frequented many times before.

The Butcher and the Boar was an expensive looking place, built of dark granite and darker wood. Imposing granite tables were surrounded by overstuffed chairs and benches of deep red leather. The lights were kept low, which pleased Snow. She walked through the foyer, without speaking to the host at his podium. He didn't seem to notice her.

Don't notice me. Don't remember me. Don't describe me.

Snow found Coyle in a booth and table combination that backed up against a glass partition wall separating the main dining area from the bar. He was just being seated, by one of the hostesses, so she paused long enough for the hostess to finish her duty and clear the immediate area. Snow stood waiting in a narrow aisle between rows of tables. Passing customers and wait staff maneuvered automatically to avoid her, without realizing they were doing it.

When the hostess had safely departed, leaving Coyle briefly alone in his booth, Snow drew a small automatic handgun from her outside coat pocket and stepped up to the opposite side of his table. She was wearing thin leather gloves on both hands.

He didn't look up from his menu.

She raised the weapon and fired four times, one silver bullet to the brain and three more into his chest. No spell, no matter how powerful, could hide that. Diners and staff screamed and backed away from Snow and the booth.

Ignoring the bystanders, she stepped halfway around the table, to examine Coyle. Assuring herself that he was dead, she ejected the automatic's magazine, cleared the unfired round from its chamber and placed those back in her pocket. Lone Ranger Loads, as they were called in the current trade lingo, were too expensive to abandon, even though they might be hard to explain if found on her. The pistol was unremarkable, untraceable, and too risky to keep. It was designed to be abandoned; a throw-down weapon, of no provenance. She dropped it in Coyle's lifeless lap and turned to exit the restaurant. She walked, not fast, but with deliberation. Everyone backed away, leaving her a clear path.

Outside of the restaurant the night had gotten darker, and the snow was falling heavier. No one immediately followed her outside. Blending into the crowd, she strolled down the rest of the block and crossed the street at 11th, going past the CVS Pharmacy. In time she could hear distant sirens, getting louder. No one took particular notice of her. She ended up walking a considerable distance before the last dregs of the spell wore off allowing her to get the attention of a passing cab.

"Notorious international terrorist killed by an assassin's bullet," Roland read from the front page (above the fold) of the next day's *Milwaukee Journal*. After retrieving her motorbike from a parking garage, well removed from the crime scene, Snow had rocketed along bad city streets, to clear the area before effective roadblocks could be set. After escaping the city environs, she'd driven through the night to make it back home. Now, exhausted by the long ride across two states, she was stretched out on the couch, attempting a nap.

"What happened to that sweet young girl who went out by the well every day to sing *Someday My Prince Will Come*?"

"That never stops being funny."

"Remind me never to piss you off," Derrek Doom said. His friends were allowed to call him Derry. He was the fourth member of their team, also recently arrived from a close protection job out of town. He was tall, sandy haired, and impeccably dressed, as per usual. His ancient mallet called the Crith Talún was locked in the gun safe. He was crouched at the moment, hanging bulbs on a modest Christmas Tree, set up in one corner of the office. As yet there were no gifts set under the tree. "All this ire, just because he spread a few rumors about hooking up with you, back in the day?"

"More than rumors," Snow said. "The disgusting stories of our so-called romantic involvement made it into published books. A whole series of them, written by that pigeon-livered what's-his-name. As if I would ever consider such a thing."

"Where's the harm? They're fictional accounts of characters who don't exist. At least that's what the great unwashed majority believes. What was the term old Lee Roy came up with, to describe the process of mortals writing about us, thinking they were making up fairytales out of whole cloth?"

"Leaking. Something about leaking," Roland said.

"Immortals Seepage," Prester John said. He'd pulled a chair up to the one window, which was cracked open to the falling snow, letting the heat out and the cold in. He held his lit cigarette out in the winter air. "A vulgar term to describe a process for which we already have a perfectly applicable word: Inspiration."

"In any case, it's all water under the bridge now," Snow said. "Any notion I'd let myself become romantically entangled with a criminal werewolf has been finally put to rest. Let that tidbit seep out to the masses. Now then, to change to a more palatable subject, are we going to get paid behind this, or do I still have to lose half of my shows?" She addressed that question directly to Roland, who'd been working the phone ever since Snow arrived in the dead of the night.

"As they often do, some of those who offered the bounties are already trying to skate out by complaining there's no way to prove who killed him."

"A testament to how well our girl did her job," Derry said. He stood up, satisfied with the work he'd done on their tree.

"But, this isn't my first day, or decade, or century. Sooner or later they'll all pony up. Lady and Gentlemen, strap in and get ready for a Merry Christmas to us, because the Black Tower Group is about to be fat in funds again."

RACHEL A. GRECO

Cinderella Next Door

A REAL ESTATE DEAL YOU CAN'T REFUSE!

THE WOLF OF REAL ESTATE IS YOUR BEST CHOICE TO SELL YOUR HAUNTED CASTLE, MANSION, HOUSE, APARTMENT OR MOTORHOME. IF YOUR PROPERTY IS NOT SOLD IN 24 HOURS, OR BEFORE YOUR CURSE TAKES HOLD... WOLF WILL BUY YOUR PROPERTY AT TOP DOLLAR!

RACHEL A. GRECO dreams of being a dragon but has settled instead for being an author, which is almost as fun. She writes about broken characters discovering their beauty. Her short story, Fairy Light, won an honorable mention in the Writer's Digest Annual Writing Competition and her dragon duology is winging to readers. When not writing, she can be found reading, kayaking, or dancing with elves in the forests of her North Carolina home. Visit her at www.rachelagreco.com

I'm pretty sure my next door neighbor is Cinderella. I know it sounds crazy, but hear me out.

When I walked by yesterday, I caught a glimpse through the window of a woman in an old-fashioned dress, with poofy topaz sleeves and a low-ruffled neckline. Her black hair was coiled on top of her head, and for a moment I thought she must be doing cosplay for *Pride and Prejudice*.

But then she picked up a slipper made entirely of glass— the thing sparkled through the window, nearly blinding me— and began polishing it. I stared until the woman finished cleaning the shoe and moved out of my line of sight.

It has to be Cinderella, right? I don't have to wait long to test my theory.

This afternoon, my Mom says, "Trixie, I think we have new neighbors. I saw a woman peek out the door this morning. Why don't you go take them these?" She hands me a plate of fresh-baked chocolate chip cookies.

Because nothing interesting happens in our small town of Nowhere, Texas (that's not the actual name, though it may as well have been), and I want to test my theory, I grab the cookies and enter the blazing-hot Texas summer. Ugh. I can't wait to get to the coast of California and start college. I've been dreaming about it and becoming a marine biologist for years now.

I ring the doorbell to the neighbor's house, wondering if my guess is correct, or if I've just been reading too many books while trying to escape my desolate existence.

A woman with frizzled red hair—not the same woman I glimpsed through the window yesterday—opens the door. She wears a pale purple dress that could have come from a Renaissance Festival: it has a scooping neckline that narrows to the smallest waist I've seen, with an apron tied over the skirt.

We stare at each other, and when I glance up from her outfit, I realize she is looking at my shorts the same way I am analyzing her dress.

I cough to break the awkward gaping and hold out the plate of cookies. "I'm Trixie, from next door, and my mother baked these for you."

The woman gazes at the cookies as if she's never seen anything like them before. "Oh, thank you," she says in an accent that I can't place, something between British and Scottish. We don't get many foreigners in this small town, so my knowledge only comes from shows.

The woman takes the plate and calls over her shoulder, "Princess, you have a guest."

Princess. The woman I saw has to be Cinderella. But whether she is or not, what royalty would ever want to come way out here, to a dusty town with a population of 1,000, where the most exciting thing to do on a Friday night is cow tipping?

I can't believe that Ralph left me here in the middle of nowhere. This place might be safer than home at the moment, but it is so strange and doesn't feel any safer. Huge metal beasts roar down the road at all times. Julia and I have had to survive on the bread, now dried and tough as toast, and pies we brought from the palace.

Neither Julia nor I have been able to figure out how to even warm up a cup of tea, nor has my fairy godmother come when I asked.

The terrible thought that pounced last night slinks back: what if there is no magic in this land?

Loneliness, hungry as a wolf, gnaws on me, and tears leak down my face. I long for Ralph's warm, familiar arms around me, hoping he's alive and well.

One year. One year of blissful marriage was all we had before our life at the castle crumbled apart. So much for dreams lasting forever and for happily-ever-afters.

A loud ringing jolts me from my thoughts, and I whirl around. "What was that?" The sound was too harsh to be the fairy's chiming language.

Julia lays down the brush she was using on my hair. "It sounded like it came from the front door. I'll go see."

I lay a hand on her arm, my nerves tight like violin strings. "Take the sword with you. Just in case they've followed us here." I nod to Ralph's sword laying near my bed. I childishly believe that it keeps Ralph near me, though he is so far away that our images flicker on the magic mirror when we communicate.

Julia shakes her head. "I don't know how to use that. And the prince said that there was nothing dangerous here."

Before I can delay her any longer, Julia leaves the room. I stand, too nervous to sit, and strain my ears for any sign of a struggle, a cry.

When Julia yells about having a guest, I bump into the chair at the mirror, and the brush falls onto the floor. A guest? We don't know anyone here.

I glance out the window, but only see parched grass and the house beside ours. I finger the hilt of Ralph's sword, but disregard taking it. The weapon would do more harm than good if the person truly is a guest, and we need all the friends we can make in this strange land.

I still hold onto the hope that we won't be here long, but that is looking less and less likely.

Reminding myself that I'm now a princess, I square my shoulders and leave the bedroom.

The princess who has to be Cinderella floats through the door in a cloud of blue silk and skirts. Gems or rhinestones embedded in the dress flash in the afternoon sunlight like stars. She's barefoot, but holds herself like I imagine a queen would: head lifted high, shoulders straight as if she practices walking with a stack of books on her head in her spare time. If she *is* Cinderella, then how did she learn to walk so perfectly poised?

The only crack in the queenly façade is when she stares at my t-shirt. At least my legs are hidden behind the tablecloth of the kitchen table that Julia had led me to.

"This young lady," Julia turns to me, "what did you say your name was again?"

"Trixie."

Julia blinks at my name, then turns to the princess. "She brought us some…" She twists back to me. "I'm sorry, what did you call them?"

"Chocolate chip cookies." I gesture at the plate. "They're very good. My mother just baked them, so they still might be warm."

I don't usually go around eating the food I take to my neighbors, but the two women stare at me and the cookies as if they've never seen the likes of them or me before. Which, judging by their outdated dresses, they haven't. So, to ease their fears, I remove the plastic wrap off the plate and take a bite of a cookie.

After swallowing the last of the treat, I smile. "Delicious. Soft and gooey and still warm, the best time to eat them."

Neither of the women returned my smile, but the princess slides onto the chair across from me and picks up a cookie. She gazes at it like *it* might bite *her*.

Julia leans toward me. "Would you care for some wine? We brought a few bottles with us. My lady and I usually have tea at this hour, but I'm afraid that neither of us can get any of the items in here working or even know what they do." She shoots a battle-wary look at the stove.

"Oh." I jump up. "I can help with that."

Thankfully, and oddly, the kitchen is well-stocked, and it doesn't take me long to find an electric tea kettle in one of the cupboards.

"You just plug this in here." I demonstrate to Julia. "Then you push this lever down to turn it on. When the lights go off and the water boils, you can pour it."

Julia leans toward the kettle, her nose almost touching the glass. "Is there a small fire in there?" She reaches out to the kettle's base, and I nudge her hand away.

"Don't touch it. It'll burn you. And no, there's no fire anywhere. The power comes from electricity."

"What's electricity?" The princess asks, the uneaten cookie still in her hand.

Oh, dear. How am I supposed to remember something a teacher taught in elementary school? My degree is going to be in marine biology, not electrical engineering. Still, I do my best. "It's power that comes from burning coal, rushing water, the wind, and other stuff. Most of ours comes from the wind. Electricity powers almost everything in here." I walk around, showing them how the lights, fridge, oven, stove, and microwave work.

Then, exhausted by their eager questions, I sink into a chair with a cup of tea I made myself from the leaves Julia gave me. I eat another cookie. And why not? I've earned it.

"There is magic here," the princess says in wonder as she flicks the lights on and off.

Well, that's one way to put it.

As I watch her and Julia express their delight and confusion to each other, nausea pummels me. Who would leave two people in a place that they clearly didn't know how to live in on their own?

"Mm." The princess groans, eyes closed. She has finally remembered her cookie and taken a bite. "These are delicious. Julia, you have to try one. They're tastier than the palace's lemon-iced biscuits." She hands her lady-in-waiting one of the treats.

Julia takes a hesitant bite, then a larger one. She grabs another cookie even as she devours the first one. "You're right. This is delicious."

I let the women continue their treats in silence for a few minutes, but when the princess grabs her third and Julia finishes her second, I pounce with my questions. "So, who actually are you? You remind me of Cinderella," I tell the princess, "but that's an old fairy tale people made up long ago."

The princess tosses a look packed with shared secrets and sorrows to Julia. "Perhaps we traveled to the future as well." She takes in the room again, her earlier wonder now replaced with grief.

She turns back to me and sighs. "I am Carolina, Princess of Lesophia. I was called Cinders not that long ago, but I try not to dwell on that part of my life." She peers into her teacup as if it can transport her somewhere happier. Maybe it can in her land.

"Were you mistreated by your stepsisters, asked your fairy godmother for help who gave you a beautiful gown and carriage, and fell in love with a prince at a ball?"

The princess gapes at me, her cup dribbling tea onto the tablecloth. "How do you know all of that?"

I'm not as shocked as Carolina or Julia that my guesses are correct (this is the part where, if I was mean, I'd say, 'I told you so', but I'm not, so I won't). But I still have a hard time imagining this woman as the same one from the fairy tale that exists only on paper or a screen.

"I told you, we have stories written about you."

"But why?" Carolina asks.

I shrug. "Everyone thinks they're just made up."

Carolina rights her teacup and says in a trembling voice, "Does it say anything about what happens after I marry the prince?"

"No. It just ends with the two of you living happily-ever-after."

Carolina's laugh is cactus-sharp as she grabs another cookie, quite possibly her fourth. "If only it were that simple. My life is far from ending, and it hasn't been very happy."

I lean forward. "What happened? Where's your prince?"

In a voice rigid like a tux, Carolina says, "My husband, Prince Ralph, is back home, engaging in important matters."

Okay... That was vague.

"Why aren't you there with him?"

Carolina sighs, smushing one of the cookies into crumbs, no longer the perfectly-poised princess. "There's been a revolt."

"Your highness, are you sure you should tell her?" Julia mutters.

Carolina gazes at me with an expression that says she'd like to be friends, but she speaks to Julia. "No one but Ralph knows where we are. I don't think Trixie will tell anyone, and she's been so helpful." She nods at me. "We are very thankful for the help with the *electisity* and for the cookies."

She glances down, realizes that she's been mauling a cookie, and lets Julia wipe the crumbs onto her hand. "We'll have to take the recipe back to Rosamund. *If* we ever return."

"Of course we will, your highness." Julia assures her. "The prince would never leave us here for good."

"Unless he dies." Carolina stares at the table, her face carved by sorrow.

Not sure how to help, I redirect the conversation. "I won't tell a soul, I promise. They wouldn't believe me anyway." I finish my now-cold tea. "How did the revolt happen?"

Carolina clenches her hands around the teacup, her gaze haunted. "It was all my fault. I forgave my stepsisters and let them live at the castle with us. And then, just a few months ago, they betrayed us. I should have expected it."

Julia prizes the teacup out of Carolina's hands before she can break the china.

"How did you know it was your stepsisters who betrayed you?" I ask.

The princess slumps back in her seat. "I found them at a secret tunnel, letting soldiers in from the country that borders ours on the east, Weseylan."

"Why would they betray you and the prince?"

"I'm sure they were bribed. They've always wanted more. Their appetites have no end, especially my eldest stepsister."

Silence burrows its nose into every nick and cranny. When I can't stand it anymore, I prompt, "What happened?"

Carolina stares straight ahead. "Death and destruction."

"The King and Queen and two of their children were murdered before Carolina and Prince Ralph could warn them," Julia tells me in a sorrow-soaked voice. "Everyone else from his family escaped, including us and Prince Ralph. He and a few soldiers tried fighting back, but they were outmaneuvered and taken by surprise. We took refuge in a fortress in the mountains. But even there we weren't safe for long." She swallows, her gaze distant.

"One day, our scouts saw some of the eastern soldiers—probably mercenaries—scrambling up the hill. We were still too weak and injured from the previous battle to fight them, so we fled to the border of our northern country. They spurned us, not wanting to get involved.

"Then the eastern mercenaries showed up again, and after a short, brutal fight, we fled again. Prince Ralph refused to give up on his country, so he sent us here with the little bit of magic he'd been able to find until he and the knights can get everything under control."

"He's always been stubborn, even when we were children," Carolina murmurs to herself.

Listening to them, it's as if I've entered the pages of a story, but a tragedy, not a fairytale. I have no words or way to comfort those lost in its pages.

This rage-choked, grief-laden young woman isn't the Cinderella I expected, living out her dreams with her hard-earned prince in a beautiful palace. No, this woman is as real as me, still fighting for her happily-ever-after.

I can't imagine suffering through a raid on the palace, fleeing for my life, and now being stuck in a place where you can't even make yourself a cup of tea, wondering if your husband is even alive. Her troubles make my longing to escape this parched, dust-clogged town seem selfish and trivial in comparison.

I decide to help these women however I can while they are here—to take their mind off their troubles and help them navigate what must be to them an alien world.

"What I don't understand," Carolina says, "is how the soldiers always knew where we were. We always covered our tracks well. And how did all their battles and plans go so smoothly? Everyone knows our soldiers are better than Weseylan's, even their mercenaries." Carolina stands and paces. "And how did they find their way into the palace? We never learned the truth from my stepsisters."

"We've been over this, your highness. Whose help could they have had? No wizard would work for the eastern country, and the giants have all moved far into the mountains."

Carolina fingers a gold necklace. "I don't know, I don't know."

I can't help them with a revolt in some far-off land, but I can help them survive this one. I stand and say, "I must get home to help my mother with dinner. Feel free to join us. We're just right next door." I jerk my thumb at the wall on our right. Surely they can find their way down the driveway to one house over. "It has pink roses out front. You do know what roses are, right?"

Carolina twirls a black ringlet around her finger. "Despite our ineptitude with your magical devices, yes, we are familiar with roses. We have many in our land. In fact, pruning them was one of the many chores I did for my stepmother." She glances down at her hands as if she can still feel the bite of the thorns.

"Great. We usually eat around six, so you can make your way over then."

Carolina takes my hands. Hers are cool and scarred, remembering the life of hard labor. "Thank you for the invitation. And thank you for the delicious cookies and all the help you've given us. Such kindness in a strange land is far better than magic."

The tears in her eyes take me aback. "Of course. I enjoyed meeting you both. And I would love to help you while you're here in any way possible. You've both been through so much."

Carolina just nods, gratitude streaking down her face in the shape of tears.

"See you soon," Julia says in a choked voice.

As I walk to the door, I feel like I am leaving behind two orphaned children.

Of course we eat tacos that night for dinner—one of the most difficult foods for anyone to eat, let alone people from another world who are also eating in fancy dresses.

Carolina is a good sport and attempts picking up the taco like my family. I wince as grease spurts onto her fiery tulle dress and half the taco falls onto her plate.

"Here, my lady." Julia stuffs a napkin into the front of Carolina's garnet-red dress, covering the pearl-studded neckline.

When the two first arrived, Carolina had said she hoped they were properly dressed; they hadn't brought anything finer. I'd replied, "You're a bit overdressed. I mean, I'm wearing this," and gestured to my t-shirt and shorts. "Dinners with my family are never fancy occasions, but it'll be okay. We'll get you some proper clothing tomorrow."

Now, the princess swallows her last bite of taco, her hands dripping grease, and tells my mom, "Even though they are messy and look disgusting, these tac-os are delicious."

My twelve-year-old sister, Amelia, snorts a laugh. She hasn't stopped staring at the women since they entered the house. If she finds out that this taco-devouring young woman is Cinderella, she will follow her around like a celebrity, asking hundreds of questions, so of course I'm not going to tell her or let her find out.

"Where are you both from?" My mom eventually asks.

"They're refugees," I blurt, thinking fast. "From eastern Europe."

I send a meaningful look at Carolina, and thankfully she's smart enough to catch on. "Yes, that's correct. Our land is at war, so we were sent here to wait it out." Her hands drop into her lap, her excitement about the meal vanishing.

Julia, who was attempting to eat her taco with a fork and knife without much success, pats her arm.

"Oh. I'm so sorry," my mother says. "We'd like to help you any way that we can."

"Thank you. Your daughter has already helped us, and this food is delicious." Carolina waves at the taco fixings, then glances at me. "Could you help me make my own?"

As I do, I turn the conversation away from the women by prattling on about my favorite topic: college and living in California.

"Oh, here we go," Amelia says, rolling her eyes.

I shoot her a glare.

Unlike my sister, Carolina and Julia are kind listeners, asking questions that sometimes make me wince, like, "What is college?" But I just steamroll through the answers, not giving my parents or sister a chance to ask anything.

I end my spiel with, "It'll be nice to live somewhere where there'll be things to do, like places to kayak and hike on the weekends. And that has more than one coffee shop." A happy sigh escapes me as I lean back in my chair.

After finishing the peanut butter chocolate cake that my mom made, I walk Carolina and Julia home. I don't need to; they made their way over fine, but I feel responsible for them, like they have been entrusted to my care.

"Ralph needs to come soon before I can't fit into any of my dresses." Carolina presses a hand to her stomach. "The food here is too scrumptious, and you don't even have hired cooks."

"Speaking of clothes, I want to take you both shopping tomorrow. We'll find you something that is more comfortable and will help you fit in better."

Carolina eyes my naked legs with a frown. "Something like those bloomers?"

I cross my arms. "They're called shorts. But no, we can find you some dresses."

The princess relaxes, leaning against the post outside their door.

"You've already been so gracious to us," Julia says, "and I fear it's not necessary. Our currency probably doesn't even work in this land."

I wave away her concern. "I don't mind. It'll be fun and give me something to do until I leave for California."

Carolina grips my arm, and I glance at her, startled. "When you spoke of traveling to that land where you will study," she says, her voice as serious as a wildfire, "you spoke as if it will make all your dreams come true."

"Well, yeah. It will. I've been wanting to be a marine biologist," remembering who I'm speaking to, I clarify, "someone who studies the ocean, since I was a child. Not to mention get out of here." I gesture at the twilit neighborhood.

"Just be careful. Once your supposed dreams come true, they have a way of shifting on you, like smoke." She lets go of me and gazes at the neighborhood, her expression hollowed out, as if everything she loves has been stripped from her. And I guess it has.

"Your dreams don't truly come true," she continues. "Or if they do, they look different than you expect. I should know." Her gaze, sharpened and scraped raw by sorrows I can't fathom, turns to mine.

"Just promise me that you won't make my mistakes, that you won't live so much in your dreams of the future that you miss out on the beauty of the present."

I frown, trying to reconcile the story I know about her with what beautiful things she could have missed out on. "Surely there wasn't anything in your life as a servant that you could enjoy. That you missed out on."

A smile as tired as a student during exam week pulls at her lips. "Oh, there were opportunities. The biggest one was my youngest stepsister. She wasn't as mean as my oldest. She tried to be kind to me in her way, but it was never enough. I let bitterness take root and missed the opportunity to befriend her. And those roses I told you about?" She peers past me to my mom's garden, where her roses glow white in the dusky evening. "I thought more about the pain from the thorns than the beauty of the blooms.

"And when my father was home, I spent more time complaining of my predicament than spending time with him, enjoying the brief moments we had together."

She draws her arms around her like she's cold, though it's got to be at least ninety degrees out here. "And then he was gone, and I was married and living a dream in a castle. But even then, I often longed for what I didn't have: a bigger garden, a baby. And now Ralph is gone and I don't know when or if I'll see him again."

She wipes her eyes, and Julia pulls her in for a hug.

After composing herself, Carolina straightens up. "You have so many good things here—a family who loves you, delicious food," her mouth tilts up, "that you soon won't have with you. Do not lose this opportunity to enjoy them. Dreams are flighty things, making you always want more. But they will never satisfy you."

She and Julia leave me there alone with the roses, feeling like a chastened child. But it's not like I'm going to lose my family; they'll just be further away. And what beauty is there in this tiny, dusty town?

"You can't wear those," I tell Carolina the next morning as I greet her and Julia at their door.

She looks down at her glass slippers. "Why not? They're surprisingly comfortable, and I wear them everywhere. They remind me of my godmother and the first time that Ralph and I danced at the balls."

Dark shadows lurk beneath her eyes, and Julia stands next her like a fierce thorn, so I decide not to press the issue. "Fine, but if lots of people stare at you, don't blame me."

"I have been the recipient of stares my entire life," Carolina says as she leads the way outside.

"Have you heard from Ralph since you've been here?" I ask.

"We connected this morning over the mirror." Carolina stops, letting me take the lead to my driveway. "The connection wasn't wonderful, but at least I could hear his voice. He and his knights have been trying to find out who's behind the attack at the palace. All they know is that some mercenaries were paid to kill Ralph's family. And now someone by the name of Tiartella rules the castle. We've never heard anyone by that name. It's a foreign, and we're not sure of the origins. At this rate—"

Carolina gasps as the garage door opens. Then, seeing my mom's sedan, she screeches and grabs Julia's hand. "You have one of those monsters?"

I probably should have explained about cars before leading them straight to it, but I'm not used to explaining everyday objects.

Julia basically holds Carolina up, but also looks as if she might faint. This will be a long day.

After I explain what a vehicle is, they both still stare at me, so I sigh and climb inside. I call through the open door, "I'm going to turn it on now. It won't do anything but make a loud noise."

I turn the car on and back up granny-slow, making sure the women don't dash behind the car. But they're as still as popsicles.

Once in the car, Carolina soon overcomes her fear, laughing like a child at an amusement park, asking to go faster. Julia just groans and covers her eyes, and I do *not* want to clean puke out of the upholstery, so I keep to the minimum speed limit.

Shopping isn't as terrible as I feared; the women both find some summery dresses they consider "decent" (meaning they stretch to their ankles), and they love the pizza we have for lunch. Julia insists on eating it with a fork and knife.

"The people here eat with their hands frequently," Carolina says, staring at her tomato and cheese-slathered fingers. "I love it."

It's weird, but as I take it upon myself the next week to show Carolina and Julia my dusty little town to take their minds off what's happening back home, I see my town through their eyes. And it doesn't look so small, dusty, or boring.

The dust slowly shakes off as we explore the town's depths—places I haven't been in years or that I've become numb too.

We try on old, elaborate hats in the antique shops on main street, stuff ourselves on popcorn while watching a chick flick that has us all bawling at the end and the other two enthralled by its "magic," walk a trail through our canyon and explore its layered, rocky face, take my sister to get our nails done, and eat as much Mexican food as possible.

I even take them to the bizarre places that only tourists visit.

"Is it... um... normal in your land to stick cars in the dirt?" Carolina gazes at the spray- painted Cadillacs half-buried in the dirt. "Is this what happens when they die?" She tentatively touches one, and a piece of paint comes off in her hand.

I haven't been here since my friends and I came to spray-paint the cars my freshman year of high school. "No. Some eccentric billionaire was bored and thought it'd be fun."

I survey the landscape stretching behind the cars until it's swallowed by the cloud-dotted sky. There's nothing beautiful here, just half-buried cars, and a dead, flat landscape. A longing for trees, for something more, rushes inside me. California's got to be better than this.

Then the sun sets behind the clouds, sending an array of melting-butter golds, six-year-old pinks, and bruise purples across the sky—a painting far better than any professional could create. The colors are so rich, so alive, so real, stretching across that endless sky, and I can't soak it up enough.

Okay, so maybe we don't have an ocean or beautiful forests or mountains, but the sunsets are something else. Something beautiful.

"Oooh," Julia murmurs. "That's magical."

"I suppose it is," I agree.

Carolina turns to me. "You do have beautiful things in this tiny town. You just need to be open to seeing them."

I nod, remembering all the fun we had this week, how magical it felt.

There's a loud pop, and we turn to where an old woman has appeared. Her dress, as shimmery as pure glass, reflects the sky above. Two men dressed in chainmail stand behind her, swords swinging from their belts.

"Carolina." Some of the woman's wrinkles smooth out when she spots the princess. "I'm so glad we finally found you."

Carolina stares at the woman. "Godmother?"

The woman nods, smiling as if she can and will wish every dream Carolina has into being. "Yes. I've been searching for you a long time, wanting to make sure you had survived the revolt."

Finally believing that the woman is real, Carolina falls into her arms. "I've tried calling for you every day, but you never answered."

The godmother lets her go and gazes at the cars in disgust. "This land doesn't work properly with my magic. That's why it took so long to find you."

Carolina glances at the two men who must be knights. "Where's Ralph? Why didn't he come with you?"

"He asked me to bring you home. He's busy setting the castle to rights."

Julia sidles over to me and murmurs, "Something about this isn't right. No one but Ralph knew where we were, as he was the one who sent us here. And last time the princess spoke to him, two days ago, he still didn't have enough men to take back the palace." She looks at the godmother as if deciding whether to throw her into a recycling or trash bin.

Hmm. It does sound sketchy. But I'm not sure why Julia told me.

"Are you ready to return to Lesophia and your prince?" The godmother asks, her smile just like a caring grandmother's. It seems too perfect to be real, as if she practices in front of a mirror every day. She stretches out a gnarled hand toward Carolina.

The princess steps toward the woman, and my stomach lurches. So much has happened to her already; I hope her godmother hasn't betrayed her.

Julia's gaze pleads with me, as if *I* can make all *her* dreams come true. But what can I do? I have no magic, no weapons, nothing.

Carolina stretches her hand toward her godmother's, and the old woman's face lights up as if all her dreams are about to come true. Something is off about the old woman—why would a godmother need a princess for her dreams to come true? And why hasn't the prince come? I don't believe that someone who loves his wife so much to send them to this unknown place wouldn't come retrieve them himself.

A foreboding creeps over me that if the godmother gets her happy ending, it won't be happy for Carolina or her prince.

And from what I know of her and her story, she deserves a chance at one.

Not knowing what else to do, I rely on my years of playing football with my dad and tackle the princess to the ground.

"What?" Carolina gasps. "Why would you do that?" She lifts her head from where she landed on the ground and looks up at me.

I'm relieved I didn't hurt her, but the relief vanishes when the knights grab me and pull me away.

"Dreams aren't always what they seem, remember?" I tell Carolina as I thrash against the knights, but their grip on my arms are like pressure cuffs.

The princess gapes at me, lying on the dirt, her new dress torn and filthy. I see the moment when she understands: her shock sours to horror. She stands and whirls around to face the elderly woman.

"Were you behind the attack on the palace?"

The woman waves a hand. "Of course not. I'm the one who gave it to you in the first place." Her smile now looks like a doll's: plastic and cheap. "Why would I take it away?"

"So you could have it," I guess, squirming against the knights. Nope, still nothing.

The godmother narrows her eyes at me, then looks at Carolina. "Very well. If the truth is what you want, then the truth is what you shall have." She whips a thin, silver rod—a wand?—out of her sleeve and waves it at the ground. Nothing happens.

The woman frowns. "This land is so primitive." Sighing, she places the wand back in her sleeve and turns to Carolina. "I gave you everything you wanted, made you a princess, and gave you your prince and palace. I only wanted a small portion of that for my granddaughter so she wouldn't end up like the rest of our race—bound to the whims of you humans."

"I thought you enjoyed helping those in need," Carolina says.

The godmother shakes her head, as if she can't believe the princess can be so naïve. "Not being compelled to help them year after year, decade after decade, century after century. Would you?"

Carolina presses a hand to her head like she's going to be sick, and Julia rushes to her side.

"I only want a better future for my granddaughter. Is that so bad?"

Carolina swallows and straightens, a princess even in her dirty clothes, and I'm proud that I've gotten to know her. But I wish she or Julia would try to release me; my arms are starting to fall asleep.

"No, but the way you did it, through duplicity and death, was terrible. Now where is Ralph?" The princess takes a step toward the godmother, a lioness on the hunt.

The old woman doesn't seem to notice or care about the hungry gleam in the princess' eyes. Her body remains as relaxed as if we're all at a tea party. "Oh, he's fine. He's alive and hidden in a fortress."

"Take me to him. I want to see with my own eyes that he's alive."

"For what purpose? So you can run away and I must send my mercenaries after you again?" The godmother clucks her tongue. "No, I don't think so. It's time to put an end to you now that you've served your purpose. Your husband will serve as an excellent bargaining chip to the other nations or even as a nice husband to my granddaughter once you're gone."

"He would never marry anyone else."

The godmother cocks an eyebrow. "I've been using magic on people for centuries. It's not that difficult of an enchantment. Besides, how do you know that his love for you isn't a spell?"

"No." Carolina sags as if she's been struck. "No, it can't be. He knew me even when we were children."

The godmother just leers at her, letting the doubts rage.

I want to hurt the woman for the harm she's done to Carolina, this sweet woman who's suffered so much. But again, I'm struck with my own helplessness. What can I do?

I glance around and notice one of Carolina's glass slippers lying next to my feet. It must have fallen when I tackled her.

As I gaze at it, understanding blossoms. This is how the old woman has been tracking Carolina—the slippers. The princess even told me she wears them everywhere.

I kick the shoe to Julia, who stands behind Carolina. At the movement, she glances down.

When she meets my eyes, I mouth, "Destroy it."

She picks up the slipper and hits it against the nearest car.

Chips of paint fly off. Nothing seems to happen to the shoe, but at least the action makes one of my guards leave. The blood rushes back into my arm as the knight grabs Julia.

The godmother laughs. "It's indestructible. Ever since Carolina received my help, she has been mine. I gave her her dreams, and I can take them away." She snaps at the guard holding me. "Finish this."

The knight lets go of me and stalks toward Carolina, his sword raised.

I'm not stupid enough to tackle him, so I run to Julia, snatch the slipper from her before the knight can figure out what I'm doing, and grab my only weapon—a bottle of spray-paint on the ground. Praying there's some inside, I spray the shoe.

A fine mist of gold spews out, covering the shoe. And then, the slipper disappears. With a cry, the same thing happens to the godmother. I can't believe that worked.

Carolina, who's backing away from the knight, stops and glances around. "Where did she go?"

"The paint must have somehow severed the magic linking the two of you," Julia explains.

"Probably some of the chemicals that you don't have in your world," I muse, staring at the spray-paint bottle.

Then, a louder, deeper shout erupts, and a young man with a thick beard and drawn face appears.

"Ralph!" Carolina tackles the man in a hug.

"I won't complain about being hugged by a beautiful woman," Ralph says, un-entangling himself from the princess, "but who are you?" Then his gaze finds the half-buried cars behind them. "And where are we?"

"A small, dusty, boring town that might not be so dusty, boring, or small after all," I tell him.

"So the fairy did put a spell on you." Carolina buries her face in her hands.

I can't understand everything that she's suffered, but she gave me words I needed to hear, and now I'll do the same. I place a hand on her shoulder. "Perhaps now you can start over, make your own dreams come true together."

One of the knights ambles over and says, "Does this mean we aren't going to be paid?"

I drive the motley gang to the women's house as Carolina fills Ralph in on everything that has happened. He remembers playing at her house as a child when visiting her father's estate, and the balls where he first met her, but not much after that.

There were holes in their future, unknowns to figure out, but Ralph lets Carolina hold his hand, so I have hope for them.

The prince promises to pay the knights after they help him root out the fairies from the palace, and I can see the happily-ever-after on the horizon, but I don't feel happy. I will miss Carolina's childish ferocity and Julia's steadfastness. They have become friends, a reason to find joy in this place. I don't want to lose them.

"How are we going to return to Lesophia?" Julia asks.

Oh, yeah, that. Maybe I won't have to lose them yet after all.

"The fairy had a magic coin with her that brought us here," one of the knights explains. "It'll take us back. I saw it on the ground." He holds up a bronze coin.

Ugh. So I will have to say goodbyes soon. I hate goodbyes.

The next few minutes pass too quickly. I dart home for my mother's recipe and rush back as Julia and Carolina finish packing.

And then I'm giving Julia one last hug, wringing a last promise from her to watch over Carolina.

Then I watch Carolina strap her suitcase closed, my recipe tucked safely inside.

She hugs me, smelling of dirt and cow manure—the smell of Texas. "Don't forget to focus on the flowers, not the thorns."

"I won't. You too as you make new dreams with your prince."

Ralph calls for her, and with one last squeeze, the group

assembles outside like something from a fairytale—breeches; tunics; long, silky dresses; and chainmail. Then the knight flips the coin, Carolina waves at me—and with a puff of smoke they're gone.

It seems like their presence was a dream, something I made up. But I still hear Julia's promise, see the outlines of their dresses, and spot a few threads of Carolina's black hair on the railing. It all happened. I met Cinderella, showed her my dusty little town, and sent her home again.

Then, the wonder steals away, lost in the everyday chirp of cicadas and the sun's steamy rays.

I'm tempted to let the emptiness smother me, to turn my thoughts to somewhere else with endless trees. But I refuse to spend my last weeks with my family missing those who aren't here and hoping for dreams that will vanish. Instead, I'll enjoy the moments between the dreams.

KEVIN HOPSON

The Wrong Suspect

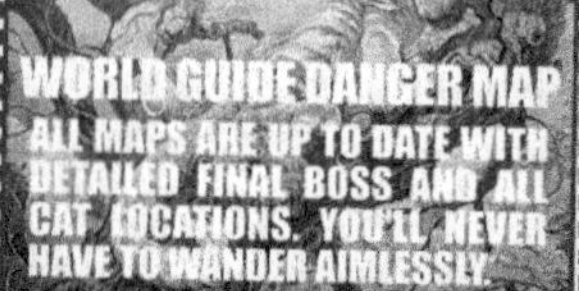

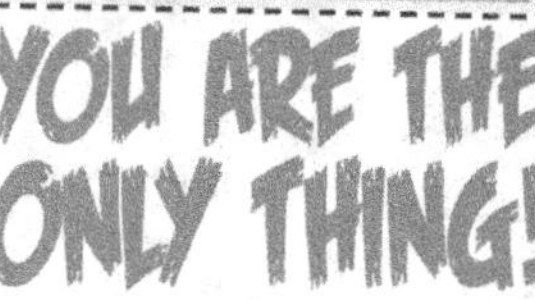

YOU ARE THE ONLY THING!

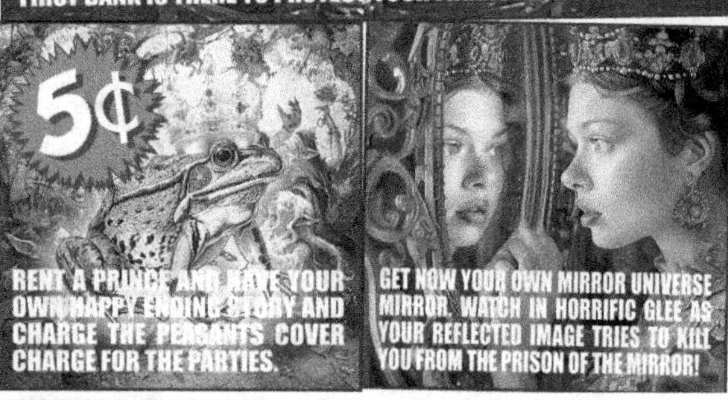

KEVIN HOPSON's work has appeared in a variety of anthologies, magazines, and e-zines, and he enjoys writing in multiple genres. You can learn more about Kevin by visiting his website at www.kmhopson.com

Geppetto was rummaging through the storage room of the pawn shop when a banging noise stole his attention. He peeked through the doorway, spotting a man at the front door. Geppetto glanced at his wristwatch, letting out a frustrated breath.

He debated whether to answer the door. When more banging ensued, Geppetto quickly lost patience and made his way toward the front of the store. As he approached, Geppetto realized that the stranger looked familiar. The man was short with thinning hair. And though Geppetto couldn't recall the man's name, he was certain he'd seen him before.

When Geppetto reached the door, he pointed to the sign hanging from it.

"I know you're closed," the man said, his voice muffled through the glass. "But this is an emergency."

Geppetto shook his head.

"Come on," the man insisted. "You open in ten minutes. Just do me this favor. Please."

Geppetto pondered for a moment.

"Look," the man said, obviously not taking *no* for an answer. "My niece's birthday party is in an hour, and I forgot to get her a gift."

There were plenty of other stores that were open at this time of the morning, so Geppetto was curious as to why the man chose his pawn shop over all of them.

"Why me?" Geppetto asked.

The man's brow furrowed. "What?"

"There are other places to shop," he elaborated.

"Yeah," the man admitted. "But I'm looking for a specific gift, and I can't get it anywhere else."

Geppetto was still wary of the man. It was a legitimate

excuse to get inside, and the man could be planning to rob Geppetto for all he knew. That being said, Geppetto noticed several people trekking the sidewalk. And since it was broad daylight, the man would be taking a huge risk if he had any ill intentions.

Geppetto huffed and pulled a set of keys from the pocket of his pants. Then he slid a cell phone from his back pocket. "No funny business. I have video surveillance, and I have 9-1-1 punched into my phone."

"Jesus," the man said. "I'm not going to rob you. I just want to buy something."

Geppetto put a key to the lock and turned it. A chiming noise followed as he pulled open the door, allowing the man

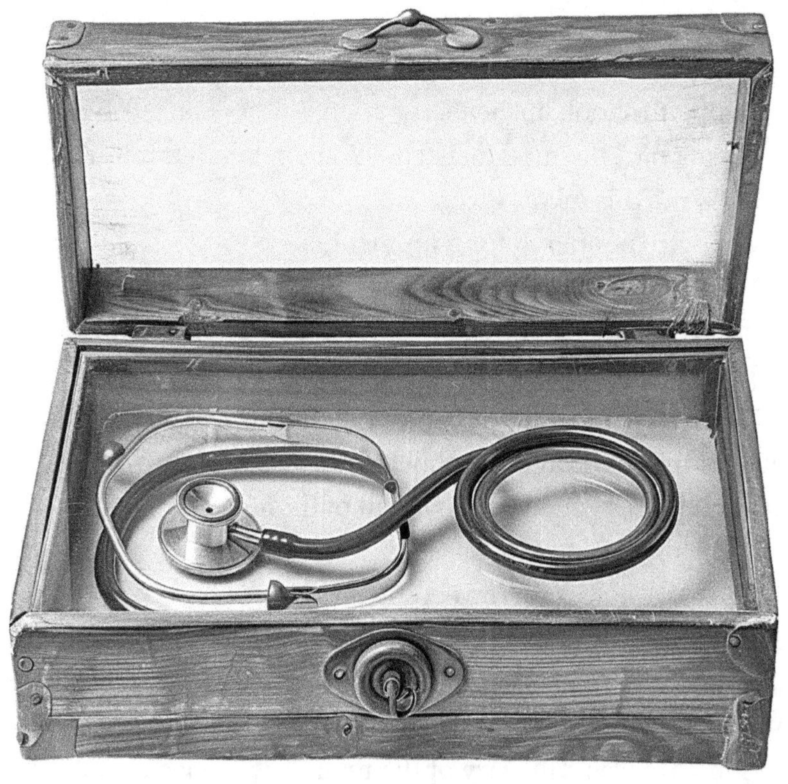

to enter. Geppetto pocketed the keys but kept the cell phone in hand. It would only take one tap of the screen for the 9-1-1 call to go through.

The man glimpsed Geppetto's phone. "Really?"

Geppetto shrugged.

"Fine," the man said. "Whatever makes you comfortable."

Geppetto closed the door and circled around the counter, standing behind it as the man approached.

"You look familiar," Geppetto said. "Have you been in before?"

"Uh-huh. I was here a couple of weeks ago. I bought a cheap watch from you." He held up his hand. "I'm actually wearing it now."

Geppetto recognized the watch.

"What is it you're looking for?" he asked, resting his phone on the stool beside him.

"My niece," the man said. "She's twelve years old, and she wants to be a doctor when she grows up. Do you have one of those devices—" He looked to the ceiling as if in thought. "I forget what they're called. One of those things the doctor uses to listen to your heartbeat."

"A stethoscope?" Geppetto said.

The man bobbed his head. "Yeah, yeah. That's it. Do you have one of those?"

"I believe I have a couple of them," Geppetto replied, moving toward the far end of the counter.

The man followed, Geppetto tracking him the entire way.

"Right here," Geppetto said, pointing a finger at the glass display case.

The man leaned over, closely examining the instruments. "They look old. What time period are these from?"

"One's from the late nineteenth century, while the other dates back to the early twentieth century."

"They're expensive."

"That's because they're vintage," Geppetto said.

"Do they work?"

"The last time I checked. Yes."

The man huffed. "I don't have the money for either of them. Can you do any better on price?"

Geppetto mulled it over. He was usually pretty firm on his asking prices. However, since the gift was for the man's niece, Geppetto was willing to make an exception.

"Give me a second," Geppetto said, walking to his computer. He hit a few keys on the keyboard, then met the man's gaze as he neared again. "The best I can do is seventy-five dollars. That's for the newer one. I'd be selling it at cost."

The man shook his head. "I still can't afford it."

"I'm sorry. I don't know what to tell you. I'm not in the business of losing money, so it's the best I can do."

The man pursed his lips.

"There is another option," Geppetto said.

The man arched an eyebrow. "What's that?"

"A loan."

"How does that work?"

"I could loan you the money to purchase the stethoscope, but you would have to repay the loan plus interest. And you'd have to pawn something of similar value."

The man shook his head again. "I don't have anything to pawn, and I don't have time to go home and come back." He eyed his watch. "How much is the watch worth?"

"Only twenty dollars or so."

He sighed. Then the man's eyes bulged. "What's that behind you?"

Geppetto spun around to look. On the shelf behind him was a wooden doll. The boy sat on the shelf, his legs dangling over the edge. And the doll was larger than most. If he had to wager a guess, Geppetto would say it was three feet in length.

"That's my favorite piece," Geppetto replied.

"How much?"

"It's not for sale. It's only for display."

"Come on. Everything's for sale. For the right price."

"Not this," Geppetto said. "It's priceless to me."

The man let out a frustrated breath.

"There is one last option," Geppetto said. "If you still want a stethoscope."

"I'm listening."

"I have some stuff in storage that hasn't been put on display yet, and I think I have a more affordable stethoscope that I recently purchased."

"Can you check?"

Geppetto nodded. "Sure. Just give me a minute."

He made his way into the storage room. It took a couple of minutes, but Geppetto eventually found what he was looking for. Then came a dinging noise. Geppetto's heart skipped a beat. When he exited the storage room, the man was gone. And his eyes bulged at the sight in front of him. The wooden doll was gone, too.

"What was stolen?" the patrol officer asked.

He was a burly, dark-skinned man, and he stood beside Geppetto near the front of the store.

"A wooden doll," Geppetto said. "A very unique one."

"Do you have a photo of it?"

Geppetto shook his head.

"Was it under the glass?" the officer inquired.

"No. Everything in the display case is under lock and key. It was on a shelf behind the counter."

The officer glanced at the far wall, then locked eyes with Geppetto. "And you know who took it?"

"I'm certain of it."

"Do you have them on video?"

"To some extent."

"What does that mean?"

"He obviously knew what he was doing. He killed the feed before he ran off with the doll, but I'm not sure how that really helps. He's still on video prior to that point."

"So, the video doesn't actually show him stealing the doll?"

"No," Geppetto admitted. "But it had to be him."

The officer nodded. "We can view the video, but a description would still be helpful."

"He's short and stocky with thinning brown hair. He was wearing jeans and a plaid shirt. I also know his name. He bought a watch from me a couple of weeks ago, so I checked my computer. His name is Conner McKay."

"Do you know where he lives?" he asked, jotting down the name.

"I have the address in my records. I can get it for you."

The officer bobbed his head. "Okay, sir. A detective should be arriving on the scene soon. They'll probably have some additional questions for you. But I have enough information to write up an incident report."

Detective Stanley Sheppard. That was the name of the detective assigned to Geppetto's case. He was a lanky bald guy dressed in a cheap brown suit, and he asked many of the same questions that the patrol officer did, with a few new ones sprinkled in.

When the two of them finished their conversation, Geppetto tried to go about his day, but he found it difficult to focus. He didn't do it often, but Geppetto decided to close up early. As tempted as he was to pay Conner McKay a visit, he thought it better to put his faith in the police.

Though he was optimistic that the case would soon be resolved, Geppetto was still surprised to see Detective Sheppard outside his store the next morning. Sheppard looked to be wearing the same brown suit, unless he had an entire wardrobe of them.

"Good morning, Mr. Belfi," Sheppard said.

"Good morning, detective."

"I have some news. Do you mind if we talk inside?"

"Not at all."

Geppetto pulled the keys from his pocket and opened the door, guiding Sheppard inside. Sheppard sidled up to Geppetto, his brow furrowing as he stared at something across the room.

"Something wrong, detective?" Geppetto asked.

"I don't know," he replied. "You tell me." Sheppard paused. "Is that the wooden doll you reported stolen?"

Geppetto pivoted to look, his eyes going wide. Atop the shelf was the missing doll. Geppetto was flabbergasted, unable to muster a response. But he needed to say something. And he had to do it quickly. Otherwise, he would draw suspicion.

"No," Geppetto finally said. "It's another doll that resembles the one that was stolen. I couldn't bear to look at the empty shelf, so I put it there until you find the other one."

Sheppard nodded, apparently buying the fib. "Well, I paid Mr. McKay a visit. Twice, actually. When I visited yesterday, there was no answer. So, I tried again this morning. This time with a search warrant. Unfortunately, I didn't find the doll. But I did find something else."

"And what's that?" Geppetto asked.

"Mr. McKay's body."

Geppetto's mouth hung agape. "Are you saying he's dead?"

"That's exactly what I'm saying."

"How?"

"A knife to the abdomen. The official cause of death will come later, but I'm pretty certain it was due to blood loss."

Geppetto shook his head in disbelief.

"It's my job," Sheppard said, "so I have to ask. Where were you last night, Mr. Belfi?"

"At home."

"Was anyone with you?"

"No. I live alone." Geppetto hesitated. "You can't possibly think I would do something like this."

Sheppard shrugged. "My gut tells me you didn't, but I've been wrong before. You had his address, so it's not out of the realm of possibility."

Geppetto let out a much-needed breath. "I'll admit that the thought crossed my mind. Visiting him and asking for the doll back," he clarified. "But I ultimately put my trust in you, detective. I figured it would be an open-and-shut case for you."

Sheppard huffed. "Apparently not."

"For what it's worth, I'm sorry to hear about Mr. McKay. I obviously didn't care for his actions, but I would never wish death upon him."

Sheppard bobbed his head. "I'm not sure if you're aware of this, but Mr. McKay had a record. A couple of domestic disturbance incidents where he got into it with some friends. Maybe he pushed someone too far this time." He pursed his lips and met Geppetto's gaze. "Anyway, I'll let you know if the doll turns up. In the meantime, I'd appreciate it if you stayed in town. In case I have any more questions for you."

"Of course, detective."

Sheppard turned and left, not even bothering to say goodbye. Geppetto quickly made his way to the door and locked it. He spun around and marched toward the doll, anger building with each step he took.

"What happened, Sebastian?" Geppetto said through clenched teeth.

The doll's head swiveled. Then its lips parted. "Besides getting kidnapped?" Sebastian replied.

"This is no time for jokes."

"Who's joking? You think I enjoyed being taken by that creep? I didn't want to create a scene in public, so I had to wait until he took me back to his house before attempting my escape. To make sure no one saw me, I waited until it was dark, too. But the guy never sleeps. Literally."

"When I tried to sneak out," Sebastian continued, "he caught me tiptoeing through the kitchen. Needless to say, he was shocked to see a living and breathing doll. He was a crazy man, and he came at me with a hammer. So, I grabbed a kitchen knife to defend myself. I didn't mean to kill him."

Geppetto needed a moment to take it all in. "He didn't give you to his niece?"

"No. Maybe that was his initial plan. I don't know. I overheard him talking to someone on his cell phone. Something about a birthday party. Apparently, he thought it was yesterday, but it's actually today. Anyway, he just took me home with him."

"Why did you come here, though? You should have come straight home. I know you can take care of yourself, but I still worry about you."

"I thought I'd surprise you," Sebastian said. "You gave me a key to the shop in case I ever needed it. Sorry if I put you in a bad situation, though. I wasn't expecting the detective to show up."

Geppetto exhaled. "And now I'm a possible suspect in a murder investigation."

Sebastian shook his head. "No way. There isn't any physical evidence that ties you to his death. And there can't be any witnesses if you were never there."

Geppetto pondered. "Did you get any blood on you?"

"No. I made certain of it. So, don't worry. We're in the clear."

Sebastian was probably right, Geppetto thought. But certain measures still needed to be taken.

"From now on, maybe I need to leave you at home when I come to work," Geppetto said.

"You know what I've said about that. I don't like being cooped up at home all alone. Even if I have to spend the day in a state of suspended animation, I prefer to be here with you."

A feeling of warmth washed over Geppetto, and he circled around the counter to embrace Sebastian.

"Fine," Geppetto said, kissing Sebastian's head. "But I'm not letting you out of my sight again."

Sebastian smiled. "Fair enough. Thanks, Uncle Geppetto."

DAMASCUS MINCEMEYER
The Song Remains the Same

ORDER BY MAGIC MIRROR

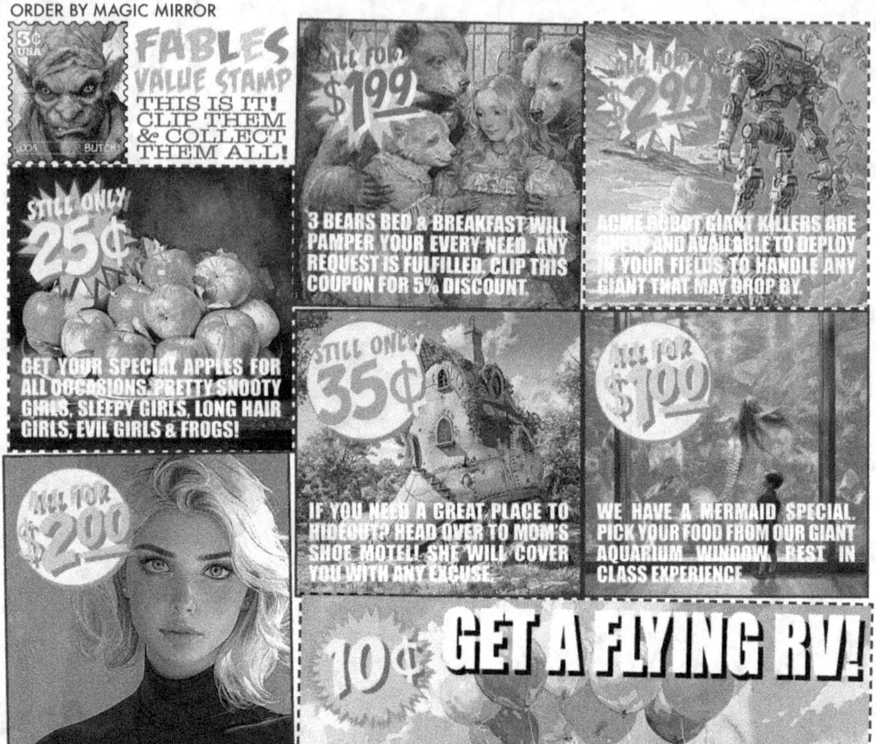

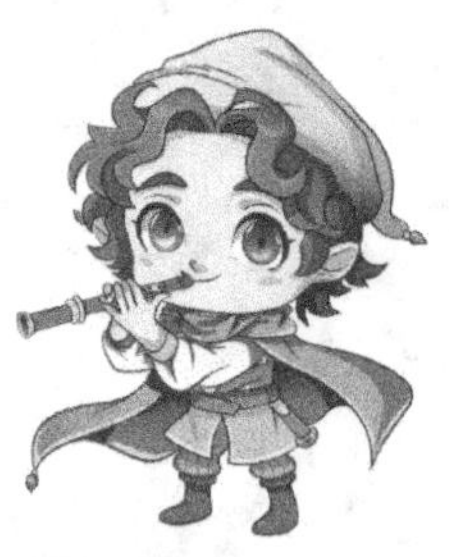

DAMASCUS MINCEMEYER was exposed to the weird worlds of horror, sci-fi and comics as a boy, and thus ruined for life. At one point he drew comics that appeared in Heavy Metal magazine, but now spends his time writing far-out fiction appearing in numerous anthologies, including Fire: Demons, Dragons and Djinn, Earth: Giants, Golems and Gargoyles, Air: Slyphs, Spirits and Swan Maidens, Monsters Vs Nazis, and many more. His first novel, By Invitation Only, is currently with The Rights Factory literary agency. Hailing from St. Louis, Missouri, U.S.A, he can usually be found posting absurd movie games on Instagram

"I don't like this, Matt," Tyler says as I open the duffel bag in my lap. From where we're parked towards the rear of The Overthrow's lot, I can see the serpentine line of fans slithering into the club. I check my watch. It's 9:24 PM.

"Dude, you know what's at stake." I sift out earplugs, a can of Mace, some zip ties and duct tape; when I withdraw the snub-nosed .38 Ruger, Tyler's eyes bulge.

"The *fuck* you get *that*?"

"My uncle's a gun nut. I kinda... *borrowed* it this morning."

"B-But I thought we were gonna just, you know, *kidnap* him and do the rest out later."

"We *are*," I slide the revolver inside my jacket. "This is just... insurance. In case things go south."

"Jesus, this is fucked up." Tyler's sweaty with nerves even though the van's heater is broken and it's twenty degrees outside. "We're gonna get a thousand years in prison for this. I'm gonna lose my butt cherry to some day-glow jumpsuit wearing gorilla because your girlfriend dumped you."

"*Don't* say that," I start getting testy. "Megan *didn't* dump me. She's under a *spell*, okay? Just like *you* were. I *told* you that."

"Yeah, I'm *still* not so sure I believe you."

I point to the nightclub. "*Look* at those people. Every single one of them is brainwashed because of that goddamn song of his. Can you imagine what'll happen if the band gets picked up by a major label? *Everyone* will be in his thrall. The whole country. The whole fucking *world*."

Tyler squirms in the passenger's seat. "But do we have to *kill* him? Can't we just, I dunno, incapacitate him?"

"No way. He's too dangerous. Imagine if you had the opportunity to off a dictator before they became too powerful to stop. That's what this is like." I hand Tyler some ear plugs. "Here. Don't forget these. I don't need you getting zombified on me in there. And *don't* take 'em out."

Tyler grumbles, but secures the tiny foam cones into his ear canal anyway. According to the packaging they've got a Noise Reduction Rating of thirty-four decibels, enough to muffle a close-quarter shot from a handgun.

Should work for a rock concert.

I glance at my watch again: 9:30.

Showtime.

I tap Tyler on the shoulder and mouth the words, *Let's go.* He hesitates and fumbles for the door, but in another minute we're racing across the parking lot. While we run, I feel a twinge of apprehension. Maybe Tyler's right. Maybe there's another solution to all this. Then I think of Megan, purple-streaked black hair, sashaying hips, sultry in her Bauhaus babydoll and fishnets; I remember of all those lonely years I'd yearned for her touch, and how the reality was so much better than the fantasy once I finally felt it. Then I envision her hanging all over *him*, moon-eyed, like she's been indoctrinated into some hippy-dippy messianic love cult, stripping naked and getting on her knees...

NO. *Fuck* no.

In that instant any reticence disappears. I run faster, thinking, *This asshole has to DIE.*

Peter. The asshole's name is Peter.

He'd moved into my subdivision's cul-de-sac that previous summer. Those first few weeks I didn't see him, though, or anyone else in his family -- only his father's van parked in their driveway.

Peter's dad was an exterminator. The advertising on the van said so:

FOR ANY SIZED PEST, PIPER IS THE BEST.

Hamelin, Ohio is a tiny burg, maybe five-thousand people, the proverbial Norman Rockwell mom-and-apple-pie American Dream bullshit. It's not a bad place *per se*, but for anyone unimpressed with mud runs and cow-tipping there isn't much to do, especially if your foremost goal is to take the music world by storm, escape to New York and *never* come back.

"I hear he's throwing a party at Tanglewood this weekend," Tyler told me one afternoon near the end of July. It was hot and we were resting between practice sessions in my garage. I use the term 'practice session' loosely: Tyler and I tuned our guitars for ten minutes waiting for our drummer Ian to show up, then chugged Miller Lites we'd swiped from my dad's stash when he failed to materialize.

"Who?" I asked. Tyler gestured over the hedgerow to the Piper's house.

"The dude next door. Uh, Peter, I think. Ian told me about it."

Tanglewood was exactly what its name implied, a rough, forested area on the edge of town where kids would go to get shitfaced. Usually our high school's preppie One Percenters funded any parties there as a way to ensure their social standing among the plebs; a newbie like Peter doing so was clearly an attempt to build street cred. *Shrewd move*, I thought.

"You wanna go?" Tyler asked hopefully; he'd emigrate to Siberia if free booze was involved. "I hear Megan might be there."

While I fostered fantasies of being in the limelight onstage, crowds and parties really weren't my thing. I'd get anxious, self-conscious, tongue-tied, and end up drinking way too much as a result. But Tyler, damn him, knew I harbored a not-so-secret hard-on for Megan Johnson since seventh grade and clearly wasn't above exploiting it to further his underage debauchery. Everyone at school called her Megan the Pagan for her outré musical tastes, cemetery cuteness and Addams Family fashion sense, but to my eyes she was pale petite perfection. In recent months she'd actually warmed up to me, partly because I let her bum vapes off me at school, but mostly because I lied and told her I was putting a band together, which is the only reason the 'practice sessions' existed to begin with.

Some simple arithmetic: Hot Girl + Lies = TROUBLE.

"If she's there, I'm there," I announced, and that Saturday night we *were* there, with a bonfire, a hundred people, music, beer, the works. True to Tyler's word, Megan made an appearance. For a while she and I sat together, drinking, talking, laughing; soon we were making out like our ship was sinking.

Around midnight I dodged further out into the woods to pee; I'd finished and was fishing a condom from my pocket when something rustled the nearby brush and a chubby white rat scuttled into the open to assess me with curious, beady black eyes.

"Get out of here," I kicked dirt in its direction, but the rat didn't move.

"Don't do that," someone behind me said. A guy stood there, tall, lean, handsome in an emo way: ragged-cut hair, tight black jeans, a Drab Majesty shirt, oozing an effortless cool I immediately envied. He knelt and started whistling softly, some melody I didn't recognize; the rat stopped, looked at him, and after some hesitation unbelievably scuttled into his awaiting palm.

My lips curled with distaste. "Rats are gross," I sneered.

"They're *not*," the stranger stood. "They're friendly, intelligent and cleaner than you'd suspect. *People* are the gross ones." He studied me as closely as the rat had. "I *know* you. You live next door."

I examined him right back. "You're...you're Peter?"

"Yeah." He stroked the rat's furry back. "You'd be Matt, right? I heard my parents mention someone named Matt. Sorry I haven't come over to introduce myself. Things have been so busy with the move. Are you in a band? I hear you playing in your garage sometimes is why I ask. It's awesome if you are."

I laughed. "*Band* implies actual skill. Dudes-twiddling-instruments would be more accurate. We're a little on the DIY side."

"*Ah*. That's *still* awesome. My dad was a musician when he was younger. I've always wanted to start a band, too, but we move around so much it's hard to establish yourself anywhere."

"Hence tonight's reputation-making Bacchanal?"

Peter smiled mischievously. "My folks would freak if they knew I'd done this. But it's like that Sisters of Mercy lyric: '*What the eye don't see won't break the heart.*'"

Stupid as it sounds, at the time I thought him referencing one of my favorite bands was a Big Cosmic Sign, like our meeting was somehow preordained. Lying would be pointless: I liked him.

Peter set the rat down; it had fallen asleep, and only woke when he nudged it. "Maybe we can hang out at my place sometime. Bring the other twiddlers. We can talk music."

"That'd be cool."

"Awesome. Enjoy yourself tonight."

"What the hell took you so long?" Megan asked once I'd found my way back to her. "I thought Bigfoot got you."

"No, no cryptid kidnapping," I answered, but something felt oddly off about the moment now that I'd returned to it; even when Megan started in kissing my neck again, I wasn't quite as into it as I'd been. All I heard was whistling, soft on the breeze.

Tyler and I visited Peter's house later that week. He'd transformed his basement bedroom into a veritable rock n' roll shrine: posters, shirts, thousands of LP's.

"Dude, this is the shit," I thumbed through a box of old obscure post-punk records: The Chameleons, Strawberry Switchblade, Lowlife, Red Lorry Yellow Lorry.

"Yeah, I'm a collector. When other kids spent their allowance on candy I was buying vinyl off eBay."

Peter had an acrylic plastic cage on a table with a rat inside. A white rat.

Tyler tapped the plexiglass. "Gnarly pet, man."

"Thanks. I call him Splinter."

"Is...is that the rat from Tanglewood?" I asked suspiciously. Peter nodded.

"He kinda followed me home, so I decided to keep him. Bought the cage yesterday."

"Isn't it, like, heresy for an exterminator's kid to fraternize with the enemy like that?"

Peter laughed. "Nah, my dad's cool with it. He used to keep rats."

"Like father, like son." Still thinking about the party, I asked, "What was that you were whistling the other night?"

"*That*? Oh, just some old folk tune. Dad taught me that, too. It's supposed to be played on a flute, but it sounds even cooler like this—" he hefted a black Epiphone Les Paul from its stand near his bed and started strumming. On a guitar the melody had the kind of infectious hook that stuck in your brain and refused to leave; I'd dropped ecstasy once at a rave the year before, and the longer Peter played, the more the sound made me feel cozy in that same way—joyful, free, at peace with the world and everyone in it.

"That was fucking awesome," Tyler marveled once Peter finished, and I could tell he was enrapt the same as me. "Dude, you are *so* in our band."

And just like that, My Recent Mania was born.

Peter suggested the name. Just having one at all made the band seem more real. Ian was just as enchanted with Peter's presence and musical ability as Tyler and I had been, and our initial jam session felt like kismet again: for the first time we actually *sounded* like a band. We started treating practice seriously, and even began writing original material instead of settling for covers. Our first real song was called 'Pay the Piper'. Peter suggested that, too.

We played a few house parties, and just before Labor Day Peter scored us some club gigs using a demo we'd recorded. By Halloween our word-of-mouth was hot. We had fans, actual fans, who bought t-shirts with our logo and knew the lyrics to 'Pay the Piper' by heart. Girls threw themselves at us. More importantly, Megan threw herself at *me*. And you can be damn sure I *wasn't* turning her down.

Even at that early point, though, something seemed... *wrong*. We were grabbing everything we'd set out to get: gigs, girls, notoriety, even whispers of local radio play, but I could sense a schism forming within the group. I'd always been the singer, but one night before a show in Columbus, Ian and Tyler abruptly informed me Peter was the new frontman, like it or lump it. While I never nurtured delusions of Jagger at the mic, the decision still stung, though the results were indisputable: the crowd responded to Peter in a way I'd never quite witnessed before, like they were enchanted by his every move, every syllable.

Yet my niggling paranoia still festered when nobody else was around. On one level I knew I was just being pissy, a Beta Wolf chafing under the rule of the new social Alpha in my midst. How bad a dude could Peter really be? He was idolized by my buddies, worshiped by fans. Fuck, even my *parents* loved him. But I couldn't shake the weird hunch a cult had suddenly formed in my midst. And cults had one commonality: a leader.

Charismatic.

Good looking.

Talented.

Peter was all those and more. I just didn't quite comprehend what that *more* was, though I had my theories...

"I think Peter's a vampire," I confessed to Tyler one day after Thanksgiving.

"A *vampire*? Seriously?"

I'd brooded on the possibility for days. Bravely, I said, "Yeah."

Tyler made a face. "I'm not so sure..."

"What? *Why*?"

"Well, first off, vampires don't exist. And then there's that thing where we've seen him in daylight. Soooo, unless he's one of the sparkly variety vampires, I'd say not."

"Well, he's *something*. He *has* to be. Vampire. Hypnotist. Swami. *Some*thing. I mean, have you seen the way Megan fawns over him?"

She did, too. In recent weeks I'd tried my best to ignore all her eyelash-batting looks sent Peter's way, the sly flirty wordplay and innuendos between them. The low point was when I dropped by his house unannounced before a gig and Megan was already there; they'd been laughing at some shared joke or other until I walked in. Then it was stone silence, like I'd intruded on their secret plans for a *coup d'etat*.

"Maybe he's just, I dunno, cooler than you," Tyler reasoned. "He *does* have a certain *je nais se quoi*."

"What*ever*," I balked. "He's controlling people. Like that rat out in the woods."

"He brainwashes rats now? What, like *Willard*?" Tyler chuckled and started humming Michael Jackson's 'Ben'.

"I'm *serious*, Ty. He's got a kind of, I don't know, power over others. Telepathy. Mind control."

I could tell Tyler wasn't buying it. "First, he's a vampire. Then he's Willard. Now he's Professor X. These are your big theories?"

I felt embarrassed and changed the subject, but the misgivings remained. Not knowing how else to handle the situation, I reverted to what I did best: avoidance. I stopped hanging out so much at Peter's place, and even started shirking practice just to get some distance. And the further from him I got, the clearer my head became. Tyler had made the crack about brainwashing, but many a truth lies in jest: the space offered clarity about how manipulative Peter was being without anyone else realizing it.

Tyler must've ratted me out to Peter, because a couple days later he called a band meeting at our new rehearsal space.

"*You're kicking me out*?" I raged when I heard the news. "I *started* this fucking band!"

Ian had initiated the conversation, but he was a wimp at confrontations, and withered once I began arguing; Tyler cowered quietly beside him, unable to look me in the eye. Peter, though, was gleaming. He'd been waiting for this.

"Don't get upset, man," he chirped. "We appreciate everything you've done. But we're going in a different direction musically and don't think you can add to the creative mix anymore."

"That's *bullshit* and you know it." I glowered at him. "You're *loving* this, aren't you?"

Peter didn't say anything, but that satisfied Cheshire smile never left his dimpled chin. I looked to Megan for reassurance; she'd accompanied me to the meeting, but all I saw on her face in that moment was thinly-veiled disgust. She withdrew from my intended touch, sauntered across the room and nestled alongside Peter.

"Babe," I pleaded, confused. "What...what are you doing?"

"I wanted a boyfriend in a band, Matt, which as of now you're officially *not*," she scorned. "We're *done*."

The rebellion complete, she snuggled into Peter's chest. I stood there, stunned.

"*Fuck* this," I snapped, and left.

Ian offered me a ride home, but I refused, saying I'd rather walk even though it was freezing outside. All night I sulked in my room, sending Megan texts that went ignored. Around midnight a light flipped on next door; from my window I could peek over the hedges into Peter's basement window. He was there, but not alone: the last thing I saw before he closed the blinds was Megan, giggling as she removed her bra.

I thought that was rock bottom, but I was so, so wrong: the following day 'Pay the Piper' debuted on WXZX, Columbus's alternative station. By that afternoon it became the most requested song they had; at week's end it was blasting from damn near every store, restaurant, and bar in half the state. I'd see people drive by, bopping their heads to its beat; everyone listening seemed so blissful, so *happy*. And that's when it hit me, all at once, like a fucking bus.

It's the song, dumbass.

Peter had even hinted as much that first day at his house: *Oh, just some old folk tune. Dad taught me that, too. It's supposed to be played on a flute.*

Hamelin. Flutes. Rats.

Like father, like son, I'd said.

God. *Damn.*

I admit, as epiphanies go, it was bugfuck insane, weirder than vampires, Willard *or* Professor X. That shit was just some fable, wasn't it? Yet how else could a seemingly ordinary kid Svengali so many so quickly? 'Pay the Piper' wasn't just a pop hook. It was a declaration of intent. And now that Peter had a taste of the dominion he truly wielded, where would he stop?

That's when I understood what must be done, right or wrong. There wasn't any other choice.

I had to *kill* him.

First Degree Murder didn't come naturally to me. I clocked a scary amount of Google research into serial killers and decided having an accomplice might be the way to go, though with everyone around me under Peter's thrall I had to be careful who I approached. I remembered Tyler's reluctance the night I'd been ousted from the band and hoped it was a sign he'd been unwillingly coerced into compliance by Peter's magical mojo. So that Saturday I swung by Ty's house on the pretense of repairing our friendship; his parents were away for the weekend, so we had the place to ourselves.

Broaching the subject of capital crime didn't seem like a good conversational lead-in, so I tried the soft approach, bullshitting about stuff Tyler was into, video games and muscle cars and *The Big Lebowski*. When I mentioned Peter, though, he grew increasingly defensive, and the longer I explained myself, the more hostile he became.

Google said serial killers favored zip ties and duct tape, so I'd brought some along, and when I saw the opportunity knocked Tyler over the head with a lamp and bound and gagged him to a chair. I had high hopes he'd calm down at some point, buuuut...

"You're fucking *CRAZY*, dude!" he shouted once I'd removed the tape from his mouth. "Peter *loves* us! His music will change the world!"

Brain: washed, rinsed, spun.

I left Tyler restrained through the night and into Sunday. After I was reasonably certain he'd detoxed enough from Peter's influence, I cut him loose.

"I feel... *empty*," he lamented. "Like I was filled with beauty and harmony and now I'm just some mongrel abandoned in the cold." His lower lip quivered; I think he wanted to cry.

Nullifying the song's effect was one thing; conspiracy to commit murder was quite another. Tyler was understandably skittish about helping me brainstorm scenarios for snuffing Peter out. There were a million ways to bump someone off, but which would be the most efficient and the least morally reprehensible? Arsenic? Defenestration? A woodchipper?

Eventually we settled on a simple kidnapping, followed by a staged suicide via an overdose of my mom's sleeping pills. My initial impulse was to snatch Peter as he left his house, but cops always interview the neighbors when shit happens, and I wanted to avoid that at all costs. Then Tyler mentioned My Recent Mania had a holiday gig that next night at a venue called The Overthrow.

"Call Peter just before showtime and tell him you're gonna be late," I advised. "That should give us some breathing room to wiggle backstage and corner him."

"What if he won't go with us?"

"Then we'll have to...persuade him."

"*How?*"

That's when I remembered my Uncle Doug and his gun collection. Sure, he was a tinfoil-hat wearing wacko who believed the CIA was stealing his memories, but he'd always been friendly at family reunions. And informing him about a diabolical mind-control plot perpetrated by a quasi-mythical figure would be *more* than enough to usher me through his front door.

With the barest bones of a plan in place, Tyler and I set about gathering the needed supplies. The whole of Monday was a blur. I drove out to my uncle's converted bomb shelter before lunch, but as the appointed hour neared, I became more nervous. I just kept thinking about the lives we'd be saving, the good we'd be doing.

We're gonna pay the piper, all right, I told myself. *And payback's a bitch.*

The floor vibrates from the opening act's set as Tyler and I dash through The Overthrow's side entrance. According to the flier they're an indie group from Columbus called The Conniption Fits; a few months ago they laughed when we'd asked if My Recent Mania could share a bill with them. Now they're just as snookered by Peter's rising star as everyone else.

I give a friendly knock on the band's dressing room door, gleefully imagining Peter's smarmy features deteriorating into regretful, frightened sobs once he gets a face full of mace, but the last person I expect to see then is Megan. Because of my earplugs I can't hear what she's saying, but reading her lips is simple enough:

"What the *fuck* are you doing here, Matt?" she snipes. "In case you didn't get the memo, you're not our guitarist anymore."

I push into the room; besides her, it's empty. "Where's Peter?"

"*That's* all you've got to say?" Megan's mouth puckers. "You know, Pete told me about your crackpot obsession with him, how you think he's Dracula or some shit." She glares at Tyler then. "And *you*. Thanks for *finally* showing up, jackass. The band almost missed curtain. You get wasted and oversleep again?"

I hold up a hand. "Wait, they're *still* playing?" I'd hedged my bet Tyler's lateness would give us enough wiggle room to wrangle Peter before showtime. But Megan's adamant.

"The Conniption Fits' bassist offered to fill in tonight. You ask me, Kyle should replace Ty. At least he looks hot in leather pants."

"*Damn it.*" This isn't how I envisioned my plan unfolding. "Look, Megan, I know you think I'm full of it, but Peter's not what he seems. There's something hidden in that song, like a subliminal message. It's how he gets others to follow him. How he made you—" the next words are bitter on my tongue. "—fall in love with him."

Megan stares at me, scowling, before swiping open her iPhone's keypad. "You're fucking *nuts*. I'm calling the cops."

"We don't have time for this." I throw her cell down the hall before yanking Tyler from the room and slamming the door in Megan's shocked face. We're bolting down the corridor when the floor, quivering from rock music heartbeats earlier, goes still.

The opening act's finished, I realize. *Peter will be onstage any second now.*

Some fans and security goons bar the entryway to the performance area, but they don't notice us until Megan bursts from the dressing room, screaming:

"*STOP THEM! THEY'RE GOING TO HURT PETER!*"

The group's attention swings like a pendulum, first to Megan, then back to me. I try pushing Tyler faster, but he only frowns and picks at his ears. "Dude, I can't *hear* you with these things in!"

I reach out to stop him, but it's too late: Tyler pops the plugs free just as the band rips into the intro for 'Pay the Piper', and his expression instantly erodes; a dreamy pall touches his brow, his eyelids droop, like he's suddenly a sleepwalker.

"Man, I forgot how awesome this song is," he swoons, and starts lip-synching the opening verse along with the crowd.

Knowing Tyler's a lost cause, I steal my chance, squirm away and squirrel onstage before anyone can wrestle me down. At the opposite end I see my replacement in the band, some hipster toady with a shag cut and skinny jeans. *So what if he knows more chords than me*, I sour. *This is* my band. *Time for Plan B.*

I barrel towards Peter, my palm so sweaty drawing the Ruger I'm afraid it'll drop. I want him to turn, to look at me, but he's so busy captivating the audience he never even sees me. Fifteen feet from him, I raise the revolver. My hand shakes. My finger lingers on the trigger.

Do it, man. Take the shot. Stop the madness.

Just then someone tackles me; hitting the stage, I assume it's one of the security guys, but I'm wrong.

It's a fan, a tatted-up chunky chick wearing a My Recent Mania t-shirt. She's not alone, either: concertgoers swarm me, and I'm dragged offstage by a hundred wrathful hands. The Ruger soon escapes my grasp; my clothes are torn; boots trample each limb. *I should've just hired a hit man.*

At some point during the beating my earplugs work loose and the full clarion call of Peter's baritone assaults my senses. His syrupy guitar riff sends a jolt of jubilation down my spine, and I start laughing despite the pain; hearing the music and feeling its energy purges all my anxiety and doubt until one thought remains:

God, I fucking love this song.

AE STUEVE
Dementia

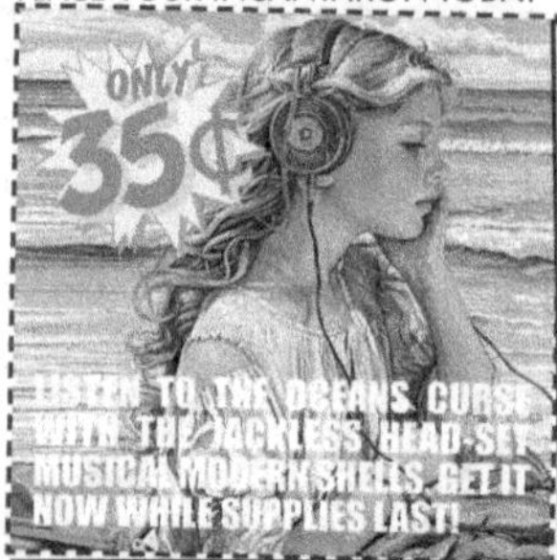

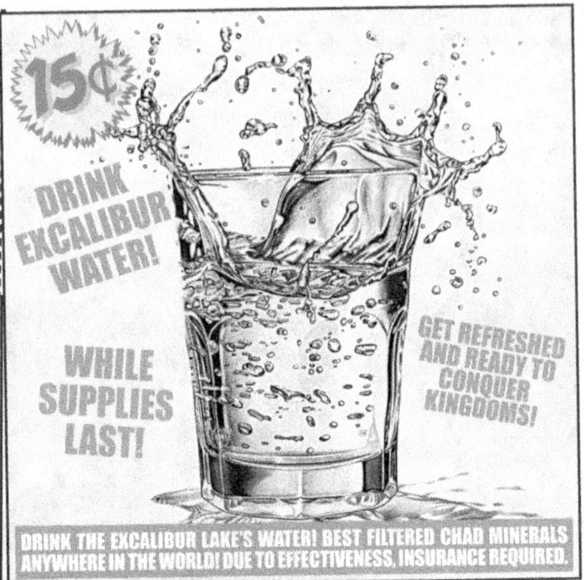

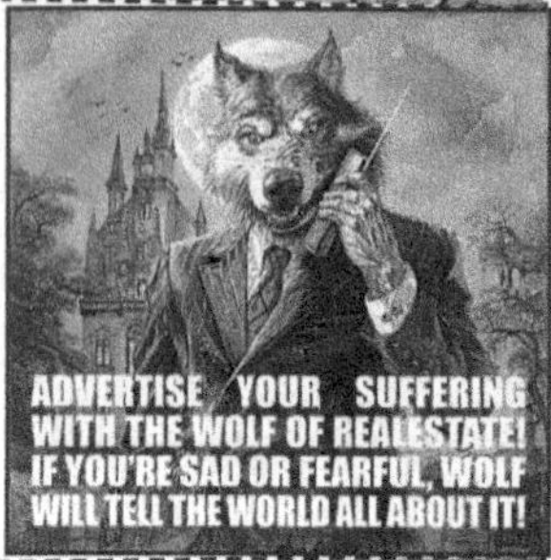

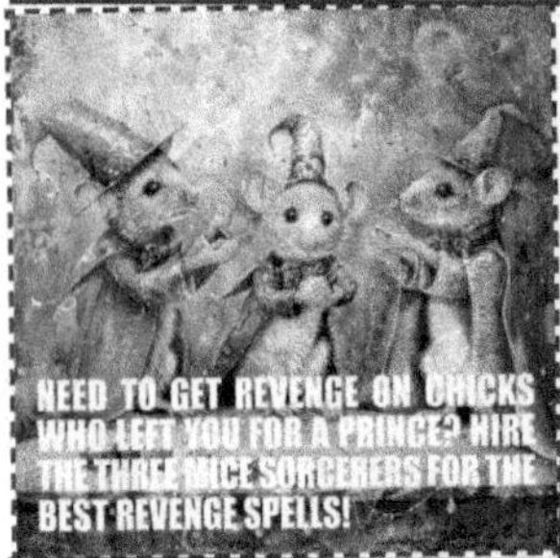

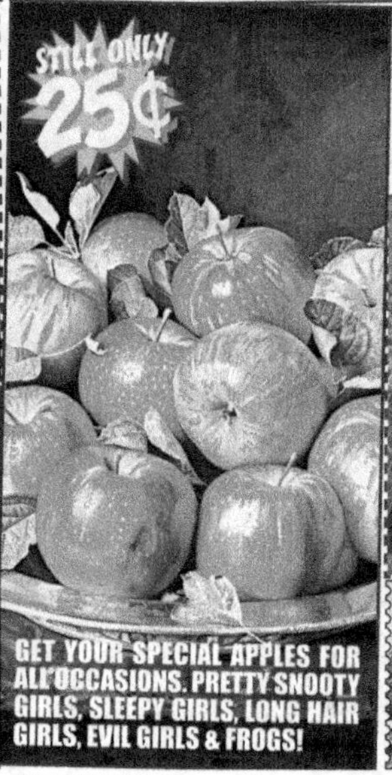

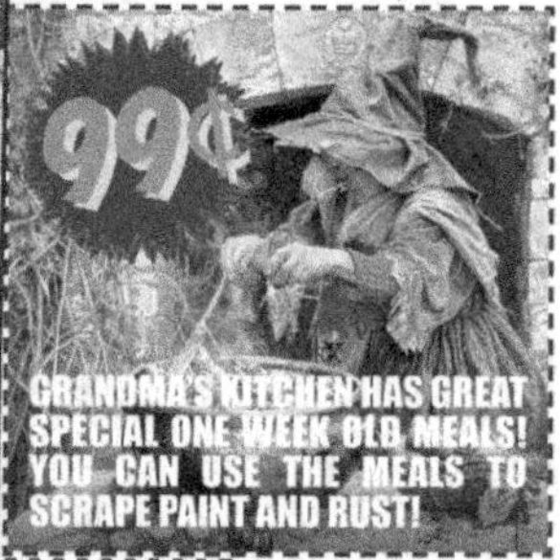

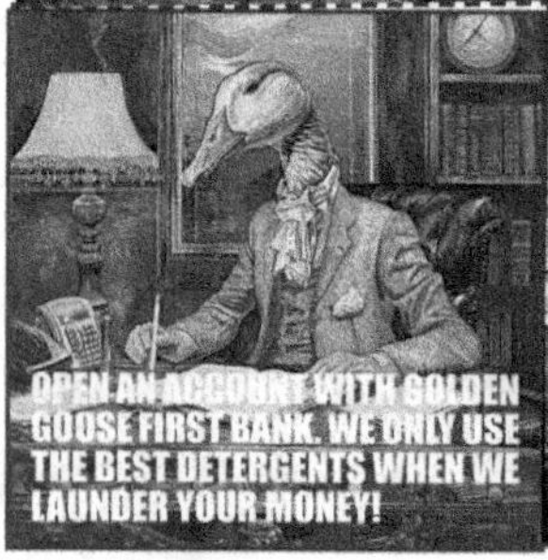

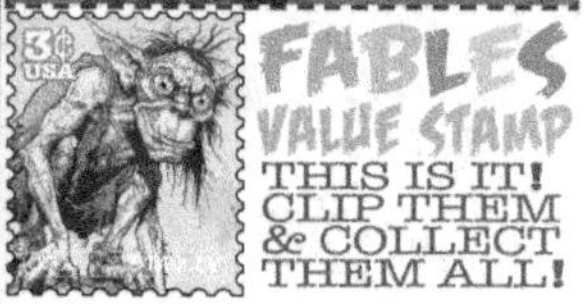

AE STUEVE teaches writing, photography, filmmaking, and design at Bellevue West High and the University of Nebraska at Omaha. His novels, short stories, poems, journalism, and essays can be found online, on podcasts, and in print. To learn more about him, check out https://linktr.ee/stueveae

Houses grew around her, poisonous like unwanted mushrooms. They invaded her territory. They took over her woods. An infection, they were, a disease.

What could she do? She was an old woman.

She accepted her fate with begrudging detachment and depleting memory. Years earlier her sisters had traveled to the most remote locations and had been incommunicado since. She didn't blame them. She couldn't remember their names. She couldn't remember *her* name. The doctors had reminded her often. What was it again?

My name is Barbara, she thought.

That didn't feel right.

The doctors said she had dementia, so she couldn't remember her past. Sometimes it fell like splashes of light through cracks in a boarded-up basement window. In her fractured memory she saw pigs rutting in mud, felt clean rain against her skin, and smelled the forest teeming with life.

Mostly, she remembered the taste of children.

And a snaggle-toothed grin that would have frightened the hardiest woodsman stretched across her face. Though there were no woodsman in this suburban land of WASPs, manicured lawns, and cookie-cutter houses. So what value was that smile?

"I was once much more than I am," she said to the house, her best friend, her *only* friend. "I know."

The house creaked; all it could do. Once it stood upon massive chicken legs and skittered through the deep woods, paying no heed to the animals and people in its path. She flew alongside it in a magic mortar that she directed with a pestle that doubled as a bludgeon. Today, her house could barely rattle in the wind. Its magic was purged from its bones by Target, public school, and the internet.

And flying? She couldn't fly. That was madness.

"No," she said, trying to remember a time when her voice was stern and wicked, not soft and weak. These ideas were not madness. She was not mad. She didn't have dementia. The doctors were mad.

An image flashed across her mind: a woman, beautiful but sad, then angry. She stood in the kitchen. Tears dripped down her cheeks.

The old woman told herself that many beautiful girls had dropped tears onto her kitchen floor. They were usually younger than the one in her mind right now.

"Bah." She waved the image away like a buzzing bottle fly and folded back the deep brown curtain before her front room window. She wasn't quite sure how she had found her way to the living room. The last thing she remembered was a heated conversation and a longing in the kitchen, but what the conversation was about and what the longing was for had escaped her.

No matter.

She loved autumn, with its chilling winds and sleeping earth, even during the day. Normally she liked darkness, but there was a familiar magic in that great orange orb that turned everything into stark black shadows.

How had she spoken with a doctor anyway? When? Where? What, exactly, was a doctor? And how was she here now in this house that she loved? A jolt of fear shot through her wizened body at knowing she did not know. The image of the beautiful woman popped into her head, popped away.

"Children," she muttered. She knew full well that seeing

children would ground her. And when she looked out the living room window this time of day at this time of year, she knew full well she would see them.

"After all," the cuckoo clock hanging above her recliner chimed, "the school bus is always on time: 3:30 PM."

In a belch of diesel smoke, the bus pulled up to the curb across the street from the old woman's house. A set of bulbous twins hopped off like bouncing bugs, giggling. They were followed by some tall child and another boy who looked

average. She didn't know how, but she knew his name was Moe. The lot of them looked delicious in their baggy, multi-colored attire, their skin soft and juicy. Not the tall one so much. He was too lanky for all of that.

"Gristle," the old woman murmured. "Disgusting."

The others? Especially those twins? They were thick. Healthy.

"Tasty," she countered softly, studying their movements as they hovered at the sidewalk. A small bubble of saliva sprouted from the corner of her mouth like a translucent weed.

What curse had befallen her to make her so weak, so powerless? So confused? A lack of nourishment? If she could get just one of them.

Just one.

"Mother!" a voice shrieked from her memory. It was recent. It was grown.

She jumped and swung her head toward the kitchen.

"Something... happened," she murmured and looked back out the window. The children on the sidewalk in the sun looked tasty.

A shout.

A whimper.

"Please," and "No."

The old woman grimaced and kept her eyes on the children. Her stomach growled.

But no. There was no way she could exit her house, trick a child into coming over, bring the child in, lead it back to the kitchen, and slaughter, dress, skin, butcher, and cook it. She didn't have the energy. Crestfallen, she watched as the children scurried off in opposite directions, headed for their homes and their computer games and their TikToks.

Strangely though, she noticed Moe wasn't heading home, which was down the street from her house. How did she know where his house was? She decided not to question that as she saw Moe heading toward her house.

She drooled openly. Using a dirty red handkerchief from her pocket, she patted her lips dry.

She gasped and let the heavy curtain fall shut. Her front room wasn't clean. It wasn't a mess either. Still, should she fold the afghan splattered across her flower-patterned couch? Should she vacuum? It had been at least a week since she had turned on that damnable noise factory and run it across the threadbare carpet. What about dust? It was too dusty in here to make a child comfortable. He'd cough up a storm and his muscles would tighten. That would never do.

What was she thinking? She couldn't have Moe over. She couldn't eat him. This new world wouldn't allow it.

"No!" a feminine voice shrieked from the edge of her memory. "Mother!"

The old woman blinked.

The doorbell rang.

Its arrogant ding-dongs danced through the house. The house seemed to enjoy the sound. Sweat sprung from the old woman's brow. She was reminded of a princess she had known. She had possessed a musical voice that had both enchanted and enraged. She had been beautiful. She had been... something important to the old woman.

Her eyes grew wide. Her head felt light. "What was that?" she whispered. "There was—" The trinkets on the shelf to her right tinkled together as the house shuddered. "Impossible," she said.

The doorbell rang again.

She hobbled toward it, pulling a faded shawl from a hook and wrapping it around her shoulders. She only had to step through an arched threshold to reach the front hall, but the journey felt like an odyssey.

"No," she muttered. "The doctor says these are dreams. She says my name is Barbara. I don't eat children. I have children. They are adults. They take care of me. I am never alone." She clacked her teeth together and rubbed her tongue over them.

Metal.

Sharp.

If she was never alone, where were her children now?

The doorbell rang a third time.

She wiped the sweat from her brow with the red handkerchief and tossed it aside. It landed on the linoleum entryway floor with an odd splat she paid no attention to. In her dirty slippers, drab sweatsuit, and dingy shawl, she opened the door only a crack. From the shadows of the house, she glared at Moe.

"What?" she growled.

Moe, a child of about seven whose features and mannerisms were as inconsequential as any, stepped back, gulping. "Grandma?" he asked, his voice struck through with childish fear.

"That's not my name," she snapped. "What do you want?"

He took a deep breath. His head swiveled as though looking for aid.

"Speak boy, speak!" she hissed.

He closed his eyes. His hands had left the book bag straps under his shoulders and were now clenched at his sides. Growing muck sweat peaked out from behind the straps.

"Mama said to meet her here today," he said so quickly she almost did not hear it.

She gulped. "Here?" she asked. "Why?" The words fell from her mouth like tumbleweeds.

Moe was short for Maurice which meant 'dark' in one of the dead languages if she wasn't mistaken, and she was never mistaken about such things no matter what the doctors said. How did she know that?

He looked at her with weak, light eyes below a mop of unimpressive black hair. "I-I don't know," he stuttered.

The old woman could feel the fear oozing out of him worse than his sweat. Her heart beat faster than it had in a century of days.

But no.

This world was a place for neighborhoods filled with fat folk who ignored their problems by falling into mundane and neutered retellings of stories from ages ago. This was a time of towering streetlamps keeping beasts at bay, revving automobiles scaring monsters into their dwindling woods. Magic was dead. Her memories were a lie. This was a place for dementia.

Modernity had won a battle her kind had never known they were fighting. This could not be.

The house rumbled enough so that Moe noticed. He stepped back.

"Why?" she asked without knowing she was asking.

Moe looked to his right and cocked his head to the side as though struggling to think.

The old woman leaned in closer, sniffing.

"I don't know!" he blurted. His cheeks reddened as he repeated himself.

She puzzled over him for a moment. He was a simple child to be sure. He could be easily fooled. With her own gulp, she settled it.

Around her she felt the house grumble loudly almost as if stretching awake. She opened the door wide and with her best grandmotherly voice, said, "Come on in. Your mother will be here soon." She had lied about being a grandmother before. She could do it again if that was needed. The flesh of children was her favorite after all. And it wasn't everyday they just walked up to your house, was it?

Moe sighed. "Did Mom bring my Switch?" he asked. "I get an hour of screen time after school."

"Switch?"

"My video game," Moe explained.

She nodded. She knew about video games and how they rotted the brain and pulled children into brightly colored worlds of make believe. She loved video games.

Time coalesced around them and formed a dome in which only the two of them stood. Nothing outside of this mattered. No sound penetrated. No smell of city life. The old woman was back in the woods of old and this child was here for... for what?

"Mother, no!" came that shrieking voice from the kitchen in her memory again. It was like a needle forcing itself into the bubble.

"Bah!" the old woman scoffed, and the needle vanished in an ironic pop. The bubble remained.

She was the witch who lived alone with only trees and birds and forest creatures and her house, her wonderful, wonderful house, as her companions. It was all there, all in this unmoving bubble. She felt the dirt beneath her cracked toes. She heard the squawking crows who lived off the remains of her victims. She tasted the pure, green air the trees had always provided.

She felt power.

"Follow me to the kitchen," she said to Moe.

The child took a few hesitant steps forward. "Okay, Grandma," he said shakily.

"Come, come," she said. "It's safe here." She turned from him, knowing full well he would follow. "Please call me Baba Yaga. My name is Baba Yaga."

Q.T. FROAME

Hare and Tortoise

New World

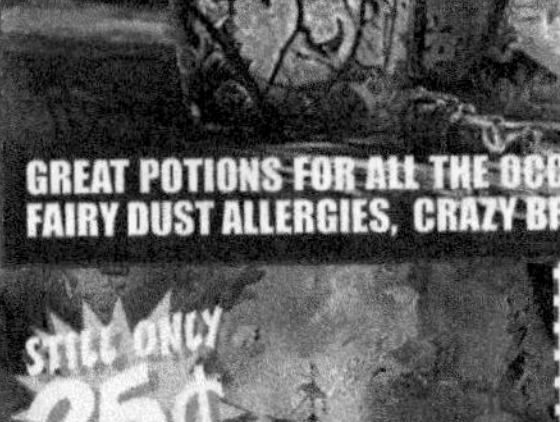

Q.T. FROAME is a young black aspiring author who wishes to create worlds that could inspire others. His favorite aspect of writing is seeing how the characters persevere. The world he wishes to explore is extraordinary, filled with tons of fun and adventure.

Being fast was natural for Hare.

It was in her nature. She wanted to speed through this world and meet all these new people. Seeing the familiar sun and heat hit her skin made her ready to go.

"These new bodies...they are quite a thing, aren't they?"

She turned around to look at the tortoise.

"So what? Let's just explore the world!"

He shook his head slowly, his face full of disappointment.

"Let's acclimate to our new environment. Figure out what happened to our world."

She didn't think much about it, but knew he was right. Still, she wanted to do something more grand.

In their old world, they were animals. It was a simple life. One in which the hare was once beaten by the tortoise. That was long past now. In a flash of light, they were transported to this world they were in now. Full of creatures moving around and buildings they had never seen before. The hare went up to the tortoise and put him on her back.

"Hey!"

She began to speed along the sidewalk. She stopped as soon as she saw a window and got a good look at herself.

She was a bit taller than most of the others around her. Her skin was deathly pale, almost white. She had long gray hair that felt good in the wind. Her eyes were brown and reminded her of the eyes she had before.

The tortoise looked funny to her.

He was shorter than her. He had wrinkles on his dark skin, making him quite old. He had dark green hair that was shaped like a bowl. Typically, she would have been on his back, but she could pick him up in this world.

Someone had come up to them.

"Are you two...new to this world?"

She was a young blonde woman in a blue dress. She seemed a bit startled by them. The hare gave her her classic grin.

"Sure are! You seem like a fancy creature, want to race?"

The tortoise put his hand on her head and pushed her down lightly.

"Stop it, Tort!"

"I've noticed that our bare bodies are exposed and yours is not. You seem like you have some idea of what is happening. Could you help us?"

The woman smiled at them. She turned around and waved for them to follow her.

"Sure can. Call me Goldilocks. It's not the first time this has happened."

They began to follow her. Hare was doing her best to walk with her instead of jogging ahead of her. She had known patience was a saving grace, but she still hated it. She could've been wherever Goldilocks wanted them to be in a flash. It took a couple of minutes, but they reached a wooden home. They walked in.

"Goldilocks, you're back!" A younger boy said. He had dirty blonde hair and was in a yellow pajama suit. He looked at the two behind Goldilocks and vibrated in excitement.

"More newcomers? I'm finally old enough to meet them!"

"Yes, yes." She picked him up and put him in the air. "But you have school now, don't you? You should be getting ready for that!"

He pouted. "That's no fun! Human boys are always so mean when I beat them!"

"Even so, you should do it anyway. Go get breakfast."

She put him down. Despite his misgivings, he went to get breakfast. Goldilocks led them to the couch, where an older man was sitting. He was big and stocky, with a head full of gray hair. He was in a brown coat and jet-black pants. He gave one look at the group and put his hand on his head.

"Goldilocks, for the love of, who are these two?"

She laughed and pointed to them.

"They're from a new group of tales, I think!"

"Did you even ask them their names?"

She shrugged. The older man grunted and pointed towards the TV, turning it off. He looked at them.

"Well, introduce yourselves. Are you two always this quiet?"

"Old man, I'm not some pushover!" Hare didn't like the tone of his voice or his attitude. "I'm usually called Hare. And the guy on my back is Tortoise!"

The older man whispered, "Aesop next..." and got up after confirming their origin. He turned to Goldilocks and gave her a thumbs up.

"Do what you will, I'll take Wee to school. "

"Thanks! You're the most helpful bear I know!"

He left and took the little kid to school. Tortoise finally spoke up.

"There's a lot happening. What's Aesop?"

She told them to sit down. Tortoise finally hopped off of the Hare's back and took a seat as she asked them. Hare did it after a little more prodding. She went upstairs quickly. She came back down and handed them clothes.

"Here! I think they fit you both. It might be a little tight on you, Hare. We need to get you two new names as well!"

"Names?"

"Yeah!" Goldilocks smiled at Tortoise. "You can't be called Hare and Tortoise. That's old school, and it's not like you guys are just animals anymore."

Goldilocks provided a mirror so they could see how they looked.

Hare loved her outfit. A black shirt that exposed her shoulders and belly, along with gray sweatpants and black sports shoes. This all felt fast to her. She knew she could go fast in this.

The tortoise also liked his outfit. He wore a huge dark green fur coat with jean pants and black boots. He had a white shirt under his coat. He felt warm and missed his shell, so this would be a decent replacement.

"So...names! I've thought of two for both of you!"

"Already?" The tortoise questioned.

"Of course! For Hare, what about Alacrity?"

"Alacrity?" She tilted her head.

"It means being eager."

"Then that's fine with me!" Alacrity nodded with a smile on her face. "Alacrity. It sounds powerful too. This new world is fun!"

"For the tortoise, Clement is kind of cute, is it not?"

"...if you wish to call me that, I have no problems."

Alacrity had started to tap her foot.

"Tort asked a question, Goldilocks. This is fun and all, but get to the point!"

Clement would typically speak up against such rash words, but it was true. She was helpful, but he did want an answer to his question. Goldilocks's face went serious, and she nodded.

"Aesop, to keep it simple, is an old storyteller. He created a collection of stories that we know now as Aesop's Fables. "

Goldilocks went to get a book with the same title. She went through them, as they weren't too long. She got to the Hare and Tortoise, both of them getting immediately more intrigued. As she went through the story, Alacrity groaned and put her face in her hands. She was doing her best to hide her face out of sheer embarrassment.

"Please tell me nobody else knows of these stories. It was already embarrassing having everyone at home know I lost to him."

"Humans tell these stories to children all the time."

Alacrity yelled in frustration. Clement couldn't help but chuckle in amusement. He figured it was a good lesson for the youth to learn. It only made him more curious.

"How did we go from this to being here now?"

Goldilocks put away the book and faced them.

"Right, okay. I'll give you the lowdown of what's happening."

She started from the beginning.

A decade ago, she was teleported into this world. She was as shocked as they were. She was human, so she wasn't out of place. She did her best to live her new life here. Still, she had no clue what was going on. She wasn't the only one, however. Many other people from the fairy tales she was a part of came with her, including the bears. They weren't the first. This was a new phenomenon being dubbed the Fairy State. A decade before even her appearing here, more fairy tales had appeared. Some were more violent than others, and they had a bounty on them even now. The world was doubtful of fairy tale creatures now. People had predicted more would show up in this decade since that was the trend the Fairy State had set, and now they appeared.

It wasn't just new looks. They had powers above what a new human would. Even she did.

"Like what? Powers?" Alacrity was getting excited. Having extraordinary abilities sounded cool. Goldilocks smiled.

"Do you think that me finding you, me getting the perfect clothes for you, and me finding the bears again was a mere coincidence? I can manipulate luck in my favor."

"Cool! I wanna race you! Can your luck beat my pure speed?"

"Alacrity, stop it," Clement said, leaning back in his seat. He was taking all of this slowly, making sure he understood it. He asked a question that was on his mind. "Did they ever find out what caused the Fairy State? Twenty years is a short time, but it seems like a quandary to focus on."

"Short?" Alacrity screeched out. "Just because you're an old fossil, Clement, doesn't mean everyone else is! I couldn't imagine being so old."

Goldilocks laughed. They were such a fun duo.

"Well, no. It's all a big unknown."

"Who cares about the details?" Alacrity got up and cracked her neck. "Let's just have some fun! Clement, if people are worried about people like us, I have the perfect idea."

"I'm sure," he sighed, knowing whatever he would hear next would be random.

"Let's take out some bounties for these creatures!"

Clement looked at her blankly.

"You mean those who have twenty or ten years on us in this world? Those bounties?"

"Yeah!" She pumped her fist in the air. "Slow and steady, right? We'll wear them down."

Clement looked at Goldilocks. "Is this as foolish as it sounds in my mind?"

"Not that foolish if I'm being honest. You won't run into anyone from the bounty list in all likelihood, so you can treat it like a big exploring adventure. Get used to the world. Grandad is cool, but he's not gonna let you live here. So, you should find your own way in this world."

Clement understood. He got up and gave her an appreciative nod.

"Thanks for the help. "

Alacrity lifted him up and put him on her back again.

"To the world! Finally! Thanks Goldi!"

She ran out of the home. Goldilocks chuckled and watched them leave. She wished them luck. The modern world was more treacherous than their old one.

Alacrity was running faster and faster. She stopped once she realized she didn't know where they were going.

"Hey Tor-Clement," she was still getting used to the new name. He hummed an affirmative sound.

"Where are we going?"

"..."

He jumped off of her. He didn't expect her to know where to go, so he was already looking at his surroundings. They were now in front of a library. People were giving them strange looks. Was it...

"Alacrity, don't go too fast while we're here."

She shook her head aggressively.

"Never! Why would I do such a thing?"

"Trust me. I'll race you again later if you agree."

"Deal!"

Her face shined with enthusiasm at the offer. He would never race her again. He told her he made his point the first time, and that any second race would be useless. Now, she could at least tie up their records!

He led her inside the library and walked up to the first person he saw who looked like they would help. It was a woman behind a counter.

"Do you have any information about the bounty list on tales?"

"It's a public list, you can check it on that computer over there."

She pointed to one of the mechanical boxes. Clement nodded.

"Can you show us how?"

"You're an older fellow, aren't you?"

"I'm only forty..."

Alacrity laughed as soon as she heard it.

"Can you believe him? He thinks he's young."

"No need to laugh, he's already going through enough as it is."

Clement didn't know why this was happening. He was young, all things considered. He let them make these jokes as the woman helped them access the list. Alacrity was excited by the bright lights, but Clement watched closely to learn what was happening.

"See here, this is the top ten and it goes down from here..."

Alacrity pointed to a large man who was number seven on the list.

"Big Bad Wolf? Totally our thing! Once we beat him, the rest of the tales will have to get a better reputation."

"You're a tale?" The woman said, gasping. Clement sighed.

"Yes, we are. "

"I have to ask you to leave then. You're not allowed in this library. Please don't harm me!"

That drastic change in attitude. What was that? Alacrity didn't want to stay there and make her afraid, so she grabbed Clement and left. There was one thing for sure, they would have to get the Big Bad Wolf. That would help their reputation. Alacrity was sure of it.

They spent the entire day learning more about how this world worked and looking for the Big Bad Wolf. Of course, they didn't find anything. They had learned not to tell people they were tales, as they often got looks of hatred, jealousy, or fear when it was revealed. They had at least learned their way around the city and would move on to the next. Clement had wanted to do something for her. She was the one who was using her powers to run them places. From this desire, a large shell appeared that covered them. Her eyes sparkled, enjoying the protection this shell had given them. He tested it out, making it large enough so she could run around in. He was able to make it small enough to fit inside the palm of his hand as well. This would be useful, he thought to himself.

As night shined and they lay outside in the forest, Alacrity decided to ask one question.

"Do you think we deserve the hatred we get?"

Clement let out a chuckle.

"Remembering the past huh? Nobody thinks you're that cocky girl anymore. We aren't being treated fairly. As long as we continue at it, we'll get the treatment we deserve."

"Right...thanks, Tort."

She didn't know what life would bring her tomorrow. All she knew was she wanted it to be exciting.

As the next day hit, Alacrity rushed them to the next city. She had gotten them inside a bakery as she was getting hungry. She didn't know if this food would be good, but it was the first thing she saw. She pointed towards one of the display cakes as she got to the front of the line.

"Give me that!"

"Sure. That'll be twenty dollars ma'am."

"And who cares about sea urchins? Just give me the cake!"

Alacrity did her best to beg this lady to give her the cake. They were in a shop that made cakes. Clement found out this was called a bakery. She didn't get it. Why didn't they just give her the cake? They made cakes! Who makes cakes and doesn't give them out to the community?

"It's currency ma'am, are you joking? I'm not in the mood."

Clement had walked up next to Alacrity. He put down twenty dollars in cash.

"Excuse her, she's a bit overactive. We have it."

"Thank you, sir."

The worker took the money. Clement grabbed her and walked over to one of the stalls. Alacrity sat down and looked at him.

"How'd you do that? What's that green stuff?"

"It's money. I asked the people behind us if they had what the person was asking for. They were very helpful. You should thank them when you're done eating."

"Sure! Just point them out!"

He pointed towards a family of four. A mom, a dad, an older brother, and a younger sister. She kept that in mind as she waited for their cake. It would be the best meal of her life until she had another. Until then, this was the best meal she could ask for.

A waiter had brought them their cake. Clement thanked them as Alacrity had already gotten herself a piece. She didn't bother to use the utensils. Clement wanted to be like her, but he wanted to learn the etiquette of this world. He tried his best to use the utensils that were given to him. It took him a while, but he finally cut himself a piece of cake. By the time he did this, Alacrity had finished her piece. She got up and went to the family of four, who were enjoying their own meals.

"Thank you guys for the money thing! Cake is great, right?"

The mother looked amused at the way she worded it. "It's no problem. I do find cake delicious."

The kids were eating their own sugary treats and ignoring the new person. The father was on his phone, watching the news. He scoffed as a tale came on screen.

"Another fairy tale phenomenon. Why do they all have to be criminals?"

"Honey, this young girl is thanking us, can you give her the time of day?"

He looked up from his phone and looked at Alacrity, who was tapping her foot impatiently. He gave her a nod and went back to his phone. The mother turned back to her and was going to apologize when she noticed something. She pointed behind Alacrity.

"Isn't that the gentleman who asked me for help?"

Alacrity turned around to see two men surrounding Clement. One was a taller man, the tallest one she'd seen. He had white hair with black tips. The other was someone who was her height with brown hair that reached his shoulders. In just a moment, they took the cake from Clement and rushed out of the store.

"Hey!"

No one would outrun Alacrity. She followed them, catching up with them quicker than even she herself expected. She grabbed the shoulders of the shorter one.

"Don't take from others!"

He punched her into the ground. Alacrity gasped, not used to the pain.

"Fox, I told you to not act rashly."

The shorter man grinned at him.

"We're nothing but evil to them, right Stork? You're talking too much, let's go before we're caught."

Stork sighed and grabbed Fox. He gained white wings with half white feathers and half black, flying them out of the city. Alacrity got up, holding her stomach. Clement finally caught up to them and watched as they flew away.

"Those two didn't hurt you too much, did they?"

She jumped up and down in anger. "No, we need to pay them back! They stole your cake, they think that's okay! It's not. "

"Do you truly think we can catch them now that they've taken flight?"

She pointed in their direction until they disappeared. She put Clement on her back and grinned.

"If I couldn't, then what good would I be? They can't fly forever. Let's go!"

They rushed through the streets. Alacrity was finally getting used to the speed she was running at. She was going faster and faster. She wanted to push herself to her absolute limit.

"Help!"

She had nearly forgotten that Clement was on her shoulders. She began to slow down to a more acceptable speed, running to where she believed they were going. It wasn't long before she had them in sight again after running halfway through the city. The two men landed somewhere in the alleyways. As they approached it, Alacrity began to slow down. She walked up to the alleyway slowly. Clement got off of her and walked with her.

Fox and Stork began to munch on the cake. Alacrity wanted to rush in and stop them, but Clement stopped her.

"Swiftness will not win this. Let them eat, and let's follow them."

She wasn't one to wait, but she knew his words had truth in them. She complied, lurking in the shadows as she watched the two eat. After devouring the cake, they walked deeper into the alleyway. Fox and Stork knocked on one of the walls, and a door appeared on the brick wall. They walked inside of it.

"What an easy nab!" Fox laughed as they walked down the stairs. Stork had a smile on his face, but he didn't respond. They were going into the deeper sewer system. Before they could go too far, however, a man had stopped them. A large, stocky man who was hairy all over. He had black hair and blue eyes. He frowned at them.

"Having too much fun out there, are you two?"

Fox bowed.

"No sir, we just had some food."

"Is that so?" The man looked at Stork. Stork gave him a knowing look.

"Getting our name up, we stole it. Our introduction to the world is going well, Wolf."

Wolf looked at both of them closely. After a moment, he turned around and walked away. Fox let out a breath.

"Guy is a wall, isn't he?"

"For someone as abrasive as you? I would imagine so."

"Don't get too cocky, Stork."

It was the right time.

Alacrity rushed and grabbed Fox, dragging him against the sewer walls.

"So, you want to be thieves?"

She tossed him into a sewer wall across the water and jumped that distance, kneeing him further into it.

"The one thing you can't steal is my speed. Give it up!"

Fox had choked up his spit. He gave her a weary smile and pushed her off of him.

"So, you're the fast hare? I should've known from when I first saw you. No one else could be this punchable" He gave her a crazed grin. "How about this? You walk out and I don't eat you."

"Catch me first, Foxy!" She went to kick him, but he caught the foot. His eyes, which were black before, were now brown like hers.

"I can. I'll show you, Hare."

She did prefer her new name now that she had been called both. She couldn't harp on it too long as she was kicked off him and into the sewer water. He began to run away at a speed that was unnatural to him. Did he really steal her speed? She jumped out of the water and caught up to him, drying herself off with her immense speed. She let out a sigh of relief. She still had her powers. It must've been a copy.

When she caught up with him, she kicked him to the ground. She planned to stomp on his face, but he rolled out of the way. He got up quickly, throwing reckless punches at her. She dodged the punches coming her way until he upped the speed out of nowhere. Catching her off guard, he uppercutted her up to the roof before jumping up and kicking her to the other side of the sewer.

She pushed herself off the wall, dodging the incoming punch coming her way. She got an idea. She started running, and Fox chased after her.

They were practically racing, side by side, running through the sewers. Alacrity was getting excited now. She didn't know if she liked fighting, but the running involved with it here made her tingle. Fox tried to get sneaky hits on her. Tripping her, hitting her in her blind spots, anything that could catch her off guard. She wasn't having any of it, dodging and jumping out of the way. She kept her momentum and sped up as she did it. Fox was getting even angrier. He was supposed to be as fast as her. How could he be losing? He decided to go even faster. With a burst of speed, he flashed through the sewers.

Before he could realize it, she had trapped him. He was running headfirst into a wall. The moment he tried to stop and steer in a different direction, she kicked him into it, cracking the wall and shaking the ground around them. She laughed.

"A wise guy told me the race is not always to the swift. Even if you could outspeed me, which you couldn't, this wasn't a race. That temper of yours is a problem."

He fell to the ground, looking up at her. He was beaten, clearly worn out, and bruised. He let out a sigh.

"You planning to...end me now?"

She looked at him incredulously.

"No! What?" She shook her head. "Just apologize! To Clement! Oh, Clement!"

She let out a gasp. She had nearly forgotten about Clement. She left him with Stork. Hopefully, he wasn't doing too badly. She reached out to Fox's hand and picked him up.

"If you need help, just ask! Even those who play tricks deserve some help."

She ran off.

Clement watched as Alacrity ran off to fight Fox. She certainly was enthusiastic about this whole thing. He would show her his gratitude later. He looked at the Stork, who was sizing him up. Stork, out of nowhere, gave him an apology.

"I'm sorry for stealing your cake."

Clement hadn't expected that.

"Apology accepted. You're Stork, right?"

"Correct. If we had known you were tales like us, we wouldn't have done so."

That was concerning.

"You should not steal from anyone. Did no one teach you proper manners?"

Stork's wings appeared in all their glory. He held his arms up to match the shape of the wings. Clement took a step back subconsciously.

"Do you really think morals are what's important here? News flash!" He grabbed Clement and slammed him on the ground. "They hate our kind. They abuse those like us, even the ones who are innocent! Why should we not pay them back in kind?" He tossed him away.

"If they didn't want to be treated the same way they treated us, then they should've opened their hearts. Now I have to open it for them!"

Clement took hit after hit. He wasn't like Alacrity. He didn't have the speed to react to such hits. Yet, not once did he ever display pain or fear. Stork was getting annoyed with how tough he actually was. It was like the hits he was landing had no effect on him. He flew into the air, his wings causing immense winds to push Clement back. Feather after feather hit him to no avail. He was still standing tall. Stork knew that, for some reason, nothing he was doing was working. It was time to try a new tactic.

He flew into Clement, grabbing his neck and holding him under the water. Stork was sure this would work if nothing else. The only thing that happened was Clement kicking him away. Stork flew back, unprepared for such strength in that little body. He took a few breaths and backed up slowly.

"What's your ability? What can you do?"

Stork was getting nervous. What type of strength was packing in this little man's body? It was unbelievable.

Clement had held out his hand.

"Join us."

With two words, Stork was officially confused. What? Why would he...why would he even offer that?

"You're not a bad person. Why don't you take a chance with us? I'm not all knowing. I don't know if humans will eventually accept us. I think that for us, and those in the future, it would be best to at least try."

Stork took it all in. He wanted to take a chance on the humans, did he? To treat them right, even after they mistreated him? Stork couldn't comprehend it. He really was just a patient turtle, wasn't he? He pushed past him, bumping his shoulder.

"Blue door, in the far east. If you wish to show me your ideals are worth fighting for, defeat the Big Bad Wolf. Show me you have what it takes to fight, win, and be unrewarded for it."

He walked off. Alacrity showed up a second later, hugging Clement.

"You're okay! Hey, is that Stork? Why is he walking away?"

"Don't worry, we have a bigger foe to fry. You know the Big Bad Wolf?"

Her face was beaming with joy. "We're gonna capture him?"

"Yeah. Follow me!"

She jumped in excitement. She let Clement get far ahead before she zipped up to him. She was bouncing around in joy. Clement had always wondered if she would ever be serious.

Clement eventually found the door Stork was talking about. Opening it, he saw the man he was looking for. He was in a small brick room, reading a book. He looked up, his blue eyes piercing them.

"Hare. Tortoise."

"You know us?" Alacrity ran behind his seat. "Yeah! Call me Alacrity now, I prefer that."

"Clement," he introduced himself as well. The wolf huffed.

"I see. You want a name like the humans have? That doesn't bother me. How did you find this place?"

"Does it matter? We're here to capture you, silly!"

He didn't seem bothered. He closed his book and got up.

"I've been in this world for twenty years. You two, a day at most. Why do you choose to go against us?"

"You're not us," Clement said. "You're you. You represent you, and you only. You've done many reprehensible crimes. Give it up. Pay for your crimes, and you'll be forgiven in the end."

"You can call me Wolf." He ripped off his shirt, showing his hairy chest. He howled loud enough that the whole sewer would hear it. Alacrity tried to kick him, but he grabbed her foot out of the air.

"After this little lesson, you'll make good recruits. "

He slammed her on the ground. Clement went to punch him, but Wolf shoulder-tackled him.

"Too slow."

He lifted Clement up and slammed him into the wall again and again. Alacrity was up now and kicked him off of Clement. She grabbed his legs and tried to throw him, but he was too heavy for her. He didn't wait for her to realize this and decided to knee her in the stomach. He grabbed her face and slammed her into the wall, making her fall to the ground.

Clement closed his eyes. He knew it was time now.

Before Wolf's punch hit his face, a green shell blocked the punch. Wolf felt the pain in his hands but didn't stop, going for a kick this time. Clement slammed the shell into Wolf, causing him to bounce on the floor and tumble to the other side of the room.

He was hurt. Clement hadn't used his shell yet, so he didn't know what it could do. It should be enough to take him down. Wolf got off the ground and cracked his neck. His eyes were now full blue. Claws came out of his hands. A barrage of attacks had started.

His attacks came faster, stronger. Clement was using his shell to block his whole body, but he was being pushed back. He eventually hit the wall and had nowhere else to go. Wolf continued to slice at him, slowly breaking down the shell. He broke it down enough to pierce the it, almost hitting Clement.

Alacrity didn't want to lay there and watch. Even with the headache she had, she wanted to at least help. She ran as fast as she could and kicked him into the wall. He ended up getting sent to the wall, breaking it on impact. He seemingly shrugged it off and went to grab her. He was gonna finish the job, but another foot kicked him off of her, sending him to the floor. He looked at the newcomers and frowned.

"You two?"

"Sir, don't look so surprised," Fox grinned down at him as he put his foot down. "I just didn't want to watch the girl I lost to lose to anyone but me."

Clement looked up to Stork. "I thought you wanted me to prove something?"

"I do," Stork got his wings ready, "but I do wish to repay the kindness I got as well. And I wouldn't be able to do that if I didn't help you here."

Wolf had gotten up at this point. He howled again and took a swipe at Fox. Fox's eyes went from brown to blue, and he withstood the attack, hissing.

"Hare!"

Alacrity didn't wait and slammed her foot into his neck. Fox, right afterward, punched him into the wall. They both jumped back as he got up and swung at them. This gave space enough for Stork to fly up and fling feathers at him. He rushed through them and was going to tackle Fox, but Clement knocked him back with his shell.

"Grab hold of him, Fox!" Clement ordered him. He nodded and ran towards Wolf, wrapping his arms around him and lifting him up. Wolf was struggling and would've gotten out of the hold had Stork not begun using his wings to make wind and push him off of the floor. Fox held him in the air. Clement held his shell towards Wolf.

"Kick it, Alacrity!"

"Got it Clement!"

She picked up speed and kicked it towards Wolf's head. She sped up and did another strong kick to the shell. Fox let go of Wolf as the shell hit him, making him crash into the wall. Only his lower body was sticking out of the wall, and he was knocked out.

Alacrity pumped her fist in the air.

"Yeah...yeah...we did it."

Clement went to make sure she didn't fall and helped her walk. His shell disappeared and reappeared on his back before disappearing again.

"Enough excitement?"

She groaned, not giving him a response. Fox and Stork carried Wolf's body as they exited the sewer.

A crowd was forming around the four. The authorities were already called and surrounded the building. Clement had figured it was due to an onlooker calling the police after witnessing Alacrity's speed. The looks of those watching were curiosity and a bit of fear. The crowd muttered about Fox and Stork doing crimes just yesterday, and worried this was all a scheme to do some evil deed. Alacrity elbowed Fox and laughed as she heard this. An officer walked up to them nervously.

"So, this is the Big Bad Wolf? Who are you two?" The officer pointed to Alacrity and Clement.

"We're just here to help, sir. Which is why we took down the Big Bad Wolf."

Clement's words had an effect. The crowd forming around whispered about the possibility of one of the biggest criminals being taken down so quietly. The officer didn't want to believe them, but he had no choice. He pointed to the other two.

"These two are coming with me as well."

Stork couldn't help but laugh.

"We helped with this job, sir. Why should we go with you?"

"That doesn't matter. You still committed crimes."

Stork couldn't believe it. He knew this would happen, but it still hit him that it did.

"That's not fair!" Alacrity stomped on the ground, frowning. "They didn't know any better, let them go free!"

Someone in the crowd had heard that and spread it around. It didn't take long for people to chant for them.

"Heroes, heroes, heroes!"

Fox couldn't help but smile. He handed Wolf to Clement, getting ready for his fate.

"Well, that's nice. Even if it's only these people who feel this way, I feel good."

He held out his hands together. Clement watched as the officer handcuffed him and the reluctant Stork next.

"Don't worry, since you were a part of taking down this guy, you'll get a reduced sentence. You won't be in there for long."

They were all taken away. The crowd began to ask the two who remained questions about how they did it, who they were, and what kind of story they came from. Clement began to relax and answer the questions. Alacrity giggled, enjoying the attention. She was used to boasting about her pride, so she couldn't help but burst out her introduction.

"I'm Alacrity! I'm the fastest around! Know the name!"

People cheered at her victorious tone. Life wouldn't be as simple now, but she would ensure she and Clement lived a life full of excitement.

ROBERT POPE
The Magic Boots

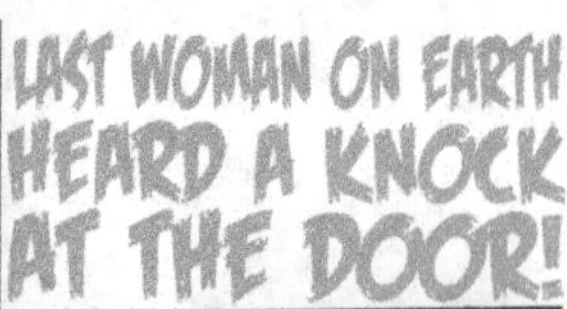

ROBERT POPE has published several collections of short stories, among them Killers & Others, with stories first appearing in Alaska Quarterly Review, Fiction International, Sequestrum, Dark Lane Anthology, and other publications.

I met an outlaw in the Arizona Territory in November of nineteen ought two who told me the strange tale of a pair of beautiful leather boots said to bring good luck to the wearer, and, more significantly, the ability to walk many miles without growing weary. Having crossed the territory visiting parishes with only my good old horse Pharaoh as company, walking much of the way to save her back, I would have welcomed such boots. But to add to their interest, the teller sat in a straight-back chair with a single pillow at his back, smoking his pipe, inside a steel cage to prevent another escape, looking more comfortable than I would have supposed possible.

The outlaw's dark hair was combed back in a sort of wave, and he had heavy eyebrows, a dark beard grizzled with gray. He wore an unsoiled white shirt and a bolo tie held in place by an onyx stone, dark slacks, no shoes at all. His feet had gotten hot, so he had taken off his well-worn boots which stood beside his toes. He appeared something more than a ne'er do well but was said to have killed thirty men.

I expected to take confession, but he lit his pipe and tried to remember what month or year he heard of a sizeable reward for anyone who brought in a bandit who held up the stagecoach by standing in the roadway flashing six-guns and wearing a pair of wonderful boots. The wanted poster said nothing about the boots, but there they were in a crude drawing by an artist who clearly knew the value of the boots on a short, heavy-set Mexican bandit, providing very few other visual clues. The outlaw had his eye on those boots, but first he must find the man. He set horse to the environs of Solomonvillle, leaving four men at the hide-out, and set out on horseback with supplies for a few days.

Arriving at the saloon, he let some locals win a few games of poker, plied them with whiskey, and asked if anyone had shown up with unexpected cash. A gap-toothed fellow leaning back in his seat asked one of his buddies about a black man he had seen at the mercantile buying up a large quantity of food and supplies. He spoke in a way they had never heard, so he must have been a foreigner. Couldn't guess where from. This information mentioned no Mexican bandit, but the outlaw determined to have a word with this fellow. After a bath and a night's sleep, he headed to the homestead where the stranger was staying with other foreigners, according to the barflies. He was met at the door by a surprised old woman, the stranger's grandmother, as it turned out, who invited him in before she knew what he wanted.

She gave him eggs, bread and butter, preserves, and coffee, talking to him the whole time about how her grandson came from Australia and was in a shed they had back there. She had cleaned it up and installed a bed. Little Pete took his blankets out there too. He had to be with his Uncle. She said someone told the man, whose name was William Igwe, that he had a visitor. He had cleaned his plate when Igwe showed up. He stood and shook the stranger's hand. The man was considerably taller than the outlaw, with a small, tight head and a small, tight grin on his face. He wore only what appeared to be pajama pants, his chest and feet and head bare.

"What, you came all this way to talk to me?"

"Yes, that's right."

"What did you wish to say?"

His grandmother brought him a cup of coffee and bread and butter, preserves. He closed his eyes and sipped deeply.

"That is welcome," he said.

"I have come to ask you if, in your travels, you have seen or heard anything about the recent stagecoach robbery that netted quite a sum."

"Why, yes, I have heard of it." His eyes were full of mirth. He took a bite of his bread, and said around it, "What have you heard?"

"No more than I have told you," the outlaw said, "but I hope to increase my knowledge in the area."

"You have a very fine intuition," the stranger said. "I was in fact there."

"I heard there was a man of color there, and when I heard of your arrival, I thought there might have been a connection."

The tall man wiped his hands on a napkin, and then he said, "Well, I am pleased to meet you. I might have made the same assumption in your position. I can't help but be a little conspicuous at times. Because of my height. Many have not seen a man so tall."

"You are quite tall."

"That comes from my father's people. I can imagine what you have heard and how you heard it. I was a passenger as well as an elderly gentleman who passed out almost immediately, though they brought him back easily enough once we got to the station house."

"And the drivers?"

He nodded. "What you have heard is probably true. A madman stood in the roadway brandishing his pistols and demanded they stop and deliver the chest of gold and currency he knew us to be carrying. When Charley went for the Winchester, the fool shot him dead, and then killed the other one who had drawn on him but not fired.

"At this point, I stepped from the carriage with my hands raised, calling out, 'Carry on, carry on. Don't mind me. I know where the chest is if you'd like a hand.' He gestured with one of the pistols, seeming to indicate I should go ahead. I did so. After getting him to shoot off two locking devices, I dug out the chest—a fairly small thing—and handed it to him. I said, 'I believe this is what you're after.'"

"He thanked me for my assistance and left my soul to God. I climbed into the driver's seat and drove the chariot into town with the old man inside. I never saw the bandit again, and I do not miss him. I leave him to God, who is already on his track, wouldn't you think?"

He laughed heartily at this and clapped his hands, rubbing them together. His grandmother laughed, and so did little Pete who had snuck in still muzzy from sleep. Another young man had come to stand in the entryway, a relative of some sort, smiling in his direction.

"Well," the outlaw said, "That pretty much meets up with half of what I heard and half of what I suspected. And you never saw the Mexican again?"

Grandmother spoke up. "He is not telling you the whole story as he told me. William is not entirely certain he was Mexican."

William did not let her continue. He said, "Sir, I do not know what he truly is, but this much I do know, he was no Mexican, though dark, sun burnt and filthy, but a white man. A pirate of the desert. I mean no disrespect. The white man was a snake in human form. I saw it in his eyes. The desert has taken him."

"What do you mean the desert has taken him?"

"The way he held his right side, crooked, like this. He had lost blood, I couldn't guess how much. There are things in that desert, when they smell blood, nothing can stop them. They are hungry, yes, but far thirstier. This is what I have heard, sir, but I have no way of knowing first-hand."

"Your grandmother said you came from Australia."

"And so I did. Many years ago. I have come to help Mama because I know there is something very bad coming. We know something is coming but do not know what, but that which comes will change everything, until we no longer recognize ourselves."

A second man came in the entryway, calling out, "Hello, sir, how are you?"

The outlaw did not respond. He did not know, after what William had said, whether or not he was off his nut or how much he could trust what he had said about the robbery. That would be a shame. He had begun to like William and his grandmother and little Pete, and however many others were about the place. He knew this wasn't the lot but wasn't certain it would serve any purpose finding out conclusively.

"So, this thing that's coming, how does it happen that you know this for a fact?"

William sat back in his chair and looked at the ceiling. He held his hands out to either side in supplication. "We come from afar. We do not even know the extent of our journey, from where we came originally, beyond the Niger, before or much more recently than that. But we do know this is not the end. We have more to do. We ask our leader to smile on our endeavors."

"Your leader? What is his name?"

He leaned on his elbows suddenly. "I have said too much already. I told you the truth about the robbery. And that the man was white and that he was wounded. Things he said made no sense. That was not Spanish."

"Did you see the boots?"

He sat back up and cocked his head at the outlaw. "You heard about the boots?"

"There was nothing of the boots on the wanted poster. I heard of them previously. From my men. But I saw them in the drawing."

"Ah, yes. They used a representation I drew for them. The man did have excellent footwear. A high shine on those boots, and they came to his calf, and they seemed to cling to him and let him move freely at the same time. And when he left..."

"Yes? When he left?"

"He ran like one possessed. Taking great strides, in spite of the wound on his side. I didn't think I could say this before, but now that you have pursued the subject, it looked at that moment as if the boots were running him rather than him running in the boots. He cried out aloud, and I thought at first it could be a victory cry, as he had gotten away with a chest of gold, but then I knew it for what it was. Pain, sir. Plain and simple. The man screamed in pain as those boots ran and ran, taking great strides, bearing him along an unwilling passenger."

"What are you saying?"

"The boots were magic, yes, but not without a sense of justice."

William looked exhausted now, slumped in his chair, staring blankly into the air, at nothing, at dreams. His grandmother clucked.

"He doesn't want to tell you the rest," she said. "This fool here took after him on one of the horses, and he got lost himself, wandering through the night into the next morning. He didn't know any more which way to go. But he saw the vulture circling overhead in the distance, and he knew what the bird was watching as it circled its prey.

"He walked toward that buzzard bird and soon came closer and closer, so he saw that man had become a skeleton with three of the big, ugly birds flying away, swarming with insects that fled at his approach. That last vulture then came for the boots. He snatched up both boots in his talons, and off he flew, into the distance, taking them back to wherever they came from."

"So, the boots are gone?"

Igwe nodded. "Back to wherever they came from."

"Where do you think they came from?"

By this time, other of his relatives had gotten comfortable enough to come in the kitchen door. "It's a nice family you've got out here, William," the outlaw said.

"Thank you, sir."

"I'm sorry about those boots."

"They didn't do anybody any good. They are bad shoes and should be avoided."

"That shed you stayed in last night, William, how many live out there?"

"Don't you worry about that. Just think about what happened to that crazy man and let those boots go where they will."

The outlaw stood and stretched his legs a little.

"I thank you kindly for the meal, ma'am. It has been a pleasure to get to know you, William Igwe. My only wish is that you prosper."

"Why thank you," William said. "How nice." He stood, extending his arms. "We part as friends!"

The outlaw hugged him back.

"We part as friends. And accomplices," he added.

Everyone laughed for a moment. The feeling was genuine. It meant something to the outlaw. It moved him deeply.

Taking his leave, the outlaw refilled his canteen at the pump, remounted, and headed back toward the hide-out, where the boys would have concocted another hare-brained scheme to make them rich for life. But he knew what this was all about. It was about getting as much as you could possibly get from this life.

And that sometimes there is honor among thieves.

At this point, the outlaw stretched in his steel cage. He reminded me he was to be hung at two o'clock the next day. I said I knew. I had seen them erecting a wall around the gallows, so only the invited would get to see him die. He said he had been thinking lately how much better it would be to be hung at three o'clock. He wondered if they might grant him a stay until three o'clock. Did it have to be two? Two had always been his favorite number.

I knew then his nerves had gotten to him at last, though I believe he did get through the entire story of the magic boots. I wondered if they had him on some kind of sedative. When I left, I told him, what is one more hour or one hour less? When we stand before the Lord the only way that hour should be spent is in repentance, and for repentance, any hour will do as well.

"Father," he said. "I do not repent. Not yet. I've got another day to go. I'll see my regular priest later on tonight and tomorrow as well, so you needn't return."

But, I did return. I had been granted a ticket to the hanging for services rendered to the county and, evidently, the hanged man. I waved at him from the gallery. In my whole life, I have never known a man so proud and brave that he gave a speech on the gallows and shook hands with friends in the crowd. He leaned close and asked me to tip the executioner.

"Don't be ridiculous," I said. "It's a serious occasion."

"No one," he said, "knows that better than me."

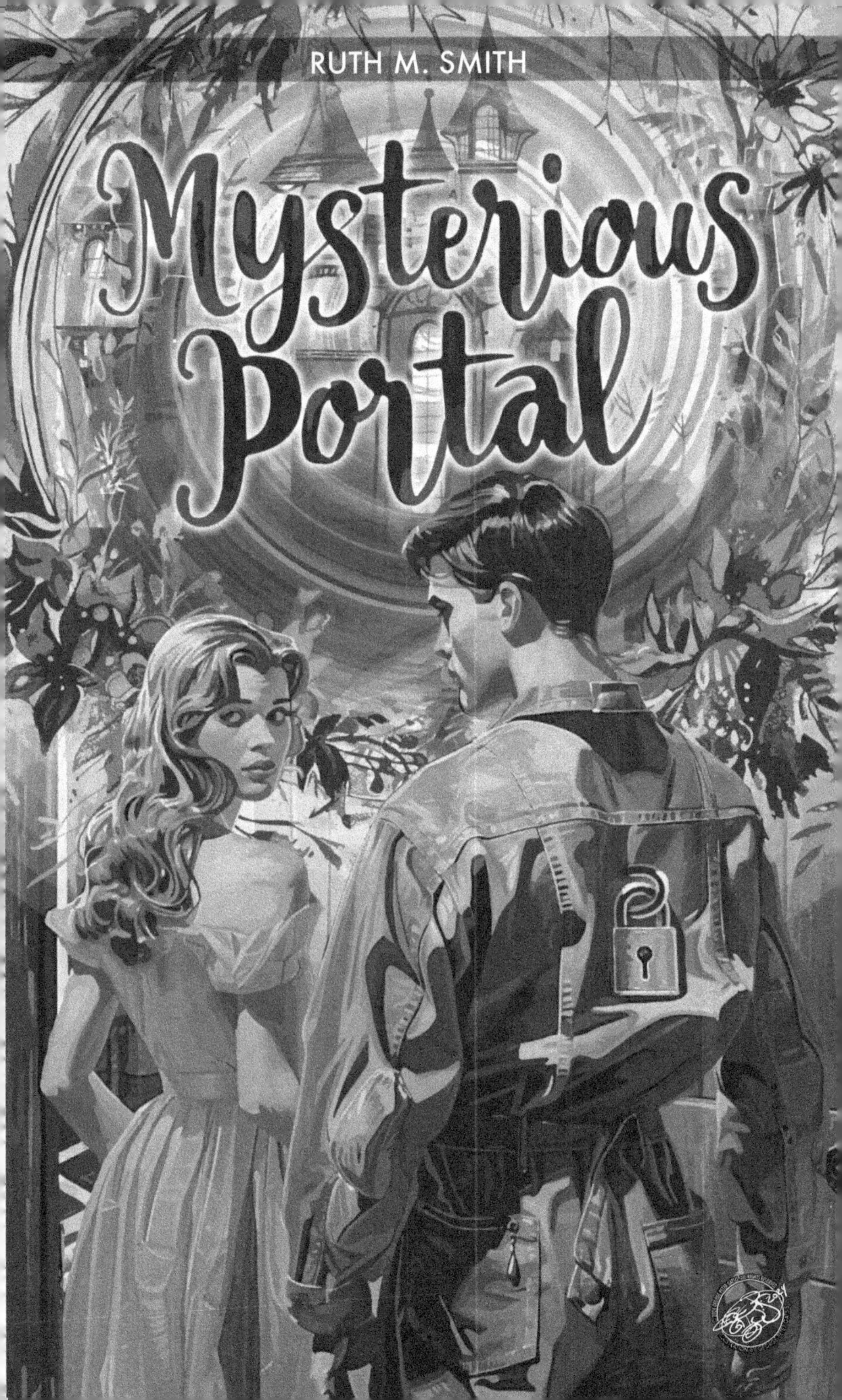

RUTH M. SMITH
Mysterious Portal

RUTH M. SMITH is a vivacious mother of three who lives on a small hobby farm in central Wisconsin with her loving husband, teen-aged daughter, a horse, and a cat. Ruth spends her time volunteering in her county 4H as a club leader, and is a 4H certified Archery Instructor, Air Rifle Instructor, and Air Pistol Instructor. She enjoys writing poetry, short stories, and has completed three novels.

Aurora stepped out of her modest house onto the front step. It was a far cry from what she was used to, but she didn't care. That life was behind her. She wanted to live in peace and quiet. She had slept away too many years. Now Aurora wanted to live her own life!

Her divorce from Phillip went better than expected. After all, who marries the first person who kisses you and still expects the marriage to last? He was attractive to look at, but as dull as a rubber ball. The nice thing about the divorce, he had given her plenty of money to start a new life.

The house Aurora had purchased was quaint. The two-bedroom, two-bath dwelling had a nice kitchen, a cozy dining room, a spacious living room, a den, and a bathroom on the main floor, with two large bedrooms on the second with walk-in closets and a full bath. There was another space on the second floor, but the access to it was locked. The realtor said they didn't have a key. A locksmith would have to be found first to get the door opened. Aurora wasn't sure yet if she was ready to see what secrets were locked behind that door. After all, curiosity was what got her into trouble in the first place. The basement was yet unfinished, but Aurora had plans for that later.

The yard was pleasant, with a large flower garden in the back and a well-manicured lawn in the front. Aurora could smell the flowers as she walked down the steps onto the walkway. She breathed in a large, deep breath and sighed. This was her bliss. She then turned towards the street.

Aurora had moved to a small town in the middle of Michigan. It was a quiet, unassuming village, inhabited by hard-working, kind, warmhearted people. She had found a job at a local flower shop where she cultivated, cut, and arranged flowers that people could purchase. Her specialty was funeral arrangements. Her arrangements were in high demand, and that kept her busy most days. Today she had an order for a large wedding to fill. The bride's mother was coming by the shop in a few hours and the bride's bouquet was not yet perfect. Aurora hurried off down the street to finish the project.

Beauty's Bouquets was a lovely shop to work at. The people were kind and friendly, and everyone loved to smile. Aurora enjoyed being there. Samantha, a tall, slim, brunette, twenty-four-year-old woman, smiled as Aurora opened the door to the shop, its merry bells announcing her entrance into the building.

"Good morning, Aurora," Samantha greeted the former queen as she walked past the cashier's desk.

"Good morning, Sam," she replied. "And how are you this beautiful day?"

Samantha blushed, then held out her left hand, a huge diamond ring perched on her ring finger. "He did it, he finally did it! Jerry proposed last night, and I said yes!" Samantha gushed excitedly. Aurora walked over to her friend and inspected the stone. "Congratulations, Samantha! My, that's a beautiful diamond! You must be so excited!"

"Oh, I am! We haven't set a date yet, and I haven't told my parents, but would you do the flower arrangements and be my Maid of Honor? Please, Aurora?"

Aurora smiled. "Of course, I will," she replied. Aurora had no idea what that entailed, but she knew how to use Google and could figure it out. Sam rushed out from behind the cashier's desk and hugged her friend enthusiastically.

"Thank you, thank you, thank you," Sam exclaimed, her excitement bursting. She refused to let Aurora go until the older woman kindly extracted herself from her friend's grasp.

"Speaking of bridal arrangements, I need to finish one for Jesselle. Her mom will be here in an hour. I'm not quite done. I will talk to you soon to hear about all of the exciting plans you and Jerry have made so far." Aurora waved to Samantha as she walked to the back of the store to her workshop.

Aurora shook her head. Marriage! How she had been disappointed in that dream. Her expectations of happily ever after had been dashed by the cruel reality of life and its monotony. She hoped Sam's future would be happier. Aurora pushed those thoughts aside and finished working on the floral arrangements for today's wedding.

After her task was completed and the bride's mother gleefully picked up the bouquet and other decorations, Aurora decided to cast all fears away and find a locksmith to open that mysterious door in her house. For all she knew, it was just another bedroom in the house that had been used for storage or something as innocent as that.

On her walk home from the florist shop, Aurora stopped off at Lock and Key, the local locksmith. Peter Lock, a tall, muscular man with thinning hair, was seated behind his desk, filling out paperwork. He smiled when Aurora came in the door. "It's nice to see you again, MS Dormant, how can I help you?" he asked.

"Good evening, Mr. Lock," Aurora replied. "I require your services to unlock a mystery door in my home."

"I'm intrigued. Tell me more about this door." Peter leaned forward in his chair and gestured for Aurora to sit across from him.

Aurora sat down and took a deep breath. "On the second floor of my house, there is a door in the middle of the hallway, across from the bathroom. When I purchased the house, the Realtor said she didn't have a key for the room. The hinges, the lock, and the knob look older than the rest of the house. They are made of polished brass. The remainder of the hardware on that floor is polished steel."

Peter nodded. "I have some experience with older locks. Do you have time for me to look at it this evening?"

A wide grin covered Aurora's face. "Definitely," she breathed. "I hadn't expected you to be available so soon."

"I may not be able to open it today. I want to look at the lock to give me an idea of what kinds of tools to bring along tomorrow when I have more time to work on it. Would that be fine with you?"

Aurora nodded. "Then let me get some things and we'll be on our way." Peter grabbed a toolbox, a tool belt, and a hat, then escorted Aurora out the door, securing it behind him. Together they walked a couple of blocks to Aurora's house. She unlocked the door, put her purse on the table near the door, and then showed Peter the door on the second floor.

Peter knelt in front of the door and looked carefully at the lock. He took a magnifying glass from his toolbox and examined the intricacies of the lock, handle, and knob. He whistled softly. "I haven't seen one this old in ages," he whispered. "This may be a bit of a conundrum to open." He rummaged in his toolbox and removed a lock pick kit. He poked around a little bit. He could feel the mechanism shift, but he couldn't get the lock to release. He shook his head. "Yes, just as I thought. This beauty is going to take a little time to figure out." He smiled. "I love challenges. Thanks for making my day!"

Aurora nodded. "What time do you think you'll be able to work on it again?" she asked as Peter stood up.

"I'll put you on the schedule for 1:00 pm. I have to do some research before I come back. There are a few aspects of this puzzle I've never seen before." Peter packed up his gear and turned towards the stairs. "This one is going to keep me up all night thinking about it," Peter smiled a gleeful smile. Aurora walked Peter Lock to the door.

"I will see you tomorrow then at 1:00," she said as he walked away.

Aurora went back into her house and returned to the mysterious door. She stared at it for a long time, thinking about whether she was sure she wanted it open. So many possibilities flew through her thoughts, most of them were negative. She wished for magical powers that would allow her to see through the portal and know if she was unlocking a simple room, or unleashing a horrid monster into the world. But this land doesn't contain the monsters of her past, was this concern unfounded? That night Aurora dreamed about a spinning wheel and a never-ending sleep.

The next morning Aurora walked past the mystery door and tried to pretend it wasn't there. The agony of not knowing, the potential for evil, the anxiety over possibilities was too much for her to bear. She had to have it opened today, good or bad, just to ease her mind. But she had to wait.

Aurora was too distracted to go to the flower shop and spent her morning in the garden tending to the flowers. Their sweet scent relaxed her and her mind to remain in the moment. By the time 1:00 rolled around, Aurora was mentally prepared for whatever was behind that mysterious entrance.

Peter Lock arrived at 1:00 sharp, a whole collection of tools in his hands. His confident smile put Aurora at ease. She led him to the door and stood back to allow him to work.

"I think this may be an antique Mortise lock. First, we will try my set of skeleton keys to see if any of them fit." He extracted a ring of about 20 keys of various lengths and styles from his bag. Slowly, he tried each key, one by one. Some of them had a little bit of a reaction, and one of them even turned halfway, but none opened the lock.

"My, this is a stubborn one," he said, putting the key-ring away. He took out his magnifying glass and inspected the lock more carefully. "Hmm," "Ahh" and "Well," were all Aurora heard as he stared at the mechanism. "Too bad there isn't a hidden switch or something," he muttered. Peter rummaged in his bag and extracted some sharp, pointed objects. "I'll try these," he said as he stooped next to the door. Aurora heard some clicking noises, but then Peter sat back, away from the lock. "It's like there are two levels to the tumblers that need to be triggered in a specific order." He turned to Aurora. "You didn't happen to find anything metal and odd lying around when you moved in, did you?"

Aurora shook her head. She had seen ancient keys before and would have recognized one. Peter sighed. "I didn't think this modern contraption would work on such an old lock, but let's try." He returned to his tool bag and pulled out a metal object, shaped like a glue gun with a sharp metal needle on one end and the handle with a trigger. He swapped the current needle from the gun with a wider, more angled one. He then knelt next to the door, inserted the needle into the keyhole, and pulled the trigger multiple times. Aurora heard the sounds of the tumblers moving before the lock was released. "Well, I'll be!" Peter exclaimed. "Never would have guessed it!" He turned to Aurora, "Do you want to see what all of the fuss has been about?"

A thrill ran through Aurora as she nodded. Peter very slowly turned the antique doorknob, then gradually opened the portal. Aurora moved next to him to see everything as it was revealed.

The room was a disappointment. There was nothing more than a drop cloth-covered bed, a desk, a chair, and a chest. Everything was laden with dust and cobwebs. Neither of them wanted to walk into the dust room. "Wow, what a letdown, after all of the build-up," Peter said. "Well, now you have another room to use as a craft room, a guest room, or a child's room if you ever have one. Although, without any windows, I'm not sure I'd put a child in it."

Aurora smiled. "And here I was afraid we'd find the skeleton of a prisoner long forgotten. Or a BDSM room filled with leather and chains and other sexually deviant torture devices. Or a room full of spinning wheels."

Peter looked at Aurora in surprise. "I wouldn't have thought your mind would go there." He shook his head, "But then again, why lock up a room like this?" He poked his head into the room and glanced around. "There doesn't appear to be anything to indicate someone sealed the door so no one would disturb a deceased person's belongings. I've seen rooms like that before. No, there is no reasonable explanation about why this room was locked in the first place." Peter turned away from the doorway and faced Aurora. "My work is done. Thank you for the most interesting puzzle I've had in a long time." He reached into his tool bag and brought out an invoice. He looked at it, then his watch, and handed it to Aurora. "And it didn't even take an hour to resolve. You can pay me anytime, no rush."

Aurora grabbed a checkbook out of her back pocket, wrote a check, and handed it to Peter. "Here you are! Thank you very much for your quick and efficient service!" Peter looked at the check and saw Aurora had tipped him $100 beyond what he had charged her. His eyes widened in surprise. Just as he was about to object, his cell phone rang. "Excuse me for a moment." He took his phone from the holster on his left hip and looked at the number. "I should take this. Thank you again!" He waved the check at Aurora as he walked down the hallway and down the stairs. Aurora followed at a respectful distance and closed the door behind him after he left.

A large sigh of relief escaped Aurora's lungs. All of that worry was for nothing! She headed to her kitchen utility closet and removed the vacuum, a face mask, a bandanna for her hair, some rubber gloves, dust towels, and a couple of garbage bags. She put on the bandanna and face mask and then hurried up the stairs to start cleaning the room.

The first thing Aurora did was plug the vacuum into the hall outlet and slowly open the door completely. She vacuumed the green carpet around the doorway, then made her way to her left, towards the bed. Once at the bed, she carefully rolled up the dust cover and put it into one of the garbage bags. The billet was made of black mahogany wood with ornamental carvings on the frame. The sheets, pillowcase, and comforter were made of light green material, silky to the touch. It reminded Aurora of one of the fairies that had protected her so long ago.

Aurora then cleaned the carpeting around and under the bed and moved toward the large wooden chest against the left wall. She vacuumed the object, then used the dust rags to clean that off. The top contained carvings similar to those on the bed frame. Aurora bent down to inspect the latch and discovered it was secured. Darn! And Peter Lock had just left! Aurora continued to vacuum around the chest and then faced the far wall where the desk was located.

She vacuumed around the desk, then took her dust rag and dusted off the top of it. The old piece of furniture was bare. She then slowly opened the drawers, fearful that she might discover a rat or mouse holed up in one of the drawers. To her relief, they were empty and dust-free except for one drawer containing an envelope. Aurora withdrew the envelope slowly. She felt it and realized it contained two metal objects. Opening the envelope revealed two keys: one for the door, the second much smaller. She glanced at the chest on the left side of the room. This may be the key to the chest.

Aurora rushed over to the chest, inserted the key into the locking mechanism, and felt a rush of relief when it fit. She turned the key. As she pried open the lid, a strange green light emitted from under the lid. Aurora slammed down the top, afraid of unleashing whatever may be inside. She inhaled deeply, suddenly aware of the sweet, floral scent emanating from the trunk. She shook her head. In her memory, evil had a foul, putrid smell to it. Aurora pried open the lid cautiously, her heart beating rapidly. As it opened, the room filled with a glowing, green light. Aurora was overwhelmed with a feeling of peace.

The once bare room was transformed into a lush, green garden. Tiny white lights sparkled everywhere. The center of the room held a pool of cool water. Aurora stared in disbelief as a being materialized in front of her.

"Greetings, Queen Aurora! I am so pleased you found a way inside here, your Destiny!" The being appeared to be male but had a feminine voice. The being was tall, over 6 feet in height, and dressed in flowing green robes. Its face was obscured by the hood of the robe, but Aurora could see soft, green eyes in the shadow. She smiled despite her concerns. A feeling of peace again overwhelmed her.

"Who are you? What do you mean by 'my Destiny'? And how do you know my name?"

The being chuckled. "My name is Sagacite. I know all, see all, am all. You, my dear Queen Aurora, were granted the gift of immortality when you were awakened from your long sleep. It's only here, in this house, where I can contact you and show you your true self."

"As an immortal, you now have a choice. Whatever path you take, good or bad, you will never die." Sagacite gestured towards a box sitting alongside the pond. It was bright blue, with knobs on it.

Aurora giggled uncomfortably, shifting from one foot to the other. "What am I supposed to do?" she hesitantly asked.

"Come here, put your hand on this box, and choose the path you wish to take for all eternity."

A loud laugh came out of Aurora, echoing through the lush garden. "Hell no!" she exclaimed. "I will NOT choose my eternal Destiny without first thinking about it. I did that once before and look where that got me." Aurora backed up away from Sagacite. She walked over to the open truck and closed the lid. Immediately the garden, pool, and the Being disappeared from the room, leaving Aurora with a half-cleaned space. She sighed deeply. "Nope, not going there today," Aurora whispered, taking the bandanna out of her blonde hair, and the mask off as she walked down the hall, down the stairs, and into the kitchen. She walked over to the refrigerator, opened the door, and removed a wine cooler from the door. Unscrewing the cap, she walked outside into her garden and sat down on a bench in the middle of her roses. She took a long drink of the beverage as a gentle breeze washed over her. "Not today," she whispered again.

MARTIN KLUBECK
Comfort
Food

PLACE YOUR INCANTATION TODAY

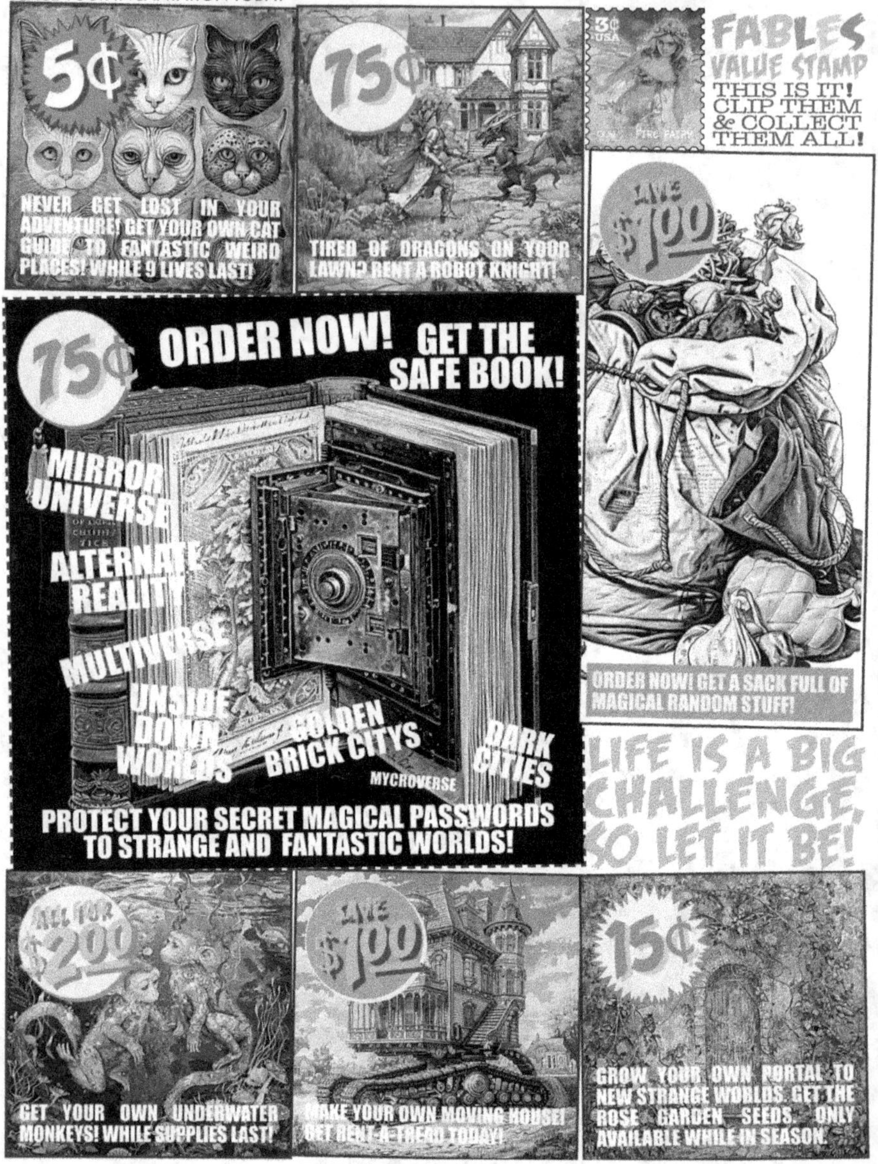

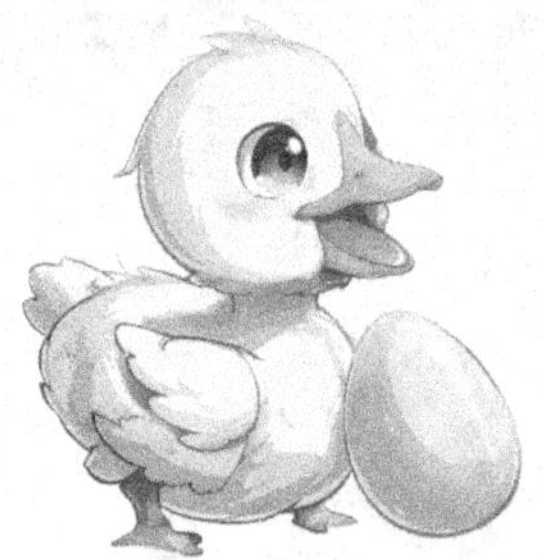

MARTIN KLUBECK struggles daily to balance his work, passions, and family life. At the best of times, the three converge. Marty is an Expert chess player, a sports enthusiast, public speaker, life coach, streamer (twitch.tv/Tiberian64), and a perpetual student. He loves playing, competing, teaching, learning, and living.

His short stories have been published in The Monsters Next Door and The Devil You Know Best, anthologies from Critical Blast. His latest work, The Adventures of Sir Locke the Gnome, is a compilation of six novellas about a gnome who wants to be the greatest detective in the world.

"You have to spend money to make money."

This was John W Richman's life motto since he was a child.

His other favorite saying was, "The gain is directly proportional to the pain." He had become a giant in the finance industry by taking the biggest risks any person could, and each time he came out ahead.

Currently he was working on the biggest deal of his life. But then again, every deal was the biggest. Tonight he was entertaining five of the wealthiest people in the world, giants in their own right. Their summer homes made his chateau seem feeble, and yet, they were coming to him. They had flown their private jets into the local airport and were on their way, in limousines he provided.

They were coming to him because he was good at what he did.

Actually, he was great. Perhaps the best ever. He would soon match their wealth and then continue on his way to exceed them. Like Midas, he wouldn't stop until he was the richest man alive. *Hell, the richest man to ever live!*

He hired on three times his normal staff including a parking valet. The extras would work the periphery. Only his most trusted workers handled the high touch-point opportunities. They all received double-pay for the night.

He finished his shower and let his valet go about the task of making him look his best.

"Like a million dollars, sir."

"Let's live a little, make it a billion," John gave his normal reply.

He liked familiar patterns. He liked having trusted staff that he could rely on. He paid very well for their services. As a bonus he gave them most of their pay in cash, so they didn't have to lose 25% to the government. He didn't think he had to buy their loyalty, but he also was happy to reward them for it. *You have to spend money to make money.* Credit made all this possible. Oh, John had a source of steady income, but not enough to live at the standard he had become accustomed to. No, it was nice for a foundation, but he consistently spent more than he had.

"Is everything in order?" John asked.

"Yes sir. Cocktails at six, hors d'oeuvres, and then dinner at seven."

"And the dessert?"

"The bakery delivered the base thirty minutes ago."

"Excellent."

"Sir, your mother, Mrs. Spriggins called again."

"Same as before?"

"Yes sir. She'd like you to visit."

"Did you put it on my calendar?"

"Yes sir, as always."

"Don't give me that look." He ran his hand through his hair. "I try. She's got everything she could ever want. I'm taking very good care of her."

"Yes sir."

Richman checked his appearance one more time in the mirror before heading downstairs. The first guests would be arriving soon. It promised to be a perfect night.

And it was progressing smoothly. His special guests came solo, no dates. This was a good sign. If they were taking his proposition seriously, they would be all business. This wasn't a social event; it was a pitch meeting.

After cocktails and appetizers (the five-bean dip was exceptional), they moved into the main room for dinner. Waiters regularly filled wine glasses, poured water, and attended to the slightest need. John's personal chef had selected an excellent menu. First a Caesar's Salad with fresh baked sourdough bread. Roast duck with cherry port sauce and a side dish followed. The duck was golden brown and crispy. The sauce had a sweet smell of cherries and honey. The roasted red potatoes were lightly seasoned and paired with beans and artichoke hearts in a rich sauce, covered with a sprinkle of Feta cheese.

"John, this is the best meal I've ever had." The CEO of the world's largest nano-tech company actually licked his lips. The other guests all nodded.

"Please, my friends call me Jack, and I think we're going to become very close friends," John said with a smile. He'd have to give his chef a raise.

He took a bite of the duck after dipping it in the sauce. It really was good. Better than good. It didn't have the gamey taste he usually associated with duck. It had a distinct rich flavor. It was succulent and indulgent. *Perfect for the occasion.* There was a hint of sweetness, beyond the cherry-honey sauce.

"Okay Jack. But seriously, this is the best I've ever had, what is it?"

He wanted to say, some kind of duck, but there was no way he wanted to come across as unknowledgeable. So he smoothly deferred.

"I'll let my chef, Manuel, give you the details," he nodded to his man-in-waiting.

"And the recipe?" the CEO smiled.

"That's up to him."

Manuel Martinez came through the double doors. He wore a pristine white chef's outfit, including a stylish toque squarely on his head. He had changed before coming out, his actual work uniform was a bit messy.

Manuel bowed to John.

"Manuel, my guests say you've outdone yourself! They want to know the details about the meal. Especially how you made the duck."

Everyone clapped.

Manuel bowed again.

"Yes, please Manuel, tell us how you did it," the CEO said.

"*Señores*, I'd be happy to share. It is a classic Chilean dish, Roast Goose with Cherry Port Sauce. The goose is marinated with a mixture of olive oil, garlic, thyme, and rosemary." The ingredients sounded exotic because of Manuel's accent. "The cherry port sauce is made with port wine, the freshest cherries, shallots, and a touch of honey. The potatoes are roasted in a thin film of avocado oil and a bed of seasoning. The beans, and artichoke hearts are sauteed with onions, garlic, and tomatoes, then topped with feta, oregano, and red pepper flakes."

"Details?" one of the guests asked. The guests all laughed.

"I just want the recipe for my cook," another said.

Manuel just smiled politely. "I must get back to the dessert, *disculpe, por favor.*"

He bowed and backed out of the room to another round of applause.

The guests got back to eating the entrée.

The CEO shook his head, "Goose? It's definitely my new favorite fowl. Do you think I can have my cook contact Manuel?"

"I'll be right back," John said, getting up from his seat. He pushed past his attentive staff, into the kitchen.

"Manuel..." John called. He saw Manuel taking off the clean uniform.

"*Si Señor?*" Manuel noticed his employer's pale face. But his neck was a bright red. "Are you alright, Sir?"

"Manuel..."

Manuel waited, *what else could he do?*

"Manuel..."

"Yes Sir?" Manuel was scared to move. He wanted to put on his working clothes and get back to the meal. He was going to use the delivered cake as a starting point. He had elaborate plans for the dessert. But something about John's demeanor made him hesitate.

"You were supposed to make duck..." Every sentence seemed to be incomplete.

"*Si Señor*. But you said you wanted a special dinner. Goose is *muy especial*."

"You said duck..."

"Yes sir."

"Where did you get the goose?"

"In the shed. Didn't you order it?" Manuel asked.

"In the shed? The locked shed?"

"*No Señor*, it was not locked."

"It's always locked! You fed me my goose?"

Manuel wisely said nothing.

"How? Who unlocked, how did you find..." John's voice kept rising in volume and the red traveled up into his face. He was actually sweating. "Out! Get out!"

"Sir?" Manuel took a step back. It seemed prudent.

"Out! You have five minutes to clear out."

Like most of his key staff, Manuel had a room in the staff quarters near the main house. There was no way he could pack and move out in five minutes.

"But sir..."

"Five minutes. If I see you after five minutes, I will not be responsible."

"Sir?"

"Manuel, clear out. Not just out of my house, but town. Take your family and go back to where you came from."

Manuel started moving backwards toward the exit, not showing John his back.

"Yes sir," Manuel said quietly, cautiously.

"If I see you, you're a dead man."

Manuel slipped out the door.

Manuel went straight to his car. It would take him the five minutes to walk to the servant parking area. There was nothing in his room worth his life. He got into his minivan and headed to where his family lived in town. They had a nice small house near the lake. Mr. Richman paid well.

Was he serious?

Manuel didn't want to risk it.

He drove home in a state of subdued shock. What would he tell his wife?

"Honey, why are you home? Isn't tonight the big party?" his wife asked.

They had recently celebrated their fifteenth wedding anniversary. He adored his wife and loved his two children. He struggled to keep his emotions out of his voice.

"I can't explain right now. We have to go."

"Go where?"

"Home."

"We *are* home sweety," she said softly. She put her hand on his cheek. After 15 years she knew when her husband was in distress.

"No, I mean home. Back to Chile. We can stay with my mom."

"What are you talking about?"

"Something happened. We have to leave the country."

"What did you do?" She knew her husband was a peaceful soul. She couldn't imagine what Manuel could have done to force them to run so far away.

"I'll tell you when we're away from here. Pack light, just one bag each. I'll grab food for the road."

"But how are we going to get to Chile? Why do we have to leave tonight?"

"Trust me, *mi amor*. We need to go. We'll lock up the house and drive to Florida. We can worry about catching a flight from there." She looked at him. "Or maybe a cruise. We've saved a lot of money so far, we can afford it."

She didn't look convinced.

"Don't worry. We can come back later. Or maybe we'll just sell this house and move somewhere else." Still she didn't move. "Don't worry, everything will be fine."

But she did worry. That was her job. But she also loved her husband, so she gathered up her two daughters and packed.

In less than an hour they were in the minivan driving away from their house.

The kids fell asleep quickly. Car rides, especially ones past their bedtimes, had that effect on them.

"Will you tell me now why we have to run away?" She asked.

"Soon."

"Are we in trouble?"

He loved her even more for the use of 'we.' She would support him, no matter what mess he had gotten them into. He smiled at her.

"I love you, *mi amor*," he said.

"I love you too Manny, but why can't you tell me what happened?"

He wasn't sure she'd believe him. He wasn't sure he believed it.

"I'll tell you everything tomorrow. In the morning."

They crossed two state lines before his wife fell asleep. Manuel wanted to put as much distance as possible between John Richman and his little family. He decided to drive through the night.

On the drive, his mind wandered. He had really messed up. He was ashamed of what he had done. All his life he had lived by his faith, trying never to sin. And when he did, he sought forgiveness. Forgiveness from whomever he wronged, and of course from God.

This time he had done neither. He had run instead.

He'd at least go to confession as soon as possible.

Around five AM, Manuel started looking for a place to stop. Luckily it was summer. He found a high end campground with family bungalows.

He unpacked the kids. He carried each in turn and put them into bed. He removed their shoes and tucked them in. He was tempted to carry his wife also, but thought better of it. Instead he pecked her cheek.

"Wake up, my love."

She came around.

"Where are we?"

"Far from Richman. We can relax a little. We'll start out again later, maybe tomorrow."

She stretched. "*Las chicas?*"

"Already in bed," he told her.

"Okay. I'll unpack the car. You go get some sleep."

"*Si, señora.*"

His wife brought in their clothes and the food. She hadn't eaten, and neither had the children. She knew that Manuel likely hadn't either as he rarely ate before Richman. Manuel and the rest of the staff usually ate after the boss went to bed. Late meals were normal, but missing dinner was a clear sign that they were in trouble.

She looked through the Bungalow's kitchen. The grounds catered to families. The kitchen had pots, pans, cooking utensils, a full set of kitchen knives, and ladles. But it also had a lazy Susan with basic seasonings. There were plates, cups, forks, knives, and spoons. She could work with this. If her children had to wake up to a total upheaval of their lives, she could make it a little easier. Her husband may be a good chef, but she was a great cook. Many times Manuel told her she was a better cook than he was.

And when she cooked there was no skimping on the calories. She didn't believe in dainty portions like they served in fancy restaurants. Her meals were robust and filling. Her family would awaken to a traditional meal. Manuel had brought enough items to make a good meal. They had potatoes, fresh vegetables, milk, butter, and flour. Funny, they only packed a couple of days' worth of clothes, but they packed the car full with food. It could have been because he was a chef, but it probably had more to do with a cultural love of good food.

Food had brought them together. Food would keep them strong.

He had a strange dream. *Can you smell in a dream?* He was serving Richman's goose to his guests. The smell was overwhelming.

Manuel woke up with a light sweat. It was before noon. He could hear his two girls playing outside. It took him a moment to remember where he was.

As if she were psychic, his wife brought him a cup of something hot.

"*Cafe?*" he asked, seeing the cup in her hands.

"*Si,* it has a full kitchen."

"I didn't pack coffee."

"No, they provide it. And not instant, they have the good stuff," she said with a smile.

"What's the smell?"

"Do you like it? *Tienes hambre?*"

"Yes, it smells delicious."

"I made us an early dinner. Mashed potatoes, sweet potatoes, broccoli, and salad."

"No bread I presume," he said half teasing.

"We have tortillas," she said.

"And no meat," he said.

She didn't answer. Instead, she kissed him and walked out of the room. He washed up in the bathroom. She had brought some basic toiletries. They had toothpaste, but no brushes. He used his finger to rub the paste across his teeth and inside his cheeks.

As he rinsed, a savory smell of roasting meat wafted over him.

His mouth instinctively watered.

He followed the smell to the kitchen. "What smells so good?"

"Dinner."

She had set up the table with four places. The salad was in bowls next to the plates. Instead of dressing, there were fresh cut lemon slices on top of each. Warmed tortilla shells were in a napkin-lined basket. The potatoes (two types) and broccoli were in separate pots sitting on hot pads in the center of the table. She had left room for the main dish.

There was a large plate with a carving knife and extra large fork sitting beside it.

"What did you make?" he asked, staring at the oven.

"I wanted to make us some comfort food, so I packed the girls into the van and was going to find the nearest town. I needed something special."

He sat down heavily into one of the chairs.

"No."

"Yes. And what a surprise the girls and I had! There was a goose in a crate in the back of the van."

"No, no, no."

"Yes!" She walked over to the oven and picked up two hot pads. She opened the oven, and the smell filled the room.

"No." Manuel laid his head on the table and began to sob.

His wife took the baster out of the oven and placed it on the top of the stove. She turned and picked up the large plate and returned to the stove.

"You still haven't told me why we had to leave in such a hurry. It must have been something terrible, but I can't imagine what you could have done."

"It doesn't matter any longer," he said.

"Why?"

"It was all for nothing." Manuel said with his head still on the table, cradled in his hands.

"Lying and stealing is rarely a good thing."

He looked up at his wife. She was standing with her hands on her hips. She wore the look reserved for chastising the children. "And keeping secrets from your wife may be worse."

He didn't know what to say.

"You'll have to return the goose," she said.

"But you…"

"I went to town and bought a turkey. Even if I didn't find this I wouldn't kill and dress a goose." She held out a solid gold goose egg.

"But…" he couldn't find the words he needed.

"Do you want to become like *Señor* Richman? The man I married, the man I love, the father of *mis chicas*, that man is nothing like that *avariento*. I want the man I love."

Manuel said nothing. He looked at the bird in the baster, really looked for the first time. It was a turkey. And the smell was clearly of a roasted turkey.

They ate dinner together and packed up. The girls were happy to hear they were going back home. Manuel said nothing other than grace over the meal. Halfway back to their home he found the courage to speak.

"I hope he doesn't kill me on sight," Manuel said.

"Perhaps you should call him and tell him what happened."

"What, that I stole his goose?"

"Yes. And ask him to forgive you."

Miles went by.

"He won't take me back." Manuel said.

"No, I guess he won't. But you'll find work elsewhere."

They drove for hours before Manuel spoke again. "And the egg?"

"Oh, *I'm keeping* that," she said.

LAUREN STOKER
Serving
the
Public

LAUREN STOKER's short stories and non-fiction have been published in the U.S., Canada, the U.K., and Australia. She lives in New England with her cat (and Chief Shreditor) Sam. Her comic fantasy, BLOOD WILL OUT (With the Proper Solvent), was published July, 2021. In November, 2022, Lauren's collection of satirical social commentary, THE POTATOES OF DEFIANCE, was released. Follow her at www.LaurenHStoker.com

Sometimes I still miss my forest. I had a sweet little cottage there, hidden away in its middle, nice and private and out of earshot. It had little windows with twinkly panes, a deep-browed thatched roof and lots of gingerbread trim. The front door was a delicious perfection in itself: cherry red, with a gum-drop of a doorknob, and a door-knocker shaped like two crossed candy canes above a mince pie. I guess I had a theme going. I've a bit of a sweet-tooth on me, or had. My home, for all its seclusion, oozed welcome. Which was nice, gave me a bit of company. From time to time, I'd get children who'd lost themselves in the forest and come knocking on my door. They were always welcome for a bite.

But you know how it is: you're getting on in years, your back starts acting up a bit; raking leaves, turning over the garden and trudging miles into town to do your shopping gets harder and harder, even for someone like me: single woman (though strong), living and making do on her own, and not the comeliest of face. A plastic surgeon's dream, if I'm honest. Never bothered the kiddies, though—my stoop and long nose or my cackle. (That's just a nervous tic, force of habit sort of thing.) Children thought I was hilarious and intriguingly old-fashioned. I still had my old, solid-fuel range in the kitchen, the kind that has ovens big enough to roast a side of ox, two turkeys, and a goose and have room for a couple of pies. Women in my day did a staggering amount of baking, and I was no exception. The kids kept asking why I had such a big stove, instead of a smart, new electric range like their mums had. They got it in the end.

Each year I'd say to myself, "Rosina, you should move closer to town, you really should. Save you more than a bit of bother." But I had my doubts. I was particular and just wasn't sure I'd have all my personal needs met in a town.

And then the town came to me. That was a shock! The kingdom's developers came and bulldozed half the forest. In short order, I was left with only a slim margin between me and their brash, new urban sprawl. There was even a mall now only a half-mile away!

At first, I thought I could work with that: malls draw children by the droves, I'd heard. But then the kingdom paved the dappled little path to my doorstep and stuck in halogen street lights, of all things, so any children who'd wandered there soon were fetched home by Mum in her mini-van. I couldn't sleep for the hideous orange glow from the lights shining in my bedroom.

When a representative from the developers, Derek he said his name was, knocked on my door and gave me an offer on my home and its acreage, I wasn't surprised. I gave *him* a surly stare but said I'd hear him out. He went over an outline of their plans. As I tapped my foot, the man sweetened the deal by including in the contract a clause that would preserve my home and the remaining 30 acres as a park. The house would become Ye Olde Sweet Shoppe with all sorts of candy and baked goods on display, quite quaint. What was left of my forest would have proper walking paths, picnic tables and barbeque stations, and a pier on the pond for boating and fishing. They'd even dedicate it me, The Rosina Leckermaul Royal Preserve.

"Very nice, but where will *I* live?" I asked him.

Derek said they were also building a housing estate right next to the kingdom complex for the likes of such as me. Displaced, I assumed he meant. Said I'd have my very own place, built to my specifications, within reason, of course. Furthermore, it would be zoned for both residential and business use, so the new owners could operate small shops and such like out of their homes, if they so wished. That sounded interesting.

"That's all very well," I said, "but won't we all be shoved in cheek-by-jowl with barely enough garden to grow a rose?"

"Not at all, my dear woman!" Derek exclaimed. ("Dear woman"? He obviously didn't know me.) "Each home will have a minimum of an acre around it. Some may have two or more, if you intend to run a business there. So, please think about it, because we'll need to know your plans as soon as possible before the building phase."

"And what about trees? What about gardens? I prefer to grow my own veg, and I like my privacy and shade, my good man!" (On my part, the "good" was sarcasm.) "Last I heard, you lot just clear cut everything to make it easy on yourselves."

"It's true," said he, "that developers have a bad rap these days, but we of the kingdom here have become more sensitive to community needs."

"Since you mowed down most of my forest, you mean?"

Derek reddened. "That, ahem, was a third-party, corporate decision. At least it didn't affect anyone's homes."

"Humans' homes, ya mean. Bugger the birds and critters."

He shrugged. "They'll still have the park's woods we're leaving."

"'Twill be a might cramped for all of 'em, I'm thinkin'."

"And," his eyebrows rose with a plea, "we've marked all the mature trees to be preserved in the new estate, so they'll be plenty of shade and curb appeal."

"Hmph. So what's this place gonna be called? I'm sure your bosses have already picked out a name for it!" (They always do, these developer types.)

Here, he smiled with pride. "It's to be called 'Magical Manors'."

Gods save us. But it made sense if it was to be plopped next to the main kingdom complex.

"Lemme think on it," I said, with a scowl and crossed arms. Didn't want to show my hand too soon.

"We'll need your decision as soon as possible. Would a fortnight give you enough time?"

"I suppose, as long as I could see the plans first."

"I'll be happy to have someone deliver those to you tomorrow, madam!" He bowed.

Bastards were prepared, I'll give 'em that.

"Sayin' I agreed to your terms—and I'm not sayin' I will—just sayin' I signed on the dotted line and such, how long would I have to clear out? How long do you reckon it'll be before the estate is built, or at least my bit of it, and I can move in?"

"In the best scenario, we hope to have completed the project in a year's time; in the worst, no more than two years," Derek said to me.

I nodded. "All right then. You deliver them plans to me tomorra, and I'll have a think on it and get back to you in a fortnight."

His shoulders went down, he tipped his hat to me and turned to leave. It was obvious he thought he'd aced the deal. I hated that. I held up a warty hand. "Just a minute, mister! Don't you be so sure I'll sign. If I don't, what then?"

He turned back, shoulders supplicating. "Er, in that event, with regrets the king is prepared to offer you a fair market lump sum for your house and its land and take the lot by eminent domain."

Now *my* shoulders rose, brushing the rim of my pointed hat. "Is that so? Well, sir, I just might have an interesting and unexpected 'counter offer' for his majesty," said I, pointing to said hat.

"I rather feel his majesty has considered that contingency and is prepared, madam," said Derek in dudgeon dwarfed only by my own. And off he trotted.

I hated myself for it but, like the others, I caved. I'd been reading the blasted developers' handwriting on the forest walls, despite its illiterate, arrogant scrawl. It was only a matter of time and I had only so much power at my summoning. So how could I refuse? My diabetes was getting the better of me anyway. Being near a hospital mightn't be such a bad thing at my time of life. And my sweet little cottage and at least some of its woods would be saved. 'Twould be a wrench but 'twas probably time to clean up my act, or at least change it up.

It ain't so bad here. A bit Theme-Park-with-McMansions sort of thing; given the location and concept, you have to expect that. Nonetheless, 'tis a pleasant retirement development for folk like me. I was genuinely surprised. I'd specified to the developers that there must be gingerbread and plenty of color on my new home—you know, the charming, Victorian variety you see in the Midwest that looks so homey and welcoming, not the edible sort. And I got it: lavender clapboard and spanking white trim, with those curly brackets on the porch posts, wavy roof trim, and attractively turned porch railings. The front door, with its little, arched window, is a luscious, glossy plum. And, true to his word, Derek ensured that the old oak in front was saved. It nicely frames the house and the path to my front door.

I have surprisingly nice neighbors up and down the road. The Sprats live just a few doors down. Their house looks like a Jacobean manor house, a là King Charles the First. I plan to have them over for dinner sometime soon.

Just across from me is Bo Peep in her thatched *faux* farmhouse. She's quite elderly now, a little senile if you must know, and has to have a caretaker, else she'll wander away again looking for her lost sheep, forgetting that their meadow was mowed down for strip malls years ago and they've long since gone to lamb chop heaven. But she's sweet, though a little thin for my taste.

Gothel, is just a few doors down past Bo. She'd been mopey ever since Rapunzel ran off with her prince—empty nest syndrome. So she moved here and has opened up quite a posh hair salon. She's said she decided to turn over a new leaf, be a kinder and gentler stepmother. Gothel's got quite an impressive clientele already, very popular with brides, what with all the roses twined in amongst the tiaras and crowns of braids. And since her new house is just a modest one-storey, with windows you can unlock, Rapunzel has felt encouraged to visit now and then. Gothel was a bit sad at first to see Rapunzel's new do, but she's come to accept it, even says the pixie cut with the blue streaks actually looks good on her stepdaughter. She's come a long way, Gothel has. She says she'll offer to do Rapunzel's hair for free next time she's in town. We'll see how that goes.

Hilda, the old lady who lived in the shoe, is at the end of my block. Don't know why she refers to herself as an old lady, she's only 55. But she's adapted to the role with gusto: always whinging about her aches and pains. Honestly, I've got decades on her and you don't hear me moaning. But anyway, she said that now all her kids have grown and buggered off (who can blame them?), she didn't see any reason to stay in the drafty, high-top sneaker, toiling up and down the spiral staircase with broth. She was quite pleased to trade it for a sensible, chic pair of flats. Says she's going to open a day-care center in one of them. I cocked an eyebrow and asked her how she thought *that* would go, given her previous lack of street cred. Airily, Hilda waved me off, told me she's a new woman and has seen the error of her ways.

And anyhow, the kiddies would only be with her weekdays, from half-past seven in the a.m. to half-past five in the evening, not all the bleedin' time. She'd even be able to buy bread for the little blighters, thanks to her nest egg from the settlement money, and that, since I was such a keen baker, maybe we could work out a deal to buy her bread from me, wholesale. I smiled at that and said it was certainly possible. It's always good to provide the right sort of nourishment to those who will come your way. I've decided that her day-care center will serve nicely as a little incubator for my future customers.

All of which brings me to my own new enterprise: I'm opening my own fitness spa and bistro! The spa has the usual sorts of weight machines and thingies, a sauna, and private massage rooms. Some restaurant critics have come by the bistro for a pre-tasting and given me quite a few raves for my innovative, fusion-style dishes. The place is quite smart, too, with intimate, little candle-lit tables and a wine bar. The adults will pour in only of an evening, likely leaving their brats behind, but I have another scheme for the kiddies, a public service, really. Daytimes will be devoted to trying out new recipes and experimenting with the different forms of local protein. My new kitchen is enormous and has all the mod-cons, as well as some un-mod ones; there's an industrial-sized double stainless sink, big enough to soak a hog in, a prep station, a carving station, and I had my huge, old range hauled over from the cottage. I also kept all my lovely copper pans and cauldrons.

The kids these days are so chunky, sitting on their arses poking at their smartphones and X boxes all the day long, it ramps up my cholesterol just *looking* at them, never mind what they'd do to my... well, never mind. So I'm planning to give a six-week cookery and nutrition course for *them*, with a tasty send-off at the end. A sort of graduation, if you like. I have it all worked out: after they've slimmed down at my spa, I'll lure them over to the bistro's kitchen for my lessons in nouvelle lean-cuisine. And won't they be surprised?

I'm sorry to say so many of the children nowadays are horrible, especially the older ones—demanding, arrogant, nasty to their mums and dads—their parents won't miss them all that much when they're away. Out of sight, out of mind. You know what parents are like these days with their latch-key kids—so much on all their calendars. Carpools that pass in the night. I'll text the parents updates on their children, when they remember to inquire, and, at the end of the course (after I've packed the leftovers in my freezers), send them a tastefully printed, signed certificate with a letter stating that their child is now a proud graduate of Rosina's School of Culinary Arts and is off to the big city to seek his/her/their fame and fortune with Gordon Ramsay and such like, and promises to write when he/she/they can.

So that's me sorted.

I hear tell Goldilocks, a bit breathlessly dotty now and wearing a girlish, curly blond wig, has opened a furniture store, just children's sized things. Limited inventory, but knowing her, I'm sure they'll be just right. And the bear family, though they themselves are greying and long in the tooth, have opened up a Teddy Bear concession next to her, in a separate shop on their lot. They had a man in, though, to install stout deadbolts and put in a security system, just in case.

I thought maybe Cinderella might be here, too, but was reminded that her new castle is in the main kingdom complex. We'll visit sometime, I'm sure. I hear, however, that her hubby, Henri, will be opening a bespoke shoe store up near the main gate, specializing in glass footwear. He's going to call it "*Chaussers pour Vous.*" (He's French, Henri.) His brother, Pierre, plans to open his own podiatry practice next to it. Makes sense: glass ain't so comfortable nor stable when you're shod in it. Stuff won't give, so corns, bunions, even broken ankles are an obvious outcome. So the prince's family will have a nice set of businesses complementing each other.

With all the sore-footed and overweight tourists and their children we'll get, at least one of us will make a killing.

ROBERT ALLEN LUPTON
Too Good to be True

ROBERT ALLEN LUPTON is retired and lives in New Mexico where he was a commercial hot air balloon pilot. Robert runs and writes every day, but not necessarily in that order. Over 200 of his short stories have been published in various anthologies, magazines, and online magazines, as well as over 2000 of his Edgar Rice Burroughs themed drabbles and articles are located on www.erbzine.com Visit amazon.com/author/luptonra, his Amazon author's page for current information about his stories and books.

I checked in with my parole officer as soon as I got off the prison bus in Fletcher, Oklahoma. I robbed a bungalow on my way to the halfway house where I'd live until I found my own place.

I'd finished three years of a five-year hitch for B and E. That means Breaking and Entering for those of you who have been living in a cave for the last hundred years. I made parole right on schedule for someone who did his time without credit for good behavior.

I didn't cause trouble, kept my head down, my mouth shut, and didn't suck up to the guards like the cons who got good behavior credit, did. Sucking up to the guards was a good way to get your ass kicked after lights out. I hated everything about prison. I hated the food, the guards, and the chains I had to wear whenever I talked to a civilian.

I was the only guilty man in prison; everyone else was innocent. I wasn't, I got caught robbing a house because I was stupid. Well, maybe not stupid, but I didn't know what the hell I was doing. My technique was simple, pick out a house and wait until the people left for the day. Always break in during the daytime. Most people aren't home during the day; they go to work, go shopping, go to school, all the other places people go. After they left, I'd walk to the back door and use my universal door key. Most people call my universal key a pry bar. Smaller than a crowbar and it works really well. On my first burglary, I used a five-pound sledgehammer for a key. The hammer worked great, but it's too big and heavy. I couldn't carry the hammer and all the loot at the same time.

After I broke into a house, I went straight to the master bedroom. That's where people keep their jewelry. If they have good prescription drugs, they usually keep them in the master bath medicine cabinet or in a bedside table. I went through all the drawers and made a blitz search of the closets. Sometimes you find guns in the closets. It's Oklahoma, almost everyone has a gun. After I finished in the master, I'd check the other bathrooms and the kitchen for drugs. I never bothered with big-screen televisions. Those things are a dime a dozen. Hard to carry, too.

Grab the stuff and get out. Never stay in the house for longer than ten minutes. I had it down to a science. It worked every time until it didn't.

I watched a house on the East side of Ponca City, Oklahoma for two mornings. The man and woman were out of the house by 7:30 on weekdays. I waited until nine. I wanted all the "go to work" traffic off the street. I didn't want to run into someone's neighbor while I was hauling stuff out of the house. I rang the doorbell to be sure that no one was at home. If anyone answered the door, I'd tell them I was selling solar electric systems. I had some business cards I lifted from "Sam's Solar World" in case I needed them. I'd rehearsed a pretty good spiel about solar systems.

No one was home and I was through the backdoor and rifling through the master bedroom a minute later. Nice jewelry, five or six watches, and a stash of hydrocodone pills. I dry-swallowed two of them. The closet was a gold mine.

There was a gun safe in the closet and it wasn't locked. I tossed three pistols in a pillowcase. One of them was a Glock. I threw in several boxes of shells. There were two hunting rifles, one shotgun and an AK-47. I took everything and headed out the door.

I always parked about a block away from my target house. I can imagine how I looked running down the street. I was a young skinny dude dressed like a solar salesman in slacks and a nice pullover shirt. That illusion fell apart because of the pillowcase full of guns, watches, and jewelry I carried over one shoulder. Or maybe, it was the four long guns that I was carrying. I was never really sure.

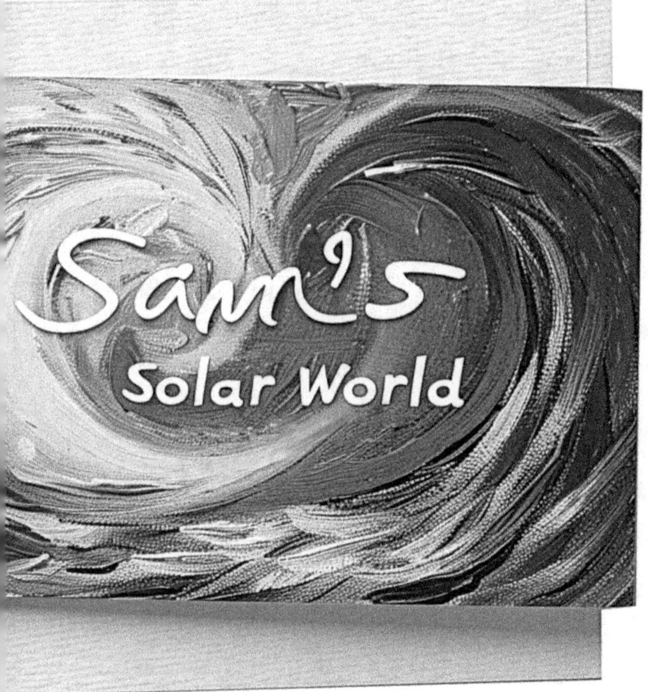

No doubt some busybody saw me hurrying down the street. I wasn't very fast because the guns kept shifting and I had to stop and adjust them every few steps. In retrospect, I should have left a couple of the guns in the house or just let them stay where I dropped them. I finally made it to my car and was loading the trunk when the police pulled up.

The police rarely turn on their lapel cameras, but these cops kept them on when they arrested me. It's hard to claim you're innocent when there's a video of you holding all the stuff you stole.

After I saw the video, I took the plea deal. My public defender said, "Jimmy, they got you on video. When the judge sees it, there's nothing you can say. The best you can hope for is to make some money from the "Stupid Criminals" television show. Don't be stupid. Take the deal."

I took the deal.

The prison in McAllister wasn't that bad. I didn't have to hide from gangs. No one assaulted my virtue. I know that sort of thing happens, but I'm pretty big and pretty ugly. Like I said, I kept my head down and did my time.

Prison is a school for criminals. Everyone is happy to tell you what they did wrong, hypothetically. Remember, everyone is innocent in prison. I was different, I was guilty. I learned that pigs get fat and hogs get slaughtered. That's a fancy way of saying don't steal more than you can carry. My cellmate, Rico, told me a story about a little boy who got his hand caught in a cookie jar. The kid couldn't get his hand out of the jar because he wouldn't let go of the cookies. Sounded a lot like me and my load of guns.

I got a new nickname out of it. Rico and everyone else called me "Cookie" for the rest of my time.

As I said, prison is educational. Especially, if you aren't going to go straight when you get out. I was going straight - straight back to robbing houses.

Prisoners had internet access during the day and Rico was a wealth of knowledge. He claimed to be a very successful burglar. He said he'd robbed over a thousand houses.

I asked why he was in jail if he was such a great burglar.

He replied, "Great burglar, bad drug dealer."

Rico's rules of burglary were pretty simple. His rules were right in line with the information on the internet. "Pick the right house. If you pick the wrong house, you might as well turn yourself into the police. Look for a house where the homeowners are away. Is the yard mowed? Are there newspapers in the driveway? Is the trash can out on trash day? Those are signs the people aren't home."

"Pick a house with lots of bushes and trees so people can't see you. A high wall or fence around the backyard is great. Homeowners like their privacy. Privacy is good for crooks, too. Stay away from corner houses, they're more exposed and it's easier for people to see you. A cul-de-sac house is the best. Less traffic."

"Even if the house looks like nobody's home," Rico continued. "I have three walk-away rules."

"What are they?"

"If there's a security system, walk away."

"I read on the internet that some homeowners just have a security system sign, not an actual security system."

"Don't take that chance, Cookie. Walk away. If there's a dog, I walk away. I don't even have to see the dog. If there's a 'beware of dog' sign, I walk away. If I see a water dish or food dish in the yard, I walk away."

"What's the third rule?"

"If the television is on, I walk away."

"Ok, so I pick a house that looks like no one has been home for a while and check the walk-away rules. Right?

"Yes, but always rob a single-story house. If you get caught upstairs in a two-story house, whatcha gonna do? Are you gonna jump out the window and break your fool neck? Fight the homeowner? Cookie, eighty-year-old ladies carry forty-five automatics these days. Don't get caught upstairs. Stay out of basements, there's only one way out of a basement. People will lock your happy ass in a basement."

We talked a lot, there wasn't much to do except talk. I learned it was a miracle I didn't get caught the first time I robbed a house. I couldn't help myself; the door was unlocked.

I listened to Rico, kept my head down, kept my mind right, and kept checking the internet.

Rico got out a couple of months before I did. I promised to look him up when I got out. He gave me a phone number.

I did a fast blitz job on my first day out to get some walking around money. I made enough from that first job to buy a junk car. The halfway house loaned me a 'pay as you go' phone. The last user left over an hour on it. Not bad. Things were looking up.

I picked a neighborhood on the outskirts of Fletcher, Oklahoma. There were three ways in and out of the subdivision and no gates or stoplights. I wouldn't be trapped without a way out of the neighborhood. I walked the streets in exercise clothes for three mornings in a row. The lady running the halfway house had a dog and I offered to walk him. Nothing says you belong in the neighborhood like a friendly dog. You'd be amazed at what people will tell you while they pet your dog. I learned the morning routine of the neighborhood. I picked a cul-de-sac and watched it like a hawk. It was free of car traffic by nine. The street was steep and the walkers skipped it.

I walked the cul-de-sac every morning and cased the houses. One house stood out, it was a single-story with faded paint. The overgrown shrubs and juniper trees blocked the view on the side of the house and the gate to the backyard. No one on the street or in a neighboring house could see me once I was on that side of the house. The gate to the backyard stood open every day. I counted ten courses in the block wall around the rear of the house. Ten courses are over six feet tall. Good enough.

There was a bonus: toys in the front yard. A portable basketball goal was rusted on its side along the driveway. One small bicycle was propped against a tree. Toys meant children. Children meant mothers, and mothers meant jewelry. Kids meant video games. Video games and jewelry are small and easy to carry. They're as good as cash. Easy money.

I arrived early the next two days. I never saw any kids, but the man and woman both left the house before eight every day. No security system, no sign of a dog, and no sounds from a radio or television.

The house met all the rules, it was too good to be true.

This was the house and Monday was the day. I parked my car a block away and walked the area in my exercise gear until nine. The neighborhood routine was perfectly normal. I hurried back to my car and pulled off the sweat suit I wore over my slacks and shirt. I put on my Goodwill jacket. I adjusted the floppy hat I wore to keep the sun off my face. It also shielded my face from view. Imagine that.

I put on my solar guy badge, walked two blocks to the house, and rang the doorbell. There was no answer. I tried the front door out of habit, but it was locked. I quickly walked around the house and stepped behind the juniper tree. In seconds, I was inside the gate and at the back door.

It was a sliding glass door. I looked and there wasn't a broomstick or anything wedged in the track to make the door secure. I tested the door before using my pry bar. The door was unlocked.

I went through the sliding door and closed it behind me. I ran through the breakfast nook, down the hall, and into the master suite. I glanced into the children's bedrooms as I went down the hall. They were decorated for a boy and a girl. Both rooms were immaculate, the beds were made and nothing was out of place. That was strange. Once in the master, I rifled through the bedside tables and didn't find much. I grabbed some costume jewelry, a couple of cheap watches, and a partial bottle of Ambien. I tossed everything in a pillowcase from the bed. I didn't find anything in the medicine cabinet except aspirin, sinus medication, and an assortment of lotions and creams.

There were two walk-in master closets. I picked the one with men's clothes. I hurried to the end farthest from the door. Always start in the rear and work your way toward the door. I pulled a double handful of hanging clothes from the top rod and threw them on the floor. I pushed the remaining clothes to one side and saw a handgun zipper case and three boxes of ammo on the shelf. I unzipped the case. It was a Chiappa Rhino Chrome with a six-inch barrel. I'd never seen one before. A Rhino is one of the most high-tech and expensive handguns in the world. I dumped the crap from the bedside tables on the floor and zipped up the gun case. The gun was all I needed to take, it was worth five or six grand, easy.

When I stepped back from the shelf with the gun case, I felt a loud click under my feet. The closet door slid closed and gas sprayed into the room. Well this sucks, I thought. I knew the police used bait cars, but I'd never heard of bait houses. Just my luck. This house looked too good to be true. Live and learn. If it's too good to be true, it's too good to be true.

I passed out. When I woke up, I was handcuffed. My feet were also cuffed and the cuffs were attached to chains dangling from the ceiling. I was in a large bathroom. I rattled the chains because that's what you do. I inspected the bathroom. There was nothing in it except the fixtures. There wasn't a single towel, not a bar of soap, and there was no toilet paper. I put my full weight on the loose chains. The hook in the ceiling was strong. I thrashed around but stopped when my wrists started to bleed.

Nothing to do but wait on the police. One thing I learned how to do in prison was wait. I actually went to sleep.

Less than an hour later I heard the door open. I swung around to face the door.

A balding old man in bifocals said. "Good morning, I hope you're not too uncomfortable? I'll bet you're thirsty. Let me give you a bottle of water. You look thirsty. Are you thirsty?"

I nodded. He took a bottle of water from his pocket and handed it to me. "They call *you* a criminal. This water comes from the Los Angeles municipal water system and the cola company that bottles it has the nerve to charge a dollar a bottle. Now, *that's* criminal behavior. Are you hungry?"

I opened the water bottle, took a drink, and nodded again.

"Excellent," he responded in his fast-paced speech. He unwrapped a plastic-wrapped ham sandwich and put it in my hand.

"You don't look like a cop," I said between bites.

"That's because I'm not the police."

I interrupted. It's hard to be courteous when you're chained in a bathroom. "If you aren't the police, why the hell am I chained up? You some kinda vigilante?"

He spoke deliberately. "It's hard to speak slowly when I'm excited. I'm not the police and I'm not a vigilante. As to why you are chained in my bathroom, it should be self-evident: It's a trap. I'm the trapper and you're the trappee. I could say that you're the trapeze because you were so easy to trap. I bet you don't think that's funny, do you?

"Hell no. You better let me out of here."

"I'll let you out soon enough. I need to wait until my sister and her children are here to help me. Once everyone's home, I'll let you out – in a manner of speaking."

"Who are you? What the hell is going on here?"

"I love this part," he said. "This is like in the movies when the hero gets the bad guy to explain his entire evil plan. I am going to destroy the world because the kids in the third grade were mean to me, my mother wore army boots, or I didn't get a sled for Christmas. Really, you think I'm going to confess everything while you digest your ham sandwich?"

He waited five heartbeats and continued, "Don't look so hurt, I'm going to tell you. I want to tell you. It will be fun to tell you. I almost never get to tell anyone."

"Once upon a time, there were two little children, a boy and a girl. Their father and stepmother were too poor to feed them. Their stepmother convinced their father, a woodcutter, to take the children into the forest and abandon them. The children wandered until just before nightfall when they found a house in the woods. The house was made of candy, cookies, cakes, and pies. The roof was marzipan frosting."

I interrupted, "I don't need to hear no Hansel and Gretel crap."

"You think not, but you don't know the entire story. You know the kids were invited into the candy house by a witch. Things after that happened differently than in the fairy tale. You were told they tricked her into her own stewpot. The kids, Hansel and Gretel, didn't kill the witch. They entered into a partnership with her. She taught them her methods and they helped her trap other children. They even lured their stepmother over for dinner one evening. They learned you don't have to hunt for food. If you make a house attractive to your prey, food will walk right in the door."

"When the kids were old enough, they kept a male victim alive long enough to get Gretel with child. She had fraternal twins, a boy and a girl. They named the kids Hansel and Gretel. My sister and I are the 20th Hansel and Gretel. Her kids are the 21st generation."

"Do I look like a kid?" I asked.

"No, you definitely do not. As the years passed we changed our hunting habits. You simply can't eat children anymore. There are Amber Alerts and pedophile watch lists. Stay-at-home parents walk their kids to and from school. The world is full of daycare centers to watch kids before and after school. The whole country is full of busybodies. People set up neighborhood watch programs. If a couple of young kids went outside and rode their bicycles for fun, someone would report the parents for child abandonment.

"The world hasn't been the same since women stopped spending their days milking cows, feeding chickens, canning food, and washing clothes. I swear the whole world went to hell with the invention of the sewing machine. People have too much free time.

"The Great Depression was good to us. Men and women riding the rails and hitchhiking across the country provided an endless supply of food. Then World War Two came along and my family had to return to their old ways, but they stopped trapping children in the early sixties. They found easier prey. With the hippies came free love, hard rock music, marijuana, LSD, and other drugs. Put a psychedelic VW Van in the driveway, aluminum foil over the windows, and a Jimi Hendrix poster or two in the windows, and let the yard go to hell. Let the paint fade and peel and leave the house in a state of disrepair. Grandma and Grandpa grew long stringy hair and wore lots of beads, tie-dyed tops, bell bottoms, and sandals. They lounged around on the front porch and always burned incense or marijuana. Mom and her sister wore thin tops with no bras.

"My granddad said that he couldn't have kept the runaway Midwestern boys away unless he'd shot 'em in the street. They fought to get inside.

"Those glory days came and went in less than ten years. My dad said that the family needed a food source that wouldn't fade away like children and hippies. He said we can't eat children anymore, not the young ones or the flower kind. He realized there will always be people who steal from other people. No one puts out an Amber Alert for a thief. There will always be criminals, and criminals will always be fair game."

I shook and pulled against my chains. "You and your kids are like, cannibals?"

His smile showed very sharp teeth. "We aren't like cannibals, we are cannibals. I can't lift and hang you over the garden tub to drain your blood and dress you out by myself. I need the wife and her kids to help lift and hang you by your feet. I'll pick the kids up from school pretty soon and the wife will be home at noon. What do you weigh, about 180 pounds? Nice! You should dress out about 120 pounds. Plenty of meat for the winter."

I snarled. "You come after me and I'll kill you." I strained against the cuffs.

"Don't be stupid. We've done this before. We could leave you chained until you're too weak to fight. Fortunately, that won't be necessary. You drank the water and ate the ham sandwich. They contain a strong sedative and you'll be asleep when I get home with the kids. You'll be pot roast by suppertime. I need to pick up some fresh carrots."

He smiled and left the room. I shook the chains, screamed, and shouted for help. I didn't feel sleepy, thank goodness. What to do? What to do? I remembered the stupid cell phone. I was able to get out of my pocket and turn it on. It had an eighty percent charge and four bars. Time to call 911 and report a residential burglary.

I didn't know the address of the house and the burner phone didn't have GPS tracking. 911 wasn't sending anyone to help.

I called Rico and got a recording. "The number that you have called has been disconnected or is no longer in service." Even if I knew any other phone numbers, I couldn't tell anyone where I was.

I started getting sleepy. I found the video recording icon on the phone and turned it on. Time for a long selfie. I pointed the phone at my face and started this recording. I can't stay awake, so I'm going to finish it now.

If you are seeing and hearing this, then you found the phone and you've already heard my story. I'm going to turn the phone off and put it in my pocket before I pass out. I hope someone sees this message. Someone needs to warn people. I hear people at the door. I hear voices. I am so tired. So tired.

Remember... if it looks too good... to be true, it's...

Too Good to be True

JANICE RIDER
The Sailor Next Door

JANICE RIDER (she/her) is an emerging writer with a background in zoology, conservation, and education. Janice has stories published in The North American Jules Verne Society's Extraordinary Visions, Speculation Publications' Beach Shorts, and Word Balloon Books' Beware the Bugs! Her work was also featured in Critical Blast's The Devil You Know Best. For fun, Janice runs a drama club for children and youth. Three of her plays for youth have been published.

A new neighbor moved into Abigail's empty house at the beginning of the winter. I can't believe that Abigail is gone. She deserved to live forever. I will never forget her kindness to my son, Simon. He is a sensitive child with a big heart, and Abigail hit it off with him from the first day I brought him home from the hospital.

A former tailor occupies the space Abigail filled with her laughter and artwork. And get this, his name is Denim Taylor! He is a fastidious man and has had renovators in to bring order to Abigail's creative chaos. As a result of his former livelihood, he designs and sews his own personal wardrobe. I have to admit that his apparel is a credit to his expertise and sense of style. Although Mr. Taylor is a slight person of less than modest height, he indulges in a large ego and talks of having defeated "seven with one blow." He even wears a golden buckled belt on special occasions imprinted with the words "Seven At One Blow." When asked the particulars of this triumph, he just winks solemnly and refuses to divulge any more. He also claims to have married well, but having tired of a wife whose illustrious birth she continually threw in his face, Denim Taylor got a divorce, and with it, an advantageous settlement. Then, he set off for the bright lights of our city. He is now a man about town.

I wouldn't miss Miss Abigail quite as keenly if Mr. Taylor was compassionate, but he's a little too self-impressed to be aware of the susceptibilities of others. As the protective mother of a son who sees the world differently from others, I fear that our new neighbor will create dissonance in our once harmonious neighborhood.

I left my life as a tailor for better things, and I left my position as a king, divorcing my queen when she told me that, had she known about my lowly birth, she would never have married me at all. A man like me has his pride, and mine would not permit me to debase myself by staying with such a one as my wife, no matter how beautiful she happened to be. Leaving my castle in Germany and its opulence was no hardship. I am, by nature, an adventurer, and my wits served to ensure that I left my queen far wealthier than I had come to her. In the past, my innate intelligence came to my aid whenever I was in need, and it will continue to do so. I have faced opponents large and small. This city, Toronto, is my latest adventure. The culture and fine dining here suit me well. As I have an eye for fashion, I set up a high-end clothing store, *Elegant Ensemble*, and hired employees to run it for me. How I love being the boss of my own business! The only clothes I wear now are my own, and that's only because no one else can replicate my fine stitches. Call me a perfectionist if you like. The truth is, looking good matters.

On the first warm day heralding the coming of spring, I went out into the backyard with my son, Simon. At eleven years of age, he was starting to look awkward, a bit out of step with his long arms and legs. Together, we studied all the plants we'd cultivated over the years and searched for signs that they were preparing to leaf out. Simon is the youngest of my sons and the only one who shares my interest in gardening. On rainy days, he collects earthworms that have been flooded out of their holes in the ground onto pavement and places them in the soil of our yard. When the sun shines, he crouches beside flowers to watch as bees forage for nectar and cheers on ants moving large pieces of debris about. He is a serious boy and not nearly as gregarious as his two older brothers, who are forever out and about with friends.

While we were inspecting plants, I glanced up and spotted Denim Taylor regarding us through binoculars from his kitchen window. The gall of that man! Eventually, he strolled out into his own yard and over to the fence dividing our properties and raised himself on tiptoe to peer over. "What are you two about?"

My son lifted his head to examine Denim's sharp, gray eyes. "We're looking for beginnings," he explained.

Our new neighbor raised his eyebrows.

"Things start again in the spring," Simon elaborated.

"Do they indeed? What are you going to do about that anthill in the middle of your lawn?"

"Well," Simon said, considering his response, "I'll probably put out the odd bit of food for the ants and watch their comings and goings as I usually do."

"That mound is unsightly. I want you to get rid of it!"

At this point, I intervened. "Mr. Taylor, this is our property, not yours. Please refrain from telling us what to do!"

"There are property standards; bylaws, you know. I want to look out my kitchen window and see well maintained premises around me, not anthills. If I wanted anthills, I'd return to the country, Mrs. Delia Maple."

"Our yard and the living things in it are well loved," I shot back, feeling the heat rising to my face. "It nurtures a variety of trees and shrubs, along with plenty of perennials that produce beautiful flowers."

Denim Taylor harrumphed and stomped back into his house as Simon's eyes filled with tears. "I want Miss Abigail back," he whispered.

"I know you do," I said, wrapping an arm around Simon and pulling him close. "I do, too."

As the spring progressed, our neighbor brought in a landscape architect and turned his backyard into a sterile space. Denim Taylor removed all of his lawn and replaced it with artificial turf, aka fake grass. Simon was appalled and agonized over what to do. I told him that, given the kind of man our tailor next door was, it would be best to avoid him.

The next thing Denim did was pepper our mailbox with suggestions as to how we could improve the look of our property, including taking down our bird feeders and baths, and draining our pond so that ducks wouldn't defecate on his splendid turf! The man is impossible! On a daily basis, I have to beg my husband not to go over and "have it out with 'Venomous Denim.'"

I am a fastidious man. Nothing irks me more than seeing complete disarray, and yet, that's what I see every time I look into the Maples' yard! My neighbors' lax standards verge on utter negligence! They allow dandelions and ants to flourish. Woodpeckers called flickers perch in their trees and drum on the side of my house. If I don't develop a severe case of tinnitus, it will be a miracle! The Maples have a pond which attracts ducks, and sometimes they make messy, odoriferous deposits on *my* lawn! Their flowers attract a myriad of bees and flies! Upon inquiring with one of the city's bylaw regulations officers, I was sorry to learn that there is a "certain amount" of leniency built into the law to accommodate "different ways of relating to home environs." As for that son of theirs, "Simpleton Simon," he glares at me every time he sees my face. I glare right back. The boy should be taught some manners.

The other day, I was reclining after a day of hard work - I fired one of my employees for not applying himself with enough diligence. Suddenly, I sensed that I was being watched. There was a magpie perched on the fence that separates my yard from the Maples' yard, but he was engaged with wiping his beak. I scanned the fenceline until I noticed a knot hole. A dark, bright eye was examining me. Simon! Rather than pulling his intrusive eye away when my eyes met his, he continued to observe me for a while longer before leaving his position. The young lad dislikes me, and my feeling for him is one of strong animosity. But how to defeat an enemy in a place where individual rights are protected?

Mr. Taylor doesn't like me. I don't like him either. Mom says to ignore him and mind my own business. The truth is, I can't. I think I could learn to hate Mr. Taylor! He thinks he knows everything. Nobody knows everything. He also thinks I'm foolish and simple. Actually, I'm very bright, but I do see the world differently, and I know that Mr. Taylor isn't the only one who sees me as foolish. Although I don't trust Mr. Taylor, my heart sometimes leads me into dangerous territory. That's what happened today.

I was outside watching the ants and warning them to keep an eye out for flickers because flickers eat ants on a regular basis. From over the fence, Mr. Taylor's face appeared, his well-trimmed, salt and pepper goatee resting on the top rail. "Young Simon," he said in a sugary voice, which didn't in the least deceive me, "there is a mouse in my house. As you know, I am averse to rodents on my premises. I believe you could catch the critter humanely and take him to a nearby field."

The man's face was not as disingenuous as he believed it to be, but he did abhor mice, and I didn't want him killing one, so I agreed to come over with a live trap to help him get it out of the house. When I walked through his front door, I knew I had made a mistake. Mr. Taylor didn't even try to disguise his look of malice. "Young man, I find your continual intrusions on my privacy a distraction; therefore, I must insist that you keep your eyes to yourself on your side of the fence. If you do not, I shall find ways and means to kill some of the creatures whom you are so fond of; for instance, I may place poisonous liquid ant baits just on the other side of your fence, or I may place mouse traps out to kill pesky rodents. I may even use illegal means to eradicate things, means which will not be discovered by anyone because I have a talent for eradicating enemies without bringing harm on myself. I have defeated giants using such means, and you are just a boy! Do you understand?"

I did understand, and as I stood in front of 'Venomous Denim,' I felt my eyes moisten before tears began to spill down my cheeks. My helplessness and vulnerability in that moment made me feel ashamed. I turned and left his house, the house which had once belonged to my friend and ally, Miss Abigail, a home in which I had once felt so welcome and loved.

It was ever so tempting to nurture my grudge against 'Venomous Denim' and feed my anger and fear with resentment, but then I thought about the collaboration that makes ants masters of remodeling the world and decided to remodel Mr. Taylor. Remodeling people is possible, you know. It just requires the right mindset. Yes! I was up for a challenge!

I began by enlisting the aid of a friend, Magpie Max. Magpies are bold, brave, and intelligent. They also love shiny objects, so I asked Max to steal something bright and precious that belonged to Mr. Taylor. While our neighbor's kitchen window was open five days later, Max stole one gold cufflink from the window ledge where Mr. Taylor had put his cufflinks down prior to rolling up his sleeves to make supper. Max's approach and theft were stealthy, but once he had hold of the cufflink, he fluttered his wings loudly before flying away. Mr. Taylor's face was a picture when he realized what had happened! He spent the rest of the day vainly searching for the cufflink. My family and I saw him out in the park next door, circling round and round while keeping his gaze fastened to the ground. When he had worked himself up into an emotional lather, I slipped out of the house to join him in the park.

"May I help you find something, Mr. Taylor?" I inquired solicitously.

Without even looking up, he said, "One of your audacious magpies has stolen a gold cufflink of mine. Do you know the brand? It is Brahmfeld and Gutruf! That small item is worth thousands of dollars!"

"Couldn't you just replace it?"

"Never! They don't make cufflinks like that anymore!"

"I may have a solution," I said.

Mr. Taylor looked at me. I kept my expression innocent and friendly. I have practice at pretending based on the way people often treat me, even if my emotions do sometimes override my ability to dissemble. "In the morning I'll have the ants look for it."

"What? You're not just a fool! You're delusional!"

"Tomorrow morning is a Saturday. You and I have the day off. Let's see if I'm delusional then, shall we?"

Saturday morning dawned. I didn't let on to my parents or my brothers what the day had in store for me and our arrogant neighbor. Fortunately, they were all involved with various projects of their own. The weather was warm, and the sun was bright. Ants revel in days such as this. Mr. Taylor arrived at ten o'clock on the dot, and I invited him to crouch with me beside the anthill in my backyard. With great reluctance, but with just a touch of curiosity, Mr. Taylor crouched beside me, perfectly outfitted in a gorgeous suit complete with bow tie and fancy shoes. I smiled at how incongruous he appeared.

To communicate with the world around me, I have to relax and clear my mind of any vexations. I imagined myself alone in the space of the yard. Soon ants swarmed to the top of the anthill, and I envisioned them heading out into the park to search for the cufflink. As they headed out in one long, dark line towards the fence on the edge of the park, I glanced at my neighbor. His eyes were definitely rounder than they'd been when he first arrived. "Now what?" he asked, just a trifle less confident than I'd ever seen him before.

"We wait," I said.

I have to give Mr. Taylor credit. He has the patience to wait. Most people I know don't. He was forced, after a time, to sit down on the ground. After two hours, just as the sun hit its zenith, a bunch of ants appeared from under the fence, struggling to carry something heavy. "My cufflink," 'Venomous Denim' breathed.

When Mr. Taylor began to rise, I grabbed his arm and urged him to sit again. "You don't want to step on any ants." Half an hour later, they'd navigated the cufflink over to me. I handed it to my neighbor, who took it from me wordlessly and left for his own home.

I saw Denim Taylor in our yard today, and I had the intuitive sense that my son, Simon, had something to do with his presence there. Mothers are like that - intuitive, I mean. Our neighbor was crouching beside our anthill and watching the ants with a certain fascination. I was astounded! Why the interest? After watching the ants for a bit, he wandered over to our flower beds, where he spent some time contemplating the bees and flies.

Simon appeared at my side, manifesting as unexpectedly as an apparition, a *Chocolove* chocolate bar in his hand.

"Mom, you won't mind if I go out to see Mr. Taylor, will you?" Simon didn't wait for an answer. This is not an uncommon thing for him to do if he fears that I will not respond in the affirmative. He left my side and bounded out the back door onto our deck.

Denim Taylor heard his feet on the wooden boards and turned. Simon held his chocolate bar aloft and queried, "Want some chocolate, Mr. Taylor?" I knew what would happen next. An offer of chocolate comes before Simon enters upon the topic of pollination of cocoa flowers. Small flies are the pollinators of the plant which we need to produce chocolate, and they are Simon's way of planting the seed of kindness for all flies in unsuspecting hearts. Days of watching Mr. Taylor through the knot hole in the fence had made Simon aware of his appetite for high-end chocolate. I smiled. My son, what a boy!

It's a strange thing. I have had many adventures and solved many dilemmas, and I consider myself a man of the world, but never has my worldview been upended, until now. It's Simon's fault. I've discovered that he is neither foolish, nor delusional, but he is dangerous. Because of him, I regret killing "seven at one blow." It now seems like a mean, despicable thing to have killed seven flies and blown this accomplishment out of all proportion to its real magnitude *and* without any regard for the flies. Of course, it did raise my worth in people's estimation. I will keep the belt to remind myself of where I've come from, but I will wear it no longer! Simon and I share an ability to navigate difficult circumstances in unique ways. I have never been a father, but going forward, I see that I could become a friend.

My son, Simon, and our new neighbor are growing close. Denim Taylor stooped to buying a pair of jeans and a T-shirt. The T-shirt has "I Stop for Things that Bug You!" stitched on the front in lovely, looping letters in vivid colors. Of course, the stitching is Denim's. Seven flies, a magpie, and lots of ants are sewn onto the front of the T-shirt, too.

Our neighbor is planning to remove his faux lawn and replace it with living, growing plants next spring! Simon has wrought a powerful change on Mr. Taylor! If Simon keeps having this kind of impact on the world, it is bound to improve! Of course, mothers always see the beauty in their children and know that they will make a difference.

DAVE D'ALESSIO
ISSUNBOUSHI
THE EXTERMINATOR

DAVE D'ALESSIO is an ex-industrial chemist, ex-TV engineer, and ex-award winning animator currently masquerading as a social scientist. His more than thirty publications include the Sidewise Award finalist The Twenty-Year Reich and Samurai Storyteller, his collection of essays on the writing lessons to be learned from anime and manga. He lives near an Ikea and enjoys assembling furniture.

Even in the 21st century, Issunboushi dressed in traditional samurai style: a dark gray *kamishono* jacket and lighter gray flowing *hakama* trousers. He tied a top knot in his hair and wore a sheathed katana on his belt. But as unusual as his appearance was, Manhattan's fine citizens generally overlooked him—possibly because he was only one inch tall.

The L train he was riding squealed to a stop, and Issunboushi laid hold of the trouser cuff of the man standing next to him. As the man stepped off he unwittingly hoisted Issunboushi across the gap between subway car and platform. Landing lightly, the inch-high samurai scrambled for the escalator, avoiding the oblivious feet of his fellow pedestrians.

At ground level Issunboushi looked up and down 14th Street, carefully eyeing the people around him. As on every other day since he'd arrived from Kyoto, he saw no sign of his quarry. "You can find anything in New York but what you're looking for," he muttered.

Cold, wet sandpaper rubbed across the back his neck. He spun, drawing his katana, and looked up into a bearded, mustachioed face four times his height.

"Yip! Yip!" A monster pink tongue lapped Issunboushi's face, wetting his head with slobber.

The dog had a master, a tall, slender woman. Her skin was dark, very dark, and her hair tied up in a topknot much like Issunboushi's except she had not shaved the front of her scalp. "Oh, it's some kind of toy," she said, plucking him up by the jacket. "It's really detailed."

Issunboushi waved his katana angrily. "I am no toy! Put me down!"

She held him close to her face. "Wow, it must be radio controlled or something." She looked around quickly and slipped him into her sweater pocket.

Kidnapped! And held in the dark! Issunboushi ground his teeth and meditated on the samurai virtue of politeness. Plucking a small samurai from the ground and depositing him in a pocket was almost unbearably rude, but so was cutting his way out with his sword.

After a brisk walk the woman ran up a short flight of stairs and unlocked a door. The pocket bobbed as she jogged up more stairs, nearly making Issunboushi motion sick in her sweater. She unlocked another door. Dishes clattered. A tea pot whistled.

She pulled him from her pocket and into the light of a studio apartment that was small even by the standards of New York City. It was crowded with the accessories of a life being fully lived, piles of worn books and manga, an ancient laptop with a cracked lid, and simple stick furniture better suited to a third-hand shop. And there was cloth in all quantities from swatches to bolts, propped in every corner and on top of every horizontal surface (except the stove top, of course).

Putting him on a table next to a steaming mug of ... deep breath ... black tea, she said, "Well. You're pretty amazing, aren't you?"

Issunboushi laid his hand on the hilt of his katana. "I would say so, yes, although it may sound less than modest. Perhaps 'interesting' would be a better word."

Her eyes widened and she looked around. "I could have sworn we were far enough away. Radio control can only go so far..."

"I am from Japan and we manufacture the finest remotely-controlled playthings in the world. However, I am not one of them." Issunboushi was tired of being treated like a toy and he had miles to go before he slept. He bowed. "I thank you for your hospitality, but now I must continue the quest that brought me to this city."

"Oh, please don't go away angry. I'm sorry," she said. "My name is Carole Livingston, and I'm on a quest, too, to be a famous clothing designer." She waved a hand around. "You can tell, right? Until then I wait tables and work in a bookstore and do whatever else I have to do to, okay? And this is ..." She picked up the dog, who nuzzled her. "... Ippudo, okay? He's just being friendly."

Returning courtesy for courtesy, Issunboushi sheathed his katana and bowed. "I am called Issunboushi."

Her nose – not quite as tall as he was – crinkled. "*Issun...* that's 'one something,' right? And isn't *Boushi* 'hat'? You're Mister One Hat?"

"One object is '*ittsu*,'" he said. "In English my name means 'One Sun Boy.' A *sun* is a unit of length of about one and a quarter inch." His parents were very loving but not very imaginative. "And now, as I am neither at nor in your service, I shall no longer impose on your hospitality." He bowed politely and strode toward the corner of the table, preparing himself to scramble down the leg.

Ippudo wiggled happily and licked Carole's face. She said, "You can go if you like, but if you want a place to stay that's warm and dry, I wouldn't mind your company. I've watched lots of anime but never met anyone from Japan before."

Issunboushi was going to say no. No one, let alone a samurai, could enjoy being picked up like a rag doll and unceremoniously deposited in a pocket, and he was not very happy with this Carole Livingston person.

But he'd already learned that New York's weather was not so kind as Kyoto's. The streets were filthy and more than once he'd been reduced to eating garbage. He counter-offered, "So long as there is something I can do to contribute to the household, then we may share. Does that agreement seem fair?"

"Fair," she said. She extended a finger to him and he tapped it with his fist.

By day Carole went to her various jobs and Issunboushi slid down the fire escape to resume his quest. He caught the subway at 1st Avenue and some days rode east into Brooklyn and on others west to Union Square, transferring to another subway car carrying him to someplace else he hadn't yet searched.

And each evening he returned to the small apartment to sup on two grains of rice or a black-eyed pea. At night they stayed up, drinking horrible American tea as Ippudo snored lightly in a padded shoebox. They spoke of many things and sometimes watched inane shows on Carole's TV, which was so old it had a picture tube.

One night Carole said, "Issunboushi, how does an inch-high samurai come to be?"

Issunboushi resisted the temptation to say, 'When a Mommy and a Daddy love each other very much ...' It would have been rude to his host. "After many childless years my mother prayed to Ojizo-san, the god who looks after babies. She asked for a baby of her own, saying she would accept any child at all even if he was only one inch tall."

"Oh."

He said, "Ojizo-san is very kind, but sometimes he is not very wise." He pondered that. "It is lonely, but I cannot be the only one."

"That makes sense. People pray for all sorts of things all the time." She yawned. "Rest well, Inch-high Samurai."

Saturdays Carole tended bar at night, so she invested the day in cleaning. She had a small single-unit washer/dryer that would have been right at home in Kyoto and a kitchen faucet that spewed slightly rusty water suitable for washing dishes if enough soap was involved; both were put to work.

Obligated to contribute to the household chores, Issunboushi declared war on hard-to-clean dust bunnies. Her bed was elevated, clearing floor space beneath it for a work table and sewing machine, and the forest of furniture legs plunked into the cheap carpet defied vacuuming. Issunboushi waded in with both hands, attacking accumulated lint as though it was the enemy of his daimyo.

Across the room in the kitchenette Carole shrieked and Ippudo yipped.

Issunboushi ran to them, katana drawn. "What is it?"

"It" was a monster. It stood as high as his knee, and had six legs and two antennae that made it as long as he was tall. Its torso was covered with scales, armoring it against the dangers of war, and it was armed with a ferocious jaw. Here was a foe worthy of his sword! Issunboushi held his katana low and stamped his foot. "Here! Meet my challenge, dragon," he shouted.

The dragon did no such thing. It turned, wiggling its tail from side to side, and scuttled toward the darkness under the refrigerator.

It was an act of cowardice Issunboushi could not abide. He sprang forward and slashed the beast's legs, severing all three on one side. As the dragon scrabbled in a circle, he drove his katana through its eye, ending the duel.

"It's a silverfish," Carole said. "They're all over these older buildings. I only yelled because it startled me."

Issunboushi peered under the refrigerator. "There are more back there. Shall I slay them or spare them?"

Carole said, "They eat books and cloth and stuff like that."

She needed say no more. The silverfish scattered and scampered, but met their fates at the edge of Issunboushi's blade.

Carole knelt, looking down at him. "Can you do that all the time?" she said.

"Of course not." He swung the katana, flinging silverfish ichor aside. "There have been battles that lasted all day, but few of the warriors in them fought the entire time. I would need to pause for nourishment, and to rest and sharpen my sword."

"Let's you and me make a deal," Carole said, and in the moments that followed the firm of Livingston and Company, Organic Exterminators, was born. The brochure Carole designed and ran off at a Duane Reade pharmacy promised, "100% Poison- and Pesticide-Free Eradication of All Household Pests!"

Flyers went up on local bulletin boards and within a day they had a client. Two floors down in Carole's building Mrs.

Wysocker owned a spaniel. "I ran him around Stuyvesant Park. He likes to do his business in the flower beds." Wolfschnagel, the spaniel, scratched miserably. Mrs. Wysocker said, "I'd just flea bomb the whole place but my asthma couldn't bear it."

Issunboushi overlooked Mrs. Wysocker's exclamation of disbelief when he was introduced to her. "Let us proceed," he said, drawing his katana.

The common flea was no taller than Issunboushi's calf, but their tough carapaces meant he had to keep his sword sharp and his strokes powerful. And the way they could jump! He cursed to himself and thought dark thoughts of Kyonshi, the hopping vampire, as one by one they fell to his blade.

He stopped in the middle of the room, breathing heavily, sword held high for the downward stroke. There was a noise, the pat of a flea landing... behind him! He spun, slashing the katana horizontally.

The flea jumped squarely on him. Issunboushi's katana plunged into its thorax, a killing blow. There was the sting of a bite, but the flea had bitten its last.

"Is that all of them?" Carole said.

Issunboushi cleaned and sheathed his sword. "That is all of them." He would undoubtedly itch horribly tomorrow, but tomorrow's winds would blow tomorrow.

Tomorrow's winds blew an ocean of calamine lotion into Issunboushi's life, but also some welcome news. "Mrs. Wysocker paid us," Carole said, holding up a check. "And she's recommended us to Mrs. Robinson on the fifth floor. Her kids came home from school with head lice."

Issunboushi thought darkly of another day lost to his quest. The lice suffered his wrath.

Employment opportunities followed as the reputation of Livingston and Company, Organic Exterminators, grew. Issunboushi annihilated ants, terminated termites, and disemboweled beetles with equal efficiency.

The work was rewarding. Carole paid her rent and saved money for her fashion school tuition. Issunboushi's futon, previously a worn-out glove, was replaced by a silk handkerchief. A maker of doll clothing was brought in to fashion him a new kimono and two sets of hakama heavy enough to protect him against bites and splinters.

He and Ippudo grew to be friends. Issunboushi fashioned a proper spear from a bamboo skewer and a wedge of tuna fish can; he climbed to Ippudo's back and the dog carried him about like the noblest of steeds as Carole laughed and clapped her hands in delight.

When Carole had to be at one of her other jobs Issunboushi continued roaming the city, searching. He found two Shinto shrines – one in Queens, the other in the Bronx – and visited them, not only to pray but also to watch the other people there. Some were migrants, some visitors, some Americans raised to Shinto; he felt confident approaching none of them, and his quest remained fruitless.

One dark, rainy day he sat in the apartment's window, looking out at the street below. This was New York, where one could find anything. But thus far he had not found that for which he searched, had found no trace of its spoor, no whiff of its scent. If he could not find it here, could he find it anywhere? What chance did an inch-high samurai have in a world of sixty-inch people?

That night Carole brought home a newspaper. "Did you see?" she said. "It's the job of a lifetime!"

Public School 19.

Kitchen.

Cockroaches.

Seven other exterminators attended the emergency School Board meeting, some from companies so large even Issunboushi had seen their ads on Carole's TV. They brought crates of equipment, kennels full of trained dogs, vats of chemicals certified 100% non-toxic to children and human beings. Carole brought her testimonials, her 100% poison- and pesticide-free guarantee, and a cost estimate one-third the size of the others.

The Board said, "You have twenty-four hours." None of them could bear to have their children at home longer than that.

By day the school's kitchen was shining bright metal and well-scrubbed tile floors, but it was also full of food, staffed by overworked and underpaid employees, and, well, in New York City, where there were seven million people and roughly one thousand times as many cockroaches. The humans fought the roaches to a draw, a parity that would hold until it came to nuclear weapons. When the roaches got the bomb, it would be all over.

Carole, Issunboushi, and Ippudo went in at night, since that was when the enemy would come out to do battle. That was the way of the cockroach: Run under cover of the night, run for cover in the light.

Issunboushi straddled Ippudo, carrying his spear upright and his katana in its sheath. The pup danced; it felt Carole's excitement and wanted please his master.

"Go get them, boys." Carole opened the door exactly one puppy-width.

Issunboushi rode his noble steed to battle.

There were only the glowing red lights of equipment plugged in but not turned on to see by, but there was a scuttling scrape in the distance. The enemy was that way! Issunboushi pulled Ippudo's head around toward the sound. "Go, my friend," he whispered. "Fly!"

The pup galloped toward the nearest enemy. Issunboushi held his spear high, and thrust with all his might when he caught a glimpse of the foe. He aimed for the roach's weak point, the back of the neck.

He slew one, then another, and another, Ippudo carrying him to where he could strike. His spear was coated with gore, the pads of Ippudo's paws caked with lymph.

As the battle raged the roaches sensed something brutal here. They scuttled for their holes, the dark, safe crannies where they hid their egg cases.

There was no room for Ippudo in those holes. When they found one Issunboushi slid down from the pup's back, unsheathed his katana, and went on alone. In the roaches' lairs he hacked their eyes and plunged his blade deep into their vitals. And when the roaches were dead he slashed open their egg cases, destroying the generations to come.

It was war and so it was brutal. Roaches ran for their lives, but he tracked them down, stabbing and slashing. Sweat dripped into his eyes and his katana grew dull from the hard work it did.

In the last hole he met an emperor, a cockroach that, when it reared up on its hind legs, stood twice as tall as Issunboushi, a king among roaches if not actually their King. It was strong and heavy and quick on its six feet. But Issunboushi had the katana, and the knowledge of how it was used. The fight was even, and it was to the death.

At the end Issunboushi pulled himself from under the King's corpse. He pushed his exhaustion aside to perform his final act of chemical-free extermination: He slashed his dull, stained katana across the nest's egg sacks again and again, until they were obliterated.

Too spent to climb, he clung to Ippudo's leg as the pup trotted back to his master.

"Issunboushi, are you okay?" Carole's voice was full of concern.

All he said was, "It is done." He slumped to the ground to rest, but when his eyes closed they stayed closed for three days.

When he woke, Carole helped him bathe in one of her thimbles. Warmth from the water soaked into his bones and put strength back into his muscles. For a few moments he could pretend he was back in Kyoto.

Eventually, Carole said, "The school board is giving us a special plaque and award for what we've done. Well, what you did."

"Ippudo is a valiant steed and bore me with great honor," he said, giving credit where it was due.

She wrinkled her nose in her usual endearing manner. "He stank so bad I had to give him a bath. He hates that. Well, anyway, they'd like you to say a few words. I think they're more interested in seeing you're actually real," she said. "We can skip it if you don't want to do it."

"No, it would be fitting to accept the honor," he said.

The school board met for a dinner meeting in PS 19's temporarily vermin-free cafeteria. To Issunboushi the food was more than adequate: There was a pea so fresh and sweet he ate almost half of it. And while he indulged in neither the bitter coffee nor the dreadful tea, there was clean water from a bottle.

The chairwoman of the school board went to great lengths to hide the fact she could see little without her glasses. "And so, we owe so much to Lowenstein and Company ..."

"Livingston," Carole said. The audience tittered appropriately.

"...and we are grateful for their service to us." She called Carole up. "Would you care to address us, Ms. Lowenstein?"

Carole said, "Yes, thank you. My name is Livingston. But you really want to hear from my partner Issunboushi, don't you?"

Issunboushi strode across the table to the microphone. As he walked he heard the usual remarks he had be subject to all his life: "Look, he's so short!" "He can't be much more than an inch high!" "How can there be a person so small?" The comments were in English here, but they did the same injury to his pride as when he heard them in Kyoto.

Pride injured or not, he spoke into the microphone. "I thank you. In truth it was nothing, and you owe me nothing."

"He means you owe the company," Carole said. There was more laughter.

Issunboushi would not be put off by Carole's byplay. "I have a question for you, if I may. I have explored the streets and subways of this city most extensively, and can say with truth that I have never ceased to be amazed by what I find.

"But, for all my searching through this, the city where all the world knows you can find anything, there is one thing I have been unable to locate. It is long past time I was married, so if you would be so kind as to tell me where there are inch-high women I may court, I would be most grateful."

Their laughter was a cruel answer, although also a sufficient one.

Issunboushi slid down the table's leg, his back stiff and his lips pressed together lest he respond to insult with insult. He climbed atop Ippudo and urged him forward. These New Yorkers, in this city where you could find anything except inch-high brides or a modicum of respect, found the sight utterly hilarious.

Together they trotted from the dining room, leaving the mockery behind.

Carole caught up with them on the sidewalk outside. "Please come back, Issunboushi," she said. She bowed in apology. "They meant no harm."

"What is meant is of no importance. What is important is what is done," Issunboushi said. "I wish you well, as you are and will always be my friend, but it is clear I must search elsewhere."

She knelt over him one last time, Ippudo wiggling in her arms. "This job paid for my schooling, so I'll always be grateful." A giant tear splashed Issunboushi's sandals. "Next time you're here I'll design you a new suit, a Livingston original."

He bowed. "Thank you very much. Your hospitality meant a great deal to me." He would not promise to return; it was a large world and he could never know where he might find a suitable bride. "Farewell."

Issunboushi scurried to the subway. At Penn Station he clung to the side of a rolling suitcase being pulled onto the Amtrak, and hung on as the case was lifted into an overhead rack. A nearby jacket served as a bed, and he drew the cloth around himself, almost able to ignore the feeling of humiliation and the sense of loss.

"Los Angeles," he muttered. "Or maybe Seattle." Both cities had large Japanese populations. Surely among them there was a mother who had also prayed to Ojizo-san for a child, even if the child was only an inch high.

ALLISTER NELSON
Gambling
with
Winter

ALLISTER NELSON is a Pushcart Prize-nominated, queer, neurodivergent author whose work has appeared in The British Fantasy Society, Apex Magazine, Eternal Haunted Summer, Renewable Energy World, Frontiers in Health Communication, The National Science Foundation, Luna Station Quarterly, Prismatica, and many other venues. By day, she's a senior technical writer/editor. By night, she dabbles in prose and poems. Find her work at allisternelson.com.

It was the taste of blood and snow on his lips that awoke him. He lay still in the first frost, letting it trace fern-like patterns over his body. Stirring, Jack clutched his staff and rose with a Chesire grin, whiskey in hand from the night before. "*Now where was I?*" he said. "*Oh yes,*" Jack smiled as a young woman passed by. He sidled over to her, cheeks red from the cold. He pecked her on the cheek furtively. The girl shivered, seeing nothing but a puff of cold air.

When the pine boughs are blanketed in downy snow and the land is ice, and all the world is a winter dream, Jack Frost dances through that eternal portal into the world of Man. Bringing blizzards and mischief, he kisses the cheeks of maidens, perhaps tickles a child's nose, making them blush with cold. He lingers in town squares, drawing sheets of ice across the cobblestones only to laugh as unsuspecting pedestrians slip in snow. And sometimes, weary, the icy trickster seeks shelter inside, tarrying in shops or dozing by the hearthside of mortals' abodes, invisible to all except cats and infants. We may have forgotten him, the Winter King of time immemorial, but old Jack likes it that way.

I watched snow fall through the smudged windowpanes, the heavy flurries chasing passersby through the quaint streets of Old Town Alexandria. They burrowed into their jackets, shielding their heads from the icy onslaught. A few tarried, taking pleasure in the white bliss as smiles danced across their lips. I tapped my fingers on the old oak counter in time to an acoustic rendition of *Lady Greensleeves* by Blackmore's Night that floated from the old speakers overhead, filling the minimally-lit King Street Coffeehouse with its melody.

Business was slow on a Sunday morning like this, with only a few patrons sitting at the antique tables on timeworn barstools and cozy armchairs, sipping their caffeinated confections with contentment. White collars read *The Post* and played table set backgammon while indie girls sat in a ring, discussing something in low voices. Closing my eyes, I inhaled the rich scent of coffee grounds and returned to reading *The Picture of Dorian Grey*, smiling at the thought I was being paid to relax.

"I'll take an iced peppermint latte with crème de menthe, my heart, with extra whipped cream," interrupted a lilting voice. Startled, I slammed my book shut and stood ramrod straight, trying my best to look like an attentive barista.

"Sorry!" I exclaimed.

Golden ringlets fell to his shoulders, framing a sharp-featured pale face and glacial blue eyes. Faint scars gleamed across his cheek and his face was flushed from the cold. He smiled craftily, dressed in a fraying white sweater, knit with snowflakes, leather boots, and torn jeans that hinted at his lean, muscled physique.

I felt as if I had stepped into a bad romance novel.

The customer laughed. "No need to panic, sweetheart, we've all been held captive by Wilde at some point," he smiled merrily, leaning up to the counter. "So, *Miss Suarez*," he said, looking at my nametag, "what pastry do you recommend? They all look so tempting, I can't decide. You see, I have a passion for lemon squares, but scones seem ideal for a winter day like this. And then there's the classic brownie, of course." He gesticulated as he spoke, and I noticed his mismatched gloves, one dun colored and the other velvet, both embroidered with silver thread.

I grinned, coming up with the most expensive dessert. "I'd have to go with the mint leaf fudge squares."

"Ah?" he murmured. "Peppermint and chocolate: the perfect combination. Yes, yes, I shall order a fudge square along with my drink."

"Well then, one iced peppermint latte coming up!" I declared, punching the prices of his order into the cash register. "That will be $6.25."

The customer fished through his pocket, withdrawing a wad of cash and placing it on the counter. "Here we are, with a generous tip for a barista with such impeccable taste in pastries," he said, laughing.

"You're too kind."

I prepared the latte, mixing the crème de menthe, espresso, and milk with the finesse that came with years of experience. Like he said, I added extra whipped cream and finished it off with peppermint shavings, presenting the latte to him in an antique coffee glass with the fudge on a small China plate. Taking his food and drink, he placed them on the bar next to the serving counter and sunk languorously into a stool, sipping the latte with pleasure.

"Mmm, you've got talent. And what a glass! I must say, I love this town; it has such *joie de vivre*, Colonial feel, such personality. It has an old-world charm. I'm especially fond of Old Town in winter when the cobblestones are blanketed in snow and the creams of Washingtonian society slip on the slush and land on their bums. Cosmic justice, I presume, or perhaps nature playing tricks on them."

I leaned against the counter, intrigued. "So, you're not from around here?"

He laughed. "Oh, I have no home, sweetheart, I'm a child of the wind and storms. I wander where I fancy, a resident of everywhere and nowhere all at once."

The crème de menthe must've gotten to his head, I thought, but nodded politely, determined not to insult a paying customer that tipped well.

"And you, Sara?"

"Huh?" I asked, lost in thought.

"From whence do you hail?" he asked with gusto, motioning off into the far distance. "Some distant castle on the sea? A forgotten wasteland abandoned by time?... Idaho?"

I smiled, playing along with him, "I'm actually the heiress to a far distant kingdom of riches and beauty, you see, but my family was overthrown by invaders who banished us to Earth."

"What kind of invaders?"

"Molepeople."

"Nasty brutes."

I laughed, and we began to talk, of distant places, of men and dreams. The stranger would pause thoughtfully to sip his latte, eyes searching the room as he drank in the sights and smells. A spell seemed to settle over the coffeehouse as the snowstorm grew feral, gales rattling the windows. The old building creaked, dark wood, bricks, and iron grinding against each other as icy cold seeped into the room thanks to the centuries-old walls. The remaining customers looked around with wild eyes, scuffling out the door to return to their toasty warm dwellings and heated cars.

Meanwhile, I set about conquering the cold drafts, excusing myself from the stranger and approaching the raised brick hearth behind the counter. Opening the glass frames, I piled a few logs into the fireplace, adding a bushel of birch bark tinder I'd collected from the old tree out back in the coffeehouse's lot. I lit a match and tossed it onto the pile, watching the smoldering tinder grow brighter as I fed them air with the bellows. I grinned as flames licked the wood, white-hot warmth radiating from the hearth and warming the dimly lit room.

I returned to the sole customer, surprised to find him grimacing mildly.

"What's wrong?"

"Nothing, I just... I enjoy the chill air. I've never been much of a fan of fire."

"Hmm, well, you know, I can do a few tricks with the flames that you'd like."

He cocked his brow. "Like what?"

I smiled. "Watch this." Grabbing a handful of powder coffee creamer from behind the counter, I hurled them into the flames. They burst into small sparks above the fire, starry and dazzling.

The stranger laughed heartily. I bowed.

"I must admit, that was amusing," he said, watching the flames lick the wood hungrily. The fire was reflected in his clear eyes, tinting them red. "Still, I'm no friend of flames. Give me the cold air over a cozy, warm hearth any day, I say! Something about the snow invigorates the spirit." He nibbled off a corner of the mint leaf fudge, mismatched gloves still on even though it was warm and toasty now with the fire roaring.

"I can see where you're coming from, you know," I pondered. "Not liking practical weather."

"Really?" he smiled crookedly, knowing.

"Yep. I love being outside during summer thunderstorms, getting soaked by torrents of rain. The water chills me but drives me wild at the same time - you should have seen me two summers ago. It was the last day of summer school and there was a humongous storm - my friend and I went wild, dancing in the rain as the lightning shot overhead! Then we had to take the final soaking wet, though. I was sitting in a pool of water from my own clothes for over an hour."

He laughed. "So, you're not afraid of being hit by lightning, then?"

"Nope! The risk makes it even more exciting."

He eyed me oddly, as if trying to discern something. Consciously, I turned my back to him and tended to the hearth, using the poker to turn the logs.

Days turned into weeks, weeks turned to months, and I began to discern that my customer wasn't mortal. We spent days creating crazy confections in the oven and out-barista-ing each other, then nights going on dates to the best spots in Old Town Alexandria.

Finally, I had the courage to ask.

"So, you're Jack Frost?"

"Bazinga."

"So, what are you? A god?"

"Sprite. Demigod. The son of the winds. Just Jack. January's my time, snow days my game," he said, stirring his sipping chocolate. He winked at me, and I felt my cheeks flush. He laughed like a bell. "Exactly. Watching blushes spread across girls' faces when I kiss them. Obviously, I have the best job in the world. Who else gets to travel the world, pressing lips with the cutest gals this old earth has to offer? Hooded crow on my shoulder, we fly together looking for adventure. I've bunked with Norwegian oil riggers, sailed seas with whalers in Alaska. Wherever the cold goes, I go. Come summertime, I vacation. I'm particularly fond of Indonesia, but Australia is my home. It's nothing like the cold fjords of Norway or snowy woods of Sweden where birds are iced on spot to trees. The outback's got Jeeps perfect for roving in, starry skies like the Milky Way I snow-skate across, and the best surfing and snorkeling you could dream of. True, I leave frost on the ground wherever I step, but no one's complaining if a few cane toads freeze over."

I contemplated my options. "Hey, Jack – I turn 18 this week with no plans tying me down. Think you have space on your magic ice beam for me? I'm sick of these seersucker fuckers."

He held me with his mismatched, gloved hands, winked a merry blue eye, and we kissed. He tasted of frosted blueberries, then pulled a magic motorcycle out from behind a bush on the walk we had meandered to by the Lee-Randolph House. "Get on, sweet snowflake. Let's go see the world. Spread mischief and merriment to the wind, winter angel."

And just like that, on a frosted storm, off we flurried – into our happy ending.

HENRY HERZ
The Troll Sons of Gryla

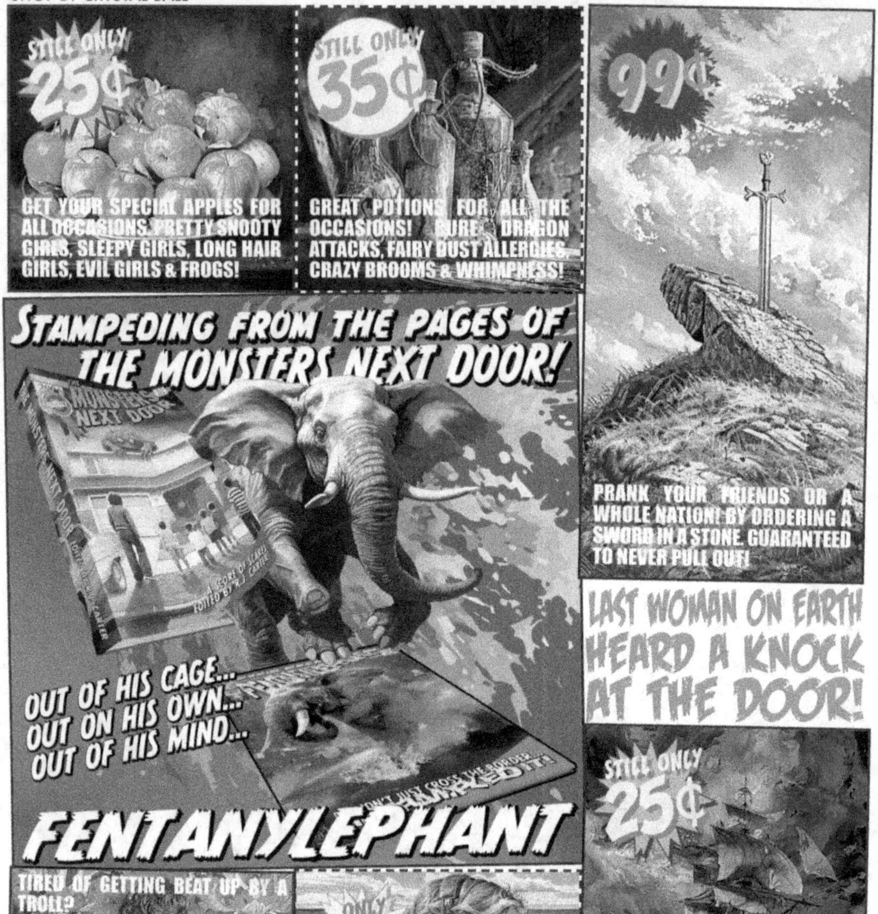

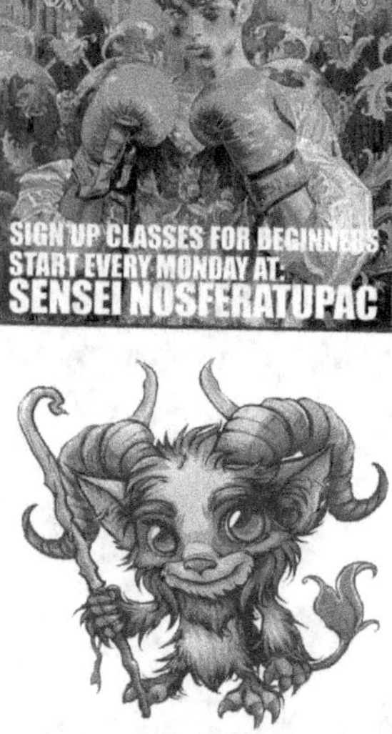

HENRY HERZ's stories will/have appeared in Daily Science Fiction, Weird Tales, Pseudopod, Metastellar, Titan Books, Highlights for Children, Ladybug Magazine, and anthologies from Albert Whitman & Co., Blackstone Publishing, Brigids Gate Press, Air and Nothingness Press, Baen Books, and elsewhere. He's edited seven anthologies and written twelve picture books. www.henryherz.com

'Tis rumored that the wizened troll Grýla ate her first two husbands, which perhaps explains the obsequious nature of her third husband, Leppalúði. Together they trod the stony halls of their dark Icelandic lava fortress, Dimmuborgir. Though gloomy and cold, Dimmuborgir never lacked noise or commotion thanks to the trolls' thirteen full-grown sons, who were so easily distracted and so eager to make mischief that they could only be relied upon to be unreliable.

"Samhain is nearly upon us," said Grýla, glancing out a narrow window at the waxing moon.

"Mannfólk now call it Halloween, dear," replied Leppalúði. "Over the centuries, their language changes and their ways meander like a frog chasing a swarm of flies."

"I trust the wisdom of the old ways," Grýla scoffed. "Come. Let us gather firewood in preparation for the Samhain bonfires."

Leppalúði sighed – softly, so as not to be overheard.

Grýla led her spouse to the entry hall, barefoot steps echoing in the rough-hewn passageways. Empty sconces left the room cloaked in menacing darkness. "Where are all the candles?" Grýla asked, turning in a slow arc. "Has Kertasníkir been at his pranks again?" She frowned. "His foolishness must stop."

"Now, dear," replied Leppalúði, as he laid a gnarled hand on his wife's shoulder. "You know how our sons love to make mischief of one kind and another. And remember, Kertasníkir has a taste for tallow. Have you ever chewed on a candle?"

"Certainly not," said Grýla with a scowl. "You know that the old ways forbid it. I can only eat naughty children that I collect on Christmas."

At Grýla's signal, Leppalúði raised the rusty portcullis. She led her husband through the front gate. Their breath fogged in the Október air.

Grýla's stomach rumbled, startling two crows into flight.

"How is your hunger, dear?" asked Leppalúði.

"Each night, I go to bed without eating anything," replied Grýla, putting her hands on her gurgling belly. "I've had no food since finishing my cauldron of kid stew at miðsumar. I snare fewer and fewer children at each Christmas. Woe is me. You have no idea what it's like to be famished for months at a time."

The corners of Leppalúði's mouth turned down. "Why do you suppose the yule time pickings have thinned?"

"I'm not certain," replied Grýla, shrugging. "But I suspect old Krampus is somehow at the root of this. Rumor has it that he relocated from Merkenstein castle in Austria to the Rock of Dunamase in Ireland. I shall send Gáttaþefur to discover what new deviltry is afoot."

Two weeks later, a travel-stained Gáttaþefur returned from his spying. "Mother, you were right," he exclaimed, wide-eyed. "Krampus abides at Dunamase and has crowned himself Horned God of the Witches. The nearby coven at Sráidbhaile does his bidding."

Grýla lurched to her feet. "I'll wager Krampus sends his witches to snatch Icelandic children on Krampusnacht. No wonder they have become scarcer." She dismissed her son from the great room with a nod.

"Did you hear that?" said Grýla, turning to her husband. "God of the Witches? Such arrogance! But the injury is worse than the insult. If his depredations continue unchecked, there will eventually be no naughty children in Iceland left for me."

Leppalúði nodded, his mouth a tight line. "But Krampus is powerful, all the more so with a coven aiding him. Do you dare oppose him?"

"On the contrary," replied Grýla, rising from a crudely carved stool. "I dare not ignore his threat since I must be able to eat. Nor am I a foe with whom to trifle." She paced the cold stone floor, rubbing a hairy wart on her chin. "Krampus may have thirteen witch minions, but I have thirteen mighty trolls."

Leppalúði reached out a thick arm to calm his wife. "You would involve our sons?"

Grýla swept aside her husband's arm. "Krampus has added pieces to the chessboard, so I shall remove them."

"But how?"

"By kidnapping," replied Grýla, eyes wild. "Each of our sons will snare a witch. Tomorrow is Samhain, when the Veil between this world and the Otherworld thins. Our elvish allies, the álfar, can guide our sons to Ireland. Gluggagægir shall lead the raid. He is the least undisciplined of our brood."

Gluggagægir strode into the room at the mention of his name.

"Snooping again, eh?" observed Leppalúði.

"I prefer to think of it as keeping abreast of developments," replied Gluggagægir with a shrug and a grin.

"Regardless, I have need of your keen eyes, son," said Grýla. "Come, sit."

"Allow me to save us time," replied Gluggagægir, grabbing a worn stool. "I overheard your plan for Krampus's witches. It seems an unnecessary risk to me."

Grýla glared. "How is eating unnecessary?"

"Not that. But instead, avail yourself of the bounty of our lands. I can get you some svið."

"I devour children's heads, not sheep heads," said Grýla.

"What about hákarl?"

"Fermented shark? You miss the point," replied Grýla, shaking her head. "The old ways require that I devour only misbehaving children."

Gluggagægir took a deep breath. "But you could avoid a conflict with Krampus by adopting some… flexibility in your diet. The local hrútspungar is delicious."

Leppalúði winced at his son's recommendation of sour ram's testicles.

Grýla stood. Her look brooked no dissent. "I cleave to the old ways. This Samhain, the álfar will take you through the Veil to Sráidbhaile. Then let the wild hunt start. Bring me back thirteen of Krampus's witches. You are dismissed."

On Samhain Day, Gluggagægir shepherded Kertasníkir, Gáttaþefur, and his other unruly siblings through the dreary lava fields and past Lake Mývatn to one of the álfar's enchanted spots. The journey to a ring of rowan saplings took longer than Gluggagægir expected, his brothers easily distracted by beetles, rabbit kits, and other fresh fare. Each troll carried a large sack, an obsidian dagger and loop of hempen rope at his belt.

Gluggagægir cleared his throat to get his brothers' attention. When that failed, he cuffed a few misshapen heads. "In order to preserve Mother's supply of yule children, we must capture Krampus's witches and lock them in the dungeon at Dimmuborgir."

"But won't the mannfólk of Sráidbhaile notice us?" asked Kertasníkir.

"No. They wear costumes on Samhain. Mother believes that is how Krampus's witches will mingle unremarked in the Sráidbhaile parade," replied Gluggagægir, looking each brother in the eyes. "We shall blend in as well. If we take care, Krampus will not know who has taken his witches and will be unable to retaliate." Gluggagægir bellowed, "We must do our best for Mother!"

His brothers roared their terrible roars and gnashed their terrible teeth, before stepping back at the sudden arrival of three álfar. Human-like in appearance, save for their pale countenance and delicately pointed ears, the álfar wore deep-hooded tunics and breeches of mottled brown and green. "Time is short," declared the tallest of the trio. "Form an inward-facing circle around me and hold hands."

Gluggagægir nodded and his brothers complied.

The other two álfar rhythmically paced around the circle of trolls, one clockwise, the other counterclockwise, chanting a deep-throated huldufólk spell to rend asunder the wan Veil between the worlds. A sudden cold wind rose. Rowan leaves swirled. An unnaturally thick roiling mist engulfed the sixteen.

The leaf rustling faded as if smothered by a thick enveloping blanket. Only the aeolian chanting of the álfar remained as they crossed into the Otherworld. Though they were told the passage would take but a few moments, it seemed to the trolls that they sailed through night and day and in and out of weeks before arriving in a copse of holly on the outskirts of Sráidbhaile.

The trolls shivered. The sound of distant Irish singing carried on the night wind.

"Our thanks," said Gluggagægir, bowing to the álfar. "As you well know, trolls cannot abide the sun. We shall return hence before dawn."

The álfar nodded slightly and vanished.

"The village is that way," said Gluggagægir, pointing in the direction of the singing. "Spread out and good hunting."

At their brother's bidding, the mischievous trolls took separate paths toward town.

Gáttaþefur entered a field of barley, crouching low to avoid being seen, but leaving a trail of trampled grain in his wake. He had nearly crossed the plot when an enticing aroma wafted past the hairy nostrils of his abnormally large nose. *Oi! Is that freshly baked bread?* he thought. Possessed of the keenest sense of smell of all his brothers, Gáttaþefur tracked the scent to a modest bakehouse.

No smoke rose from the chimney and no light shone from the window, offering Gáttaþefur all the invitation he needed. He forced open the flimsy door with one heave of a heavily muscled shoulder and soon busied himself stuffing one loaf of barley bread into his smiling jagged-toothed maw and the remaining loaves into his sack.

Giljagaur clomped toward a nearby farm. The split rail pasture fence broke under his weight as he attempted to vault over it. The sharp crack of snapping wood startled a few head of cattle. He landed in a heap.

Giljagaur picked himself up and shook off the fence fragments. He spied a full-uddered Kerry cow. *Warm milk!* he thought. The thirsty troll gave chase and the cow fled toward the barn. Breathing heavily, Giljagaur entered the building and pulled up short. He smiled at two rows of milk jugs.

Bjúgnakrækir headed straight for town. But he forgot his orders when his gaze fell upon a tall shack with no windows. *What could be in there?* He moved to investigate, soon salivating at the smell of smoke. *A smokehouse!* He forced his way through the door without so much as a knock. His jaw dropped, for from the rafters hung more sausages than the simpleminded troll could count.

Grýla paced to and fro in the great room at Dimmuborgir, her brow furrowed. "What is taking them so long?" she asked Leppalúði. "I fear our impetuous sons are off indulging themselves rather than following orders. I must see this done with my own eyes."

Leppalúði nodded, possessing the wisdom and sense of self-preservation not to gainsay his strong-willed wife on so important a matter.

Grýla bid the álfar bring her to Sráidbhaile.

Grinding her stumpy stained teeth, she raced through the countryside, gathering up the unruly trolls with a series of increasingly agitated ear pulls, rump kicks, and head cuffs. Grýla's face flushed redder with each son, for while some hefted full sacks, none held a captured witch. She marched them to a nearby field.

They mumbled their excuses.

"Be still!" Grýla ordered, staring into all their yellow eyes without blinking once. "Do you want your dear mother to starve?"

The thirteen trolls swung their downcast heads from side to side.

"Now, listen. Time is short," said Grýla, hands on her hips. "We shall join the rear of the Samhain parade, acting like mannfólk dressed in large troll costumes. From there, I will send you forward one at a time. Grab the first witch you see, toss her in a sack, and bring her to the copse where we first arrived. Any questions?"

No one spoke.

Grýla force-marched her sons into town, where they soon joined the tail of the costumed, torch-waving procession.

"Gluggagægir, you first," whispered Grýla, the ancient troll sweating and huffing from exertion.

Her son nodded and loped forward, sifting through the townsfolk for a witch.

The crowd wound through the narrow village streets and Grýla quickly lost sight of Gluggagægir. "Kertasníkir," she whispered. "Now you. Go."

Grýla deployed her sons in this manner until she marched alone at the tail of the parade. She slowed her pace and slipped away, making for their rendezvous point.

Gluggagægir hurried through the drunken revelers. He spied ahead a woman in a long black dress, wearing a pointed hat and brandishing a broom. *She's a witch!* He maneuvered directly behind her. As they passed an alleyway, he looped an arm around her waist and clamped a hand over her mouth. Gluggagægir pulled her out of the crowd and into the dark lane. He tugged his large sack over the witch and tied it shut. Heaving the sack over his shoulder, he weaved through the darkness toward the enchanted spot, a smile on his craggy face.

Kertasníkir advanced along the left edge of the boisterous crowd. Craning his neck, he spotted a witch directly ahead. He hurried forward.

As if warned by a sixth sense, the witch looked over her shoulder just as Kertasníkir approached. Her gleeful expression soured. She spun and gestured at the troll with a slim wand of alder wood.

Kertasníkir's muscles suddenly stopped obeying his will. He collapsed in a heap at the side of the road.

Celebrants, assuming he was simply overcome with drink, laughed and paid no further heed.

Someone pulled a hood over Kertasníkir's head. He felt himself dragged into a side street and his arms and feet bound, whether with thick rope or by magic he could not tell. A sharp blow struck the back of his head and he knew no more.

Stúfur, the shortest of Grýla's offspring, worked his way through the jostling crowd, eager to do his mother's bidding. Out of the corner of his eye, he noticed the dark shape of a witch eyeing him from an open doorway. He swerved from the crowd toward her.

The woman took two steps back into the building, the amused expression never leaving her face. The implication of the witch's lack of surprise or fear of a troll charge did not occur to Stúfur until he crossed the threshold, triggering a blinding flash of red light before all went dark for him.

Grýla paced back and forth at the enchanted spot in the copse, her heavy steps flattening the turf.

After a time, Gluggagægir, Giljagaur, Bjúgnakrækir, and Gáttaþefur joined her, breathing hard from carrying heavy bulging sacks.

"What have you brung me?" asked Grýla, rubbing her hands together.

Gluggagægir grinned. "A witch." He untied the rope securing his sack and dumped its contents onto the ground.

The woman in the long black dress sat up and shook her head to clear it. When she noticed five real trolls surrounding her, she fainted straightaway.

"An odd reaction from a witch," observed Grýla, scowling. She bent down for a closer look. "And that's not her real nose. It's a false one. This is no witch!" she cried.

"What have YOU brung me?" Grýla growled at her other sons.

They wilted under her glare. Finally, Giljagaur summoned the courage to speak. "Just jugs of milk I stole."

Bjúgnakrækir and Gáttaþefur offered similarly disappointing tales.

Her face the color of an Icelandic beet, Grýla raised her hand. But before she struck, her son Askasleikir burst through the bushes.

"They have seized Skyrgámur," he cried. "From a distance, I saw two witches cast a spell on him. He vanished."

Grýla's expression changed from anger to concern. She moaned and held her head in her hands. "And since they have not joined us, my other sons are also likely captives of the witches. How did they discover us?" Her eyes widened with realization. "Krampus! He helps the coven. We need aid as well."

With the thick fingers of her left hand, Grýla grasped a copper amulet hung around her neck and chanted in a tongue unrecognizable to her sons.

The three álfar appeared.

Grýla turned to them. "Kindly conduct my five sons home to Dimmuborgir, then rejoin me here."

The álfar bowed and repeated the Veil-piercing ritual. They soon reappeared, though it felt like hours to Grýla.

She straightened her bowed back. "I need your aid to rescue my sons held by Krampus at the Rock of Dunamase."

"We know of an enchanted spot in the dungeon there," replied the tallest álfar with unearthly calm.

"I bid you take me," replied Grýla. "You hidden folk can move unseen to locate my sons. I shall break their shackles and then you can return us to Dimmuborgir."

Two álfar circled Grýla and the four passed through the Otherworld to a dank dungeon, reeking with despair. The tallest álfar signaled Grýla to remain still. The álfar vanished.

The dawn arrives soon, thought Grýla, struggling not to race down the dark corridors calling for her brood.

Eventually, the álfar reappeared. "We found your eight sons. They appear to have been whipped and are chained to the wall of a large cavern."

Grýla's eyes narrowed. Her fists clenched of their own accord. "Take me there."

The álfar vanished. An invisible hand guided Grýla.

She crept with all the stealth an old troll can summon, cringing at the soft patter when her foot disturbed an unseen pebble. Sputtering torches periodically lit the stone passageways through a series of turnings that Grýla committed to memory.

At last, they passed through an archway, entering a high-vaulted cavern. Grýla's bloodied sons stood chained to the far wall, their arms shackled over their heads.

A low gasp escaped Grýla's mouth and she raced to her trolls, hope returning to their faces. Grýla enclosed her copper amulet within a wrinkled fist and muttered a spell.

The thick iron chains binding the trolls rusted and crumbled, as if five centuries passed in an instant. Her sons collapsed to the floor.

"Hurry," Grýla whispered, a solitary snail of a tear meandering down her leathery cheek. "I will treat your injuries later. First, we must escape. Follow as quietly as you can."

Her sons struggled to their feet and staggered after Grýla.

A booming voice brought the trolls up short. "Who do we have here?" said Krampus, bending his goat legs so that his horned head could pass under the archway. Thirteen black cloaked witches filed into the cavern behind him. "Well, if it isn't Grýla."

Her shoulders fell. "Save yourselves," Grýla breathed to the álfar, knowing there was nothing the hidden folk could do for the trolls now. Her sons huddled behind her.

"I planned to make a stew of these eight trolls," said Krampus. "But I'm sure my cauldron can accommodate one more."

"I thought you only ate mannfólk," Grýla replied, her mind racing to find a way to save her sons.

"And so I did. But I have discovered the advantages of straying from the old ways," he added gesturing toward his new witch allies.

I am lost, but at least I can save my sons, thought Grýla. Her face hardened. She yanked the copper amulet from her neck, snapping the fine chain. She began chanting, summoning the deep magic.

Krampus's eyes widened as he recognized a spell to conjure a lake of lava that would engulf the castle and all within. "You would destroy yourself *and* your sons?"

Grýla paused. "If I cannot save them, then I shall take you and your coven with us to Hel. Unless –"

"Ah. I'd hoped there was an unless," replied Krampus.

"If you let us go, I will snatch no more ill-behaved children. They are all yours, from now to the breaking of the world." *I will starve*, she thought. *But my sons will survive.*

"Hmmm. Far more preferable to being consumed in fire. Will you *swear* to it?" Krampus asked, raising his eyebrows.

"I tell you three times," replied Grýla.

"I hear you three times," said Krampus, completing the ritual. He gestured toward the archway. "You may go."

The witches parted to make way for the trolls.

Home at Dimmuborgir, Grýla's sons honored her by preparing a celebration with the food stolen from Ireland.

Grýla eyed the banquet ravenously. *But the old ways...* she thought, the weight of her immense age pressing down upon her. She smelled good things to eat from far away across the world. Her empty belly rumbled.

"Try some sausage, Mother," pleaded Bjúgnakrækir. "Please."

She sighed. *I must change if I am to survive. And I swore a solemn oath.* Grýla took a tentative nibble. Her eyebrows rose and a fissure of a smile cracked her stony face. Like a loose pebble on a mountainside, the sausage triggered an avalanche of eating. An hour later, a thunderous belch echoed in the halls of Dimmuborgir, signaling the long overdue end to Grýla's fasting.

And from that day to this, Grýla never ate children again.

Author's Note

Krampus is described in Central European folklore as a chain wielding half-goat, half-demon who swats misbehaving children with birch branches and kidnaps others during the Christmas season. In some regions, he is considered a companion of Saint Nicholas.

This story contains seven references to *Where the Wild Things Are* as an homage to Maurice Sendak's trolls.

The castle names and Icelandic foods mentioned are authentic. Grýla, Leppalúði, and their thirteen troll sons (the Yule Lads) are widely known in Icelandic folklore. They're even featured on postage stamps. Grýla is reputed to kidnap and eat misbehaving children during yule time. Her sons commit oddly specific mischief in the thirteen days leading to Christmas:

Stekkjastaur (Sheep-Cote Clod) – His stiff peg legs impair his ability to catch and eat sheep.

Giljagaur (Gully Gawk) – He hides in gullies, awaiting opportunities to sneak into cowsheds and steal milk.

Stúfur (Stubby) – He's very short and steals pans to eat any leftover crumbs.

Þvörusleikir (Spoon-Licker) – As his name suggests, he steals and licks wooden spoons. But apparently, he's not good at it, for he is very thin.

Pottaskefill (Pot-Scraper) – He does to pots what *Stúfur* does to pans.

Askasleikir (Bowl-Licker) – He lurks under beds awaiting opportunities to steal food bowls.

Hurðaskellir (Door-Slammer) – He slams doors, particularly at night.

Skyrgámur (Skyr-Gobbler) – Skyr is Icelandic yogurt and this fellow gobbles it down.

Bjúgnakrækir (Sausage-Swiper) – He lurks in rafters to swipe sausages being smoked.

Gluggagægir (Window-Peeper) – Restraining orders don't stop this troll from peering through windows in search of items to steal.

Gáttaþefur (Doorway Sniffer) – His large nose gives him an acute sense of smell with which he seeks laufabrauð (leaf bread).

Ketkrókur (Meat-Hook) – He uses a hook to steal meat. Not creepy at all.

Kertasníkir (Candle Beggar) – He steals candles from children and eats them (the candles, that is).

-(261)-

The Troll Sons of Gryla

J. NEIRA
NO
Thanks,
Yallery
Brown

READING IS 40 TO LIFE!

J. NEIRA is the child of a Mexican immigrant, who now lives in Minnesota. Neira occasionally writes fantasy but focuses mostly on Science-Gothic tales. Neira's stories tend to have a compassionate side (think Mike Flannagan.) Neira's most recent novel is Lola's Haunter, a YA sci-goth novel inspired by the Wednesday show.

The first time I saw him was when I was twelve years old.

It was a couple of nights before Halloween, and the air was tinged with the smell of pumpkin spice and wet leaves. I was late walking home from school, and dusk was beginning to fall, painting the sky in shades of blood and amber.

Houses and windows were decorated with fake cobwebs and plastic decorations, and pumpkins lit by candle-flame sat grinning at me from porch steps, their faces grotesque and hollow in the growing darkness.

I kept stopping on my way home to admire all the Halloween displays, growing increasingly more excited for the night of enchantment and disguise, when the dead intertwined with the living, and monsters and humans became one and the same. I was planning on going trick-or-treating around the neighborhood with some of my friends, like we did every year.

Dry leaves crunched under my boots as I skipped down the sidewalk, a chill wind tangling through my dark hair. The breeze steadily picked up, rustling through the trees and making their dark, barren branches reach for me as I passed beneath them, scraping against the top of my head.

The streets were oddly quiet as I walked. I could hear nothing but the wailing wind and the rustling leaves and the distant caw of a crow as it took flight. Goosebumps spread along the back of my legs, which began to tremble in the cold.

I hurried my pace, wrapping my arms around my chest to ward off the chill. These dark autumn nights sure fell fast. The sun had disappeared behind the rows of terracotta rooftops, and the shadows gathered at the edges of the street. A heavy fog rolled down the street, hanging like a veil over the houses.

Behind me, I heard the soft whisper of footsteps. The sound cut through my thoughts, and I glanced back, but there was nobody there. Nothing but a distant echo, distorted by the mist.

I wasn't normally out this late. Not used to being chased by shadows and mist and echoing footfalls. I told myself I was being paranoid. Nobody was watching me. I was just a kid walking home from school, like I did every day. It wasn't my fault I'd been assigned to help clean up after classes had finished, taking me well past the last bell.

A dozen plastic doll heads hung from one of the trees outside a house, swinging in the wind with the creak of a rope.

I rolled my eyes. Those kinds of decoration were too tacky for my taste, and they were far from scary.

A black bin bag full of trash toppled over as I walked past it. For a second, I thought I glimpsed something else; movement, a tiny shadow darting away behind the trashcans, but when I looked again, it was gone. Probably just a bird, scavenging for scraps.

I shook my head, telling myself to stop being so jumpy. I was almost home, anyway. Just a couple more streets to go, and I would be out of this bone-numbing mist.

I climbed to the top of the hill, where a dark, shrouded house sat up a long gravel drive. Like the rest of the street, it had been decked out for Halloween, fake cobwebs and bat-shaped banners fluttering in the wind. But that isn't what caught my attention.

Half a dozen faces grinned at me from the porch, their faces twisted and grotesque, flickering with lamplight.

Jack-o'-lanterns.

There was something uncanny and realistic about their faces, like they had been carved from human flesh.

I hurried past, but there were even more pumpkins ahead. One of the houses had a pumpkin patch in their front lawn, tangled with long green vines. There was an assortment of large, round ones and tall skinny ones and ones with lumps and warts and strange dark bruises.

At any other time, I would have paused to admire the display, but with the fog and shadows thickening around me, I was reluctant to linger.

As I stepped past the pumpkins, something stirred, stepping out of the undergrowth. At first I thought it was one of the pumpkins, coming to life, the shadows elongating around it. But this was no pumpkin. No larger than a potato, with yellow-brown skin protruding with lumps and warts, it was a tiny man. It hopped out from behind the pumpkins, dusting itself off with small, bony hands, and looked up at me.

The moment its small black eyes met mine, a scream tore from my throat and I stumbled back, almost tripping over the sidewalk and falling onto the road.

I caught my footing, releasing a short, sharp breath as my heart thundered in my chest. *What was that?!*

It started moving towards me—tottering forward on stick-thin legs—and with another panicked scream, I turned and ran down the street, the wind streaming my hair out behind me.

The soft pat of footsteps echoed in the quiet between my own, and I knew without turning around that it was following me. It was laughing too. I could hear its wild, manic laughter whipping around me.

Reaching the end of the street, I threw a glance behind me to see the small yellow creature still chasing after me, darting between the decorations and ducking beneath overhanging branches, still cackling loudly.

I averted my eyes, and almost tripped over an empty can rolling around in the gutter, leaves crunching beneath the sharp heel of my boots.

The small, semi-detached house that I shared with my parents came into sight, and I put on another burst of speed, sweat beading my forehead despite the autumn chill in the air.

I grabbed the door handle with a trembling hand and threw open the door, half-stumbling inside. My mom was just coming down the stairs. She immediately saw the wild, panicked look on my face as I stood in the doorway, panting heavily.

"Socorro, what happened? Have you been running?"

I ignored her and turned around, gazing back out to the street.

The strange creature was gone. It had been right behind me, so I knew it couldn't have gone far.

"Corro, what's the matter?" my mom asked again, softening her voice.

It took me a moment to gather my thoughts enough to tell her what had happened. "It chased me all the way here," I told her, pointing down the street. "I've never seen anything like it before."

My father poked his head out of the kitchen at this point to listen, and I saw him share a concerned glance with my mom.

"Perhaps it was just one of the Halloween decorations. Some of those things look so realistic these days," my mom said, putting a gentle hand on my shoulder and closing the front door, shutting out the wind and the fog rolling up the drive.

"It wasn't a decoration," I told her, my tone insistent. "It was real."

"It's getting dark out there, and there's all sorts of stories going 'round this time of year. You probably just imagined it," my dad said, and I knew there was no point trying to argue. They wouldn't believe me, no matter what I said.

But I knew I hadn't imagined him. Whatever he was, he had been real, and he had chased me that night, for some reason or other.

Halloween came and went that year without another glimpse of the strange creature, and I had almost forgotten about the entire experience, until October the following year, when I saw him again. I had been trick-or-treating with my friends when I saw him watching me from behind a gnarled tree-stump near the entrance to the park. I dragged one of my friends over to see if it had been real, but by then, he had already disappeared. Like a phantom.

For the next six years, I saw him every Halloween. Most of the time, it was nothing more than a glimpse out of the corner of my eye; a flicker of movement, a darting shadow, but I always knew it was him. The mysterious creature with the lumpy yellow body and bony hands.

So the years went by, until I started college.

It was the night of Halloween. I was staying late at the library to study with some of my friends when I overheard some students saying that agents from ICE were on campus, looking for undocumented immigrants. My family had moved to the US from Mexico when I was a child, and I knew I didn't have the documentation to prove it had been legal, so I was afraid that they might come looking for me.

We left the library just after ten o'clock that evening, when it was good and dark out. The campus was lit with security lights and there were other students walking around, but something about the chill in the air made me feel uneasy, and I drew my jacket tighter around my body.

I said goodbye to my friends, since they lived in dorms on-campus, and started to walk home, keeping my arms huddled around me.

Every time someone glanced my way, I averted my eyes, worried they would be undercover immigration agents, but nobody approached me.

I was almost off campus when I saw them. There were two of them standing together, their jackets printed in big white letters with 'POLICE ICE'.

Fear struck me hard, my heart pounding in my chest as I looked for some way to get around them.

If I got caught now, I didn't even want to think what might happen to me, or my family.

Swallowing back the lump in my throat, I turned around and started walking, quickening my pace. I heard one of them shuffle their feet, but I didn't dare to glance back in case I drew attention to myself.

As I rounded the corner, I stifled a short gasp. More ICE agents were hanging around one of the buildings, right where I was supposed to be heading.

My eyes darted across the campus, trying to remember the other exits, but my mind was drawing a blank from panic. Calm down, Socorro. They might not stop you.

It was a risk, walking straight past them, but it was dark and there were other students, so I figured I might be able to slip past them.

Taking in a deep breath, I pulled up the hood of my jacket, obscuring my face, and shoved my hands into my pockets, walking hunched, like I was trying to ward off the cold.

I kept my pace casual, but there was a feeling of urgency biting at my heels as I walked past the loitering agents.

I didn't release my pent-up breath until I was safely past them, stepping off campus and onto the street.

Without stopping, I walked towards the bus stop before remembering that the last bus had already gone. I shouldn't have stayed at the library so late.

With a sigh, I kept walking. It would take at least twenty minutes to get home, maybe longer if my route was congested by all the trick-or-treaters out on the streets tonight, celebrating Halloween.

After five minutes of walking, I realized I was being followed.

I stopped walking and bent down to pretend to tie my shoelace, throwing a quick glance behind me.

My heart stuttered in my chest. It was one of the ICE agents. He wasn't looking at me, but at something on his phone. Maybe I was just being paranoid. Maybe he wasn't following me after all.

I stood back up and crossed the street, my heart pounding in my chest. I needed to find somewhere to hide.

Lifting my gaze, I shivered with relief. A church spire blotted the dusk, a few streets away. My parents had always told me that churches were sanctuaries; perhaps I would be safe there.

I hurried towards the church, stepping around children dressed in Halloween costumes, toting bags and buckets full of candy.

When I finally reached the church, I opened the doors noiselessly and slipped inside, shutting out the sound of the wind. It was quiet inside, and warm, the room lit with orange candlelight. I immediately felt at ease. I would be safe here.

I pulled down my hood and sat in one of the pews at the back of the room, taking a few deep breaths. It was almost eleven o'clock, and I felt drained. I wanted nothing more than to get home and soak in a hot bath. I had long since grown out of the tradition of trick-or-treating, but I could at least cozy up on the couch and watch a movie until I fell asleep and forget all about the ICE agents.

For the next hour, I sat in the quiet solitude of the church, listening to the distant shouts and laughter of the trick-or-treaters, and the wailing cries of the wind. I was almost starting to doze, when I heard the soft shuffle of footsteps approaching me.

I snapped awake, glancing up with a start. An older woman was shuffling up the aisle, towards the doors. She must have been sitting in one of the pews at the front of the church, unseen. She caught my eye with a faint smile before leaving, the doors shutting firmly behind her.

I was alone.

I checked the time. It was almost midnight. Surely those ICE agents would have moved on by now. I bit my lip, hesitating. It was getting late. I couldn't stay here all night. At some point, I would have to leave and make my way back home.

Bolstering my resolve, I stood up with a stretch and made my way to the doors. I threw a curious glance behind me, but there really was nobody else here.

The heavy wooden door creaked as I pulled it open. While I had been inside the church, a heavy fog had settled over the night, mist swirling along the sidewalks like something alive.

I shivered against the chill, and closed the doors behind me, stepping back out into the night.

I had barely made it past the bushes at the front of the church when a figure stepped out of the shadows. It was the ICE agent who had been following me earlier.

"Socorro, I presume? You're under arrest for lacking lawful immigration status," the agent said, retrieving a pair of handcuffs from his belt and grabbing me forcefully by the arm.

"B-but how did you know I was in there?" I blurted, my eyes going wide. I swear he hadn't been following me before; had he seen me go inside the church? Then why didn't he come in after me?

The agent sneered as he pulled my arms behind me. I tried to struggle, but he was older, bigger than me, and my attempts were futile. "A little friend helped me," he said, and before I could ask who he was talking about, the bushes rustled and a small figure jumped out.

My heart plummeted down to my stomach.

It was the potato-creature. He looked just the same as he had that night, six years ago, and every Halloween night since, with his small yellowish-brown body and bony hands, his black eyes glittering mischievously.

"Y-you," I gasped as he barked out a laugh.

"Yes, 'tis I," he said, his voice low and gravelly as he bowed.

The ICE agent turned to the little man and smirked. "Thanks for your help."

To my surprise, the creature's face twisted into a portrait of rage, his eyes flashing red beneath the sallow moon. "I warned you to never, ever thank me!" he screeched, waving his hands frantically. "For I am Yallery Brown!"

I stuttered in surprise, and the ICE agent seemed to cower back, loosening his grip on my wrists, but not enough for me to pull free.

Without warning, the creature—Yallery Brown—broke into a jig, bending his crooked little legs and swinging his arms side to side as he sang,

"Wokk's tha will,
tha'll nivver do well,
Wokk's tha mowt,
tha'll nivver gain owt,
For harm an' mischance an' Yallery-Bro-wun,
Tha's let out theesen from unner the sto-wun!"

He finished his song and dance and twirled around into a bow, then hooked a gnarled finger towards the ICE agent. "I warned you, boy, and you didn't listen. Now you will be cursed with ill fortune 'til the day you die."

The ICE agent scoffed, but I could see the sliver of doubt in his eyes at Yallery's words.

Taking advantage of the agent's distraction, I went to pull myself free of his grasp, but he managed to tighten his hands around my wrist before I could manage to wrench myself away.

With a frustrated cry, I wrestled against him, twisting and writhing against his hold. He grunted in effort, his nails digging into my skin as he reached once more for his handcuffs, tugging them free from his belt.

Before he could snap them around my wrists, he let out a sharp cry and stumbled back, twisting his ankle. He dropped the handcuffs and let go of my wrist, his knees buckling in pain.

I had no idea what had happened, but I yanked myself away and watched as he cradled his leg in his hands, wailing in pain.

Beside me, Yallery Brown laughed. "I made good on my word, didn't I?"

I nodded wordlessly, rubbing my wrists.

The creature turned its gaze to me, its dark eyes still glistening. "Well? Are you going to thank me?"

I shook my head fervently. "No thanks, Yallery Brown," I said, before turning away and running off down the street, Yallery's laughter following me on the wind.

IAN BENTWOOD
Roscoe
and the
Beanstalk

PLACE YOUR INCANTATION TODAY

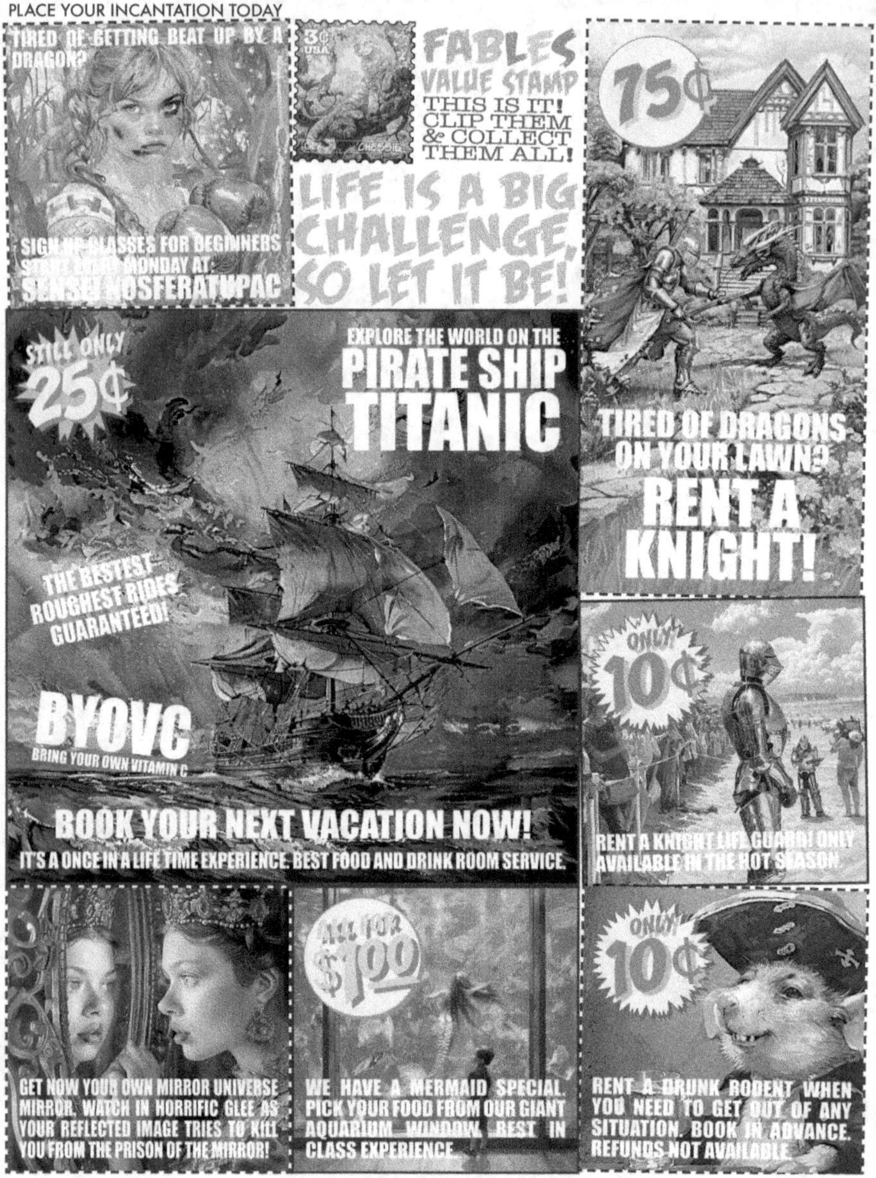

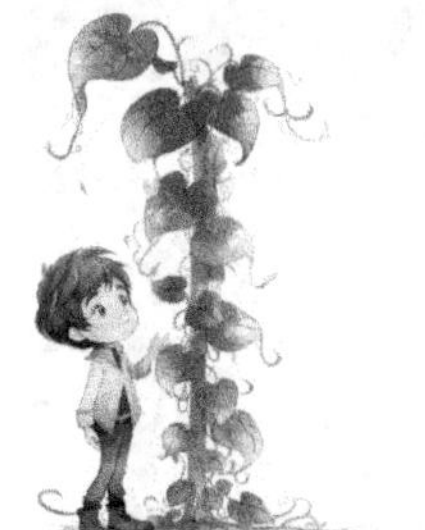

IAN BENTWOOD is a retired UK lawyer and engineer and Imperial College graduate who caught the writing bug from his author-wife, and has a particular interest in science fiction and science fantasy, specialising in aliens and imaginary inventions.
His Amazon author page is located at:
www.amazon.com/Tom-Howard/e/B00E6HRVSC/

"Roscoe! Bring me a glass of water!

I groaned. My bed-ridden Grandpa Jack was getting more and more demanding.

"Game Over!" My avatar had died as I was distracted by the call and my last credit had been used up. I pushed the chair back and slowly got to my feet.

Grandpa's coughing became more serious and prolonged as I grabbed a glass and hurried into his bedroom where he was leaning on his side, having lost his balance. I helped him to sit up straight, adjusted his cushions and handed him the glass, which he gratefully sipped and his coughing slowed.

"Thanks. Now sit down, Roscoe, I need to talk to you."

"Oh no," I thought. Another long reminiscence about how successful he had been at my age and why couldn't I go out and get a job since leaving university in the summer. I was wrong.

"Roscoe, you're a good kid, but I know I have let you down."

"No Grandpa," I protested, but he held up a hand to stop me.

"Look, I know we are poor and have almost nothing left each week. My pension just does not stretch far enough for anything more than survival. We cannot go on like this."

Grandpa could see I wanted to interrupt again, but a glance was enough to stop me. His face was etched with worry-lines and a vitality glowed within him that I had not noticed for many years, certainly not since he was bed-ridden following a fall the previous summer.

"You may not believe this, but my grandfather was also named Jack, and gave me something for times like these. He made me promise not to use them unless I had no other choice. I think we have reached that point."

He handed me the empty glass and rummaged under his pillow for something, eventually producing a small, sealed, transparent plastic envelope with what looked a seed inside. He held it up in front of him with a flourish and smiled, expecting me to know what it was and be as excited as he clearly was. I looked baffled.

"It's a seed. So what?"

"Not just any seed." He shook it violently. "It's a magic seed."

I shook my head. "What do you mean, magic seed."

Grandpa shook his head in despair. "Don't they teach you anything at school these days?" Don't you know the story of Jack and the Beanstalk?"

I scratched my head. "You mean the boy who planted a seed and it grew into an enormous tree that reached into the clouds. And at the top was a castle with a giant guarding loads of gold. That story?"

"Grandpa was nodding furiously, and his pillows toppled over. I helped him straighten them again and he continued," Yes. The Jack in the story was my grandfather."

"That was just a fairy tale, Grandpa, it was not real. In any case, didn't he chop the tree down at the end and burn it to kill the giant? How can this seed be connected?"

Grandpa shook his head in despair again. "It's all true. Before chopping the tree he took some seeds from the flowers and gave one to each of his grandchildren. They all died before they were able to plant them and their seeds were never found, but I kept mine securely, just in case we ever fell on hard times. "He looked around the sparsely furnished room." I think we have reached that point now."

"That's all nonsense, Grandpa. You don't believe those fairy tales, do you?"

Grandpa looked deadly serious. "I am telling you to plant it, Roscoe, it's our last chance to make some money and provide some comfort for my last few years and help you get started in your life."

"But Grandpa, we are on the sixth floor of an apartment block, we don't even have a balcony, let alone a garden!" I looked round the tiny one room flat we shared and shook my head at the absurdity of the situation.

"Look, Roscoe, I am too ill to do it myself. Go and find a patch of garden in the communal area and plant it there. Plant it at night so you cannot be seen, and water it regularly. Keep an eye on it. Promise me this one request of an old man." He grabbed my hand, squeezed tightly and looked me in the eyes.

"Okay, okay," I shook his hand off. And took the seed packet. "If it will make you happy, I'll do it."

He slumped back onto the pillows and sighed.

"That's a good boy. Now let me sleep. I am tired after all that coughing."

He closed his eyes and was soon snoring noisily, so I stood up and returned to my desk and shut the door partially muting the annoying sound, and held up the packet to the light of the window and shook my head. "Crazy fairy tales! I muttered to myself.

I had an idea. Maybe other people would believe the myth.

I leaned forward and clicked on the eBay logo and the window opened, asking what I wanted to sell today. I looked down the options and selected 'Seeds', another list appeared, and I scrolled down, but 'Magic' was not one of the options. I grinned to myself, and clicked on 'Other'. I rapidly completed the listing for a 'Magic" Seed, related my grandpa's story into the description field, and added a footnote saying that I offered no money-back guarantee on the existence of a fortune at the top of the beanstalk, added a photo taken with my web-cam and submitted the auction, with a starting price of $10, and a time period of seven days. Let's see how many suckers out there actually believed this nonsense.

A week later, I logged on again, and was delighted to see an email confirming that the magic seed had been sold. I opened the account and saw that the auction had been competitive, bidding up to $150 as the winning bid! "Suckers!" I thought to myself, as I checked the winner's address - Geoff Hadstock, Butterfree Island. I knew the place, only about fifteen minutes by bike along the coast, although only accessible at low tide. I checked the tide times and emailed Mr. Hadstock, suggesting I hand-deliver the seed and he could pay me in cash that afternoon between 3 and 6pm.

He replied soon afterwards, and that afternoon, having checked that Grandpa was asleep, I carried my bike down the six flights of stairs and cycled along the coast. I could see that the tide was out, and the muddy causeway was visible, as I cycled down the coastal path and across the beach toward it. I slowly cycled across the muddy path, surrounded by pools of seawater on either side, and then after around 100m, the slope upwards became more substantial and I cycled to the door of a small cottage, perched on the top of the low hill at the center of the island, and the only building visible.

I stared at the large door, at least 3m high, and could not see a buzzer, so I knocked on the door as loudly as I could. After a few seconds, the door creaked open and an extremely tall, but bent over man stood there leaning on a walking stick and smiled down at me. He had straggly white hair and a wizened face and appeared to be older than my grandpa.

"Roscoe?" He inquired? I nodded.

"Do you have the seed?" He looked concerned for a moment, and then his face smiled broadly as I held up the packet, which he snatched euphorically from my outstretched hand.

"At last!" He boomed, so loudly that I had to put my fingers in my ears. He stepped backwards into the hallway and turned away from the door.

I was concerned that he would slam the door in my face and stepped forward, blocking the closing door with my foot, and cleared my throat.

"Excuse me, Mr. Hadstock. You promised to pay $150 for the seed."

He turned back to face me and paused to stare at me as if surprised for a moment, before putting his hand inside his jacket and pulled out a bundle of notes and handed them to me. I counted them quickly to confirm the amount was correct.

He looked down at me and his head tilted slightly.

"You really don't know what you have here, do you?" He laughed at me, almost sneeringly.

"I know my grandpa believed it was a magic bean, and it had been handed to him by his grandfather, the original Jack from the Jack and the Beanstalk fairy tale."

"It was not a fairy tale, Roscoe. It was true." His facial expression became serious.

I laughed. "Yeah right. So how do you know it was true? Were you there?" I laughed again at the preposterous idea, but Mr Hadstock looked me in the eye and nodded.

"Yes. I was there." He was somber and glanced down at the walking stick. "I am the giant in the so-called fairy tale."

I shook my head in disbelief.

"But you can't be. The giant died when Jack cut down the beanstalk. That's how the fairy tale ended; in any case it was over 100 years ago. You couldn't possibly be the same person."

"Roscoe, my young naive disbelieving friend, I am a giant. Giants live longer than humans. Yes, I fell badly from a great height when the beanstalk collapsed and was knocked unconscious, broke my leg, damaged my hips and shoulder, so I now am a hunchback and struggle with a limp, but I did not die. I have been trying to return to my castle in the sky and my family and friends ever since. I heard that Jack had given seeds to his grandchildren, but having tracked them all down, they refused to tell me the whereabouts of the seed even under threats, and they all died before revealing their secret... except for your grandfather, who I was never able to find... until now!"

He waved the seed packet triumphantly.

"I will plant it immediately. You can stay and watch if you wish." I nodded, barely able to believe what I was witnessing. The giant stepped back into the hallway, temporarily disappearing into the gloom before reappearing with a spade and a bucket and pushed past me into the garden. For a centenarian he dug swiftly and easily, and after a few minutes was satisfied with the hole, threw down the spade, ripped open the bag and gingerly handled the seed before bending down and placing it carefully at the bottom of the hole, then brushed the heap of earth back over the seed with his bare hands and patted it down. He grabbed the bucket of water and poured the contents over the mound.

"Should I come back tomorrow?" I inquired looking at the giant, but he shook his head and pointed. A green shoot was already moving upwards, and the growth rate was astonishing. Within a short period, it was taller than the house.

"I must collect my things. I'll be just a few minutes." He disappeared inside again, and I watched the green trunk thickening and soaring skywards in amazement at the speed of growth.

By the time the giant returned with a rucksack strapped to his enormous back, the tip of the stem had disappeared into the clouds.

He shook my hand and started climbing upwards and I watched him moving nimbly for someone of his advanced age, the profile slowly shrinking as he climbed higher.

Suddenly, the stem started shaking violently and I looked up higher. Dozens of giants were climbing down the trunk, carrying what appeared to be weapons. They were invading!

I panicked, looked around and saw an axe leaning against the cottage wall, and I grabbed it and started chopping the trunk, which swayed ominously. Glancing upwards at the rapidly descending army of giants, I thought about burning the beanstalk, but wondered how I could produce a fire. Then I remembered my cigarette lighter and reached into my pocket and removed it, quickly flicked the trigger to create a flame and held it near to the bottom leaves to ignite them. The flame soon took hold as the sea breeze encouraged the flames, which roared furiously, and the wind carried the flames upwards as I continued to chop. Eventually the combination of fire and chopping caused the trunk to collapse into the sea with a tremendous crashing sound and a tidal wave swept back towards the shore. I dropped the axe and rushed into the giant's cottage and slammed the door just in time as the wave hammered against the outside of the building, but it withstood the shock and soon passed.

I collapsed on the floor inside the door to get my breath back and calm my fractured nerves. After a few minutes of heavy breathing, I stood up and slowly opened the door to gaze out to sea and scanned the visible horizon for survivors. I was relieved to see nothing but debris floating on the turbulent sea. My bike had somehow stayed near the wall, surviving the tidal wave, and I picked it up and cycled back to grandpa's house.

He was awake and shouting for me in the familiar angry tone, when I lazily delayed responding for more than a few seconds. As I opened his door, the angry face shouted at me,

"Where have you been? Did you plant the magic seed?"

My face betrayed my feelings, and he calmed down, realizing that I had followed his orders.

"Come on, son, tell me what happened?"

I waved the fistful of dollar bills and proudly told him the amount I had received.

He shook his head in disappointment.

"I was really hoping that you would make something of your life with the magic seed, maybe save the planet or something, when all you got was a lousy $150."

TOM HOWARD
Dorothy

TOM HOWARD is a science fiction and fantasy short story writer with over one hundred and forty short stories sold. He lives in Little Rock, Arkansas, USA and retired from working around the world as a banking software consultant. He has four children who, along with his grandson, provide him with many story ideas.

Dorothy Gale stood with her friend and fellow pilot, Em, in the maintenance bay. Dorothy was short and blonde, and brunette Em towered over her. Her friend's tailored teal jumpsuit brought out the blue in her eyes, while Dorothy's olive-green attire made her skin look sallow. Dorothy wasn't jealous; they'd been friends since flight school.

Em eyed the ship at the end of the dock. "Are you sure about this? The ship's not much to look at."

The cargo ship *Golden Way* had recently become Dorothy's property. A bequest from her estranged father, the ship had hauled cargo within the Alixis systems for decades.

"I'm certified to pilot interstellar," Dorothy said. "According to the will, I only need to make one run before I can sell it."

"I'm surprised Saleba gave you time off. The witch thinks her planetary transport business is top priority."

"Yeah, so she tells us." Saleba had reluctantly approved Dorothy's sabbatical; without pay, of course.

Em crossed her arms. "Why are you doing this? You hated your dad."

"All the more reason to take his money. He couldn't be bothered to return for Mom's funeral." She hadn't seen her father for years. No birthday greetings, no vids of his travels. She'd been surprised when his lawyer contacted her about his death and the will.

"It could use a coat of paint," Em said.

The *Way* looked like a giant melon with thrusters at the rear and a small cockpit at the front. Most of the interior space was for shuttling goods and people between the neighboring star systems. The once yellow exterior was now a dull brown, but Dorothy's credit balance couldn't afford a new paint job. It took almost everything she had for fuel.

A man in a blue uniform approached. "Captain Gale."

Dorothy had never been called that. "That's me."

"Sign here for the mail we loaded." He handed her an electronic clipboard and looked at the *Way* skeptically. "Will you make it to Bennok on time?"

"No problem." The old ship was space worthy. Dorothy placed her fingertip on the clipboard and handed it back.

"Are you two the crew? This mail has to be there in forty-eight hours, or your payment will be reduced."

"I'm the only crew," Dorothy said.

Em smiled at the man. "Are you escorting the mail?"

"No." He grinned and walked away.

"Too bad," Em told Dorothy. "He could make the lonely hours between gates interesting. How long since Bozo?"

"Bonzo." Dorothy didn't like thinking of her former boyfriend since he'd moved onto Saleba and was getting the best routes. "Not long enough. I'm looking forward to some peace and quiet."

Em laughed. "You want to hammer that last nail into your father's coffin. I'd go with you, but I've a new co-pilot. He wears pants tighter than that mailman."

Dorothy hugged Em and boarded her ship. One profitable run, and she'd never have to think about her father again.

The odd-looking man on the screen stared at her. She'd spent hours on the *Way* to the first jump gate repairing an oxygen recycler. She was tired and didn't respond well to his bad news.

"What do you mean, the gate is closed?" she asked.

The jump gate hung before her, visible through the forward windows. The shimmering gold circle looked fine. It transported ships between star systems and served as the link between planets. Several ships waited near the adjoining space station.

"I'm sorry for the inconvenience, Captain," he said. "We were unaware of your scheduled arrival."

She had forgotten to reserve a transit time. The paperwork associated with cargo vessel operation was new to her.

The man's face was a mishmash of different skin tones and textures. Dark lines of demarcation crisscrossed his skin and continued down his neck. Had he been in an accident?

"Before you ask," he said, "I suffer from a wasting disease from the Clockwork Wars. Most of my parts are hand-me-downs."

"I apologize. I didn't mean to be rude."

"No problem. I'm familiar with your family and your ship. I was sorry to hear about your father."

Dorothy wasn't surprised. Her father probably came through this jump gate frequently. "Thank you. How long until the gate is open?"

"I'll check with my superiors." He glanced at a man standing behind him. "Please wait."

"I'll be here." She signed off and leaned back in her chair. Two ships waited with her.

Dorothy activated the ship's AI, the Tactical Oversight and Technical Operator, for the first time since she'd boarded. "TOTO, I need information."

"Hello, Captain Gale. How may I help you?" The computer sounded like her father.

"Can you identify the ships waiting to go through the gate? They're crowding us." It might be her imagination, but they did appear closer. Pirate vessels found cargo ships easy targets. She didn't want to lose the *Way* on her first time out or get herself killed trying to satisfy her father's last wishes.

TOTO beeped and whirred. "I've scanned them. Neither ship is registered in my databanks. They're either new vessels or obscuring their identities."

Had pirates taken over the gate? "TOTO, are they waiting for someone to come through? Check the station's database."

"Accessing information from other databases is illegal," TOTO said, "unless it's an emergency."

Nice loophole her father had used. "This is an emergency. Who is scheduled to come through the gate?" If the ships

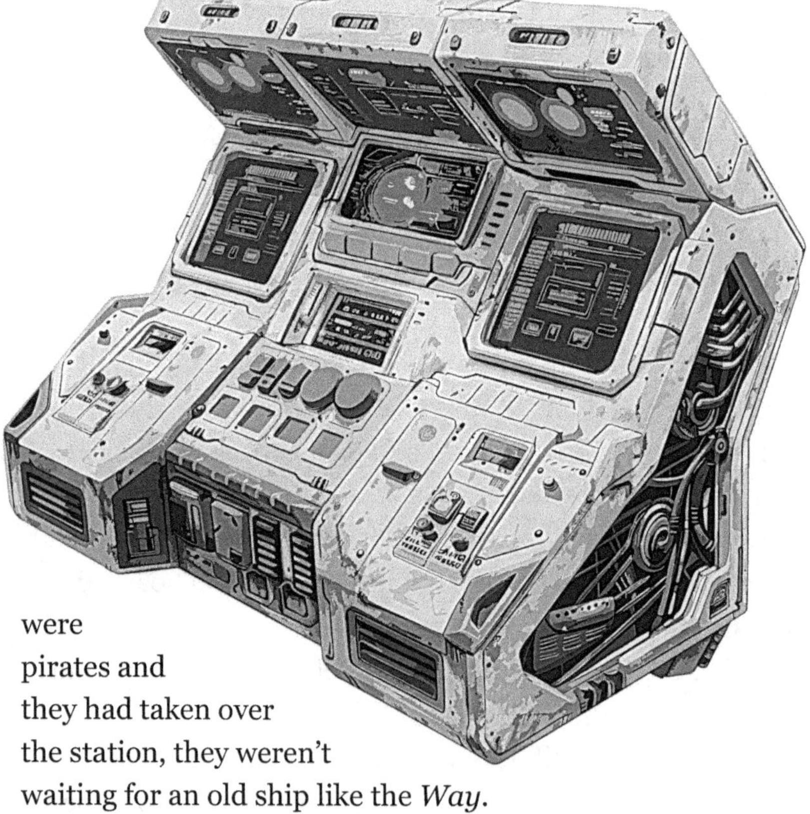

were
pirates and
they had taken over
the station, they weren't
waiting for an old ship like the *Way*.

While TOTO searched, Dorothy scanned the station. It had

a small crew. She pinpointed the patchwork man by his scrambled bio-readings. According to station schematics, the station master was accompanied by two men, and the other six crewmembers appeared with guards like the one she'd seen behind the gate controller.

"TOTO, do we have weapons aboard?"

"Handheld blasters are available. I've identified the incoming vessel. I see you did not reserve a transit time for us."

"Noted. Who are these mysterious ships waiting for?"

"A cargo vessel, the *Spearhead*, belonging to the Jolan Consortium."

The rich and powerful Jolan family were not her concern. Whatever the pirates were planning, she'd mind her own business. No one would pay her ransom or insurance money to rebuild her ship. If she survived.

"Captain, the two ships beside us are closing in. They've armed weapons."

Damn. So much for sitting this one out. "Back us away slowly."

Alarms rang throughout the ship. "Now what?" she asked.

"A delivery tube from the station. It's carrying one person. I've opened a docking port."

"Wait!" Why were they sending someone? Was it a pirate?

"The delivery tube has docked. We are backing from the gate. The pirates are not following."

She checked the cameras in the hold. The patchwork man crawled out of the delivery tube.

"Permission to come aboard, Captain," he said into the intercom.

"What are you doing here?"

"I worked with your father. I slipped away to warn you the pirates want the *Spearhead* and will destroy the *Way* to get it. I thought you might need some help."

"The pirate vessels are approaching the gate," TOTO said. "The *Spearhead* is their target."

"I can help," the man said. "Without me, you're a sitting duck. With me, we can save your ship."

"Permission granted." If the man had worked with her father, maybe he knew secrets about her ship she didn't.

The man scampered up the ladder and took the co-pilot's seat. "You've interrupted a robbery. Because you didn't have a scheduled appointment, the pirates didn't expect you."

"Can you really help, Mister..."

"Syn. Christopher Syn. Your father talked about you often when I helped him on an occasional run." He turned to the console and activated the controls. "I can't believe his heart exploded on a solo run. It must have been too much for his auto-doc to stabilize."

She hadn't realized her father had died alone in space. "What are you doing?"

"Some of your father's operations were illegal. The *Way* has upgrades you may not know about. I'm arming the ship's external weapons."

"My father was a smuggler?" Her mother hadn't talked about Dorothy's father. "We have external weapons?"

Before Mr. Syn answered, the two pirate ships fired at a large cargo vessel coming through the gate.

"The *Spearhead's* shields are down," TOTO said.

"What could they be carrying that would attract pirates?" Dorothy asked.

Syn chuckled. "The *Spearhead* carries many destructive and expensive things not listed on the manifest."

The pirates continued firing on the *Spearhead*, and the cargo vessel fired back. Like the *Golden Way*, it should not have had weapons.

One of the pirate ships exploded in a ball of fire. The *Way* moved toward the remaining ship.

"What are you doing?" Dorothy asked.

"Preventing the destruction of the station, the gate, and us," Syn said.

TOTO interrupted. "The *Spearhead* is severely damaged. Two of its crew have taken a lifepod to the station. The pirates aboard the station have retreated to the remaining pirate ship."

The *Way* shuddered as the pirate ship fired on them.

"Don't be alarmed at what we do next," Syn said.

Alarmed? Her father had been a smuggler who died from a heart attack. Pirates were firing at her ship. An assistant station manager knew her ship better than she did.

Gravity plates squealed as the *Way* twisted to evade the pirate ship's blaster fire. The *Spearhead* appeared dead in space.

Dorothy clutched the arms of her chair as the *Way* slammed sideways.

"Give me fire control, TOTO," Syn said. A panel above his seat opened, and a scope with handles dropped down. He grabbed them.

He turned to Dorothy. "I can't handle evasive maneuvers and armament at the same time. Could you take over as pilot?"

She wanted to retort that she was the pilot, but the *Way* shook again from another hit. Taking the controls, she backed the ship away on an erratic course.

"Steady," Syn said and fired.

A beam shot from the *Way* and hit the pirate. Before it could return fire, Syn hit it with another blast. It vented atmosphere and spun away from the gate.

"Good flying." Syn pushed the scope into the ceiling.

"Thank you. Good job on taking out their engines with armaments I didn't know I had. TOTO, why didn't you tell me about the armament when I asked?"

"Apologies, Captain. I was waiting for the right time."

"Being fired upon isn't the right time? And why does Mr. Syn know so much about the ship?"

"Mr. Syn has prior authorization."

Syn smiled at her with half his face. "We'll dock at the station and get the gate open." He pressed a panel on the cabin wall, and it swung open to reveal several blasters. "You may need one of these."

Her father had talked about her? After working so hard to get her pilot's certification to impress him, she'd never heard from him.

Dorothy took a blaster and followed Syn through an umbilical the station attached to their airlock. Inside the station, *Spearhead's* two crew members talked to the staff. She recognized Elso Jolan from news vids. Tall and muscular, he had the tawny mane and amber eyes of the Jolan clan.

"I must return to my ship to begin repairs," Elso said.

His cyborg companion stepped forward. "I need to ensure the ship is safe, sir."

Dorothy had encountered cyborgs before, but she'd never seen such a high-end version. It wore the Jolan lion lock above its heart, signifying it had biological components and was not a Clockwork assassin. After the war, mechanical beings had been outlawed in human space. The lock proved the cyborg was safe.

"Nonsense, Mission-7," Elso said. "I've contacted the family. She'll send a ship."

A massive explosion rocked the station, and alarms rang out.

"Did the pirate ship explode?" Dorothy asked.

Syn checked a nearby monitor. "It was the *Spearhead*. It must have been severely damaged. The *Way*, the station, and the gate are unharmed."

"The potential for loss overcame the gains," Mission-7 said.

"No!" Elso shouted. "They wouldn't have activated the self-destruct. I could have been on the ship."

"We must leave the station," Mission-7 said. "Your family may consider further action."

Elso ran his claws through his head of hair. "How can we leave? Our ship is gone."

Syn turned from the monitor. "For a reasonable fee, I'm sure Captain Gale will take you to Bennok. She's delivering mail there."

Dorothy was taken aback by Mr. Syn's offer. He had no authority to offer her ship's services. But, she could charge Elso and Mission-7 double the usual rates to transport them somewhere she was already headed. She nodded.

The cyborg handed Dorothy a credit chit. "Captain, please book passage to Bennok for Mr. Jolan and me."

Elso scowled. "From Bennok, we can seek more suitable transport."

"Or perhaps the Scholar can help us," Mission-7 said.

"Stop talking," Elso said and led the cyborg to the umbilical.

"I'm coming with you, Dorothy," Syn said. "I can familiarize you with the *Golden Way's* systems."

The systems her father had added to make a cargo vessel able to destroy pirates.

Syn's mismatched eyes had widened at the mention of the individual called the Scholar.

She handed him the Jolan credit chit. "Tell TOTO to charge twice my father's regular fee. And why do you think you can join my crew?"

"I owe it to your father to keep you safe from jackals like Jolan," he said, "and the Scholar."

"All right." Who the hell was the Scholar, and why had Mr. Syn decided to join her when he heard the name?

Aboard her ship, Elso confronted her about his room assignment. "What do you mean all the cabins are the same size?"

"Just what I said." Dorothy and her passengers stood on the platform overlooking the hold, and Syn sat in the cockpit behind them. "There are no VIP suites on this ship."

He smiled. "Then I'll take your cabin."

"Fine, but it's the same size as the other cabins and has my dirty underwear scattered everywhere." She lied. She hadn't had time to unpack, and she didn't want to give him the satisfaction of forcing her to vacate her cabin. *It was* larger.

He scowled and walked away.

"Since we're on such a short trip," she called after him, "we're on galley rations. Self-service." If he expected fancy meals at times he dictated, he had a long wait coming.

She leaned against the railing. Below her, crates of postal deliverables were neatly stacked in rows.

"I apologize for Mr. Jolan's rudeness," Mission-7 said. He hadn't followed his boss. "His family destroyed his ship without warning him. He's upset."

She looked into his black plastic eyes. "What cargo was so dangerous that it had to be destroyed before the pirates found it?"

"I don't know." He leaned against the railing beside her. "We weren't told of the cargo."

White armor covered portions of his frame. Joints of polished steel peeked from beneath the armor.

"You weren't always a cyborg?" she asked. "Some of you is still human?"

"Yes and yes. During the war, the doctors replaced my damaged anatomy with mechanical parts. Eventually, only my organic brain remained."

"Is Mission-7 your real name?"

He shook his head. "No. The Jolans own eight cyborgs. We were given numbers to identify us."

"Own? Isn't that illegal?"

"We're under contract until we pay off the cost of our cybernetics."

Mission-7's mannerisms and deportment seemed as natural as Dorothy's own. She had no trouble believing he'd been a breathing human once. "Who were you when you were 100% human?"

"I don't like to think about it. How did you end up piloting an old scow like this?"

She told him of her father's death and her unexpected inheritance. She didn't tell him she'd been surprised to discover the ship had blasters strong enough to deal with pirates. "I'm making a mail run before I sell the *Golden Way*. I didn't expect to encounter pirates and take on passengers."

The ship shuddered as they transited the first gate. Syn plotted a course to the next one. Although they were a little behind schedule, they should make it to their destination before the deadline.

"Is the Scholar a Bennok leader?" she asked.

"Yes, but he's not part of the government. He approves all planetary trade. Elso hopes the Scholar can get him back in the family's good graces. They may blame him for losing the cargo."

"Why would they worry more about what they're hauling than their son?"

"Good question," Mission-7 said. "I hope the Scholar can set things right."

Syn called from the cockpit, "Captain, we're approaching the next jump gate. I apologized for not having a reservation."

Dorothy sighed. "Any pirate ships?"

"No. We're scheduled to go through in an hour. I'm off to find those rations." He unbuckled his belt and climbed out of the cockpit.

"I'll go with you," she said. "You can tell me what else my ship is hiding."

Syn nodded. "I'll show you the hidden bar. With His Highness aboard, we may need a few drinks."

Mission-7's face flowed into a happy expression. "That's what gets me through the day."

"You drink?" Dorothy asked.

"Wouldn't you? Let's find the bar before Elso commands me to turn his rations into a five-star meal."

Later, she rejoined Syn in the cockpit. "Okay, what's up with the Scholar? You didn't seem happy when Elso mentioned contacting him."

Syn sighed. "He's bad news. I refused to work with your father on his last run because it was a job for the Scholar."

"Why didn't he use his own ships?" She'd eaten with Syn but had declined a drink. She needed her wits with passengers aboard.

"I guess the job was too small or too dangerous. Ships that don't do what the Scholar wants tend to disappear. I wouldn't be surprised if your father's heart attack had been arranged. The auto-doc was definitely tampered with."

Dorothy didn't know her father well enough to be angry that he might have been killed, but she didn't intend to take her ship into the clutches of the man who might have engineered her father's death.

This run was more trouble than it was worth. "We'll deliver the mail, drop off Elso and Mission, and avoid the Scholar. If he asks me to make a delivery for him, I'll refuse on the grounds I'm selling the *Way*." A paying cargo on the way home would be nice, but it wasn't necessary to prove the ship was marketable. Let the next owner deal with the Scholar. She had no intention of dying alone in space.

She slammed into the bulkhead and fell onto the deck beside her bunk. Stunned, she opened her eyes to flashing red lights. Sirens wailed through the ship. "What the hell?"

Scrambling into her robe, she reached the door as the ship shook again. Her elbow hurt from where she'd hit the floor, and the sound of her pounding heart drowned the klaxon alarm.

She raced barefoot up the ladder to the cockpit.

Syn pulled at the steering column, sending the ship sideways. She clutched the back of the pilot's seat and stared out the window. Outside, lights spun and ricocheted off one another. "Are we hitting asteroids?" she asked.

Syn swerved again. "No. We've hit a Clockwork minefield. One of the mines penetrated our hull."

"We're not losing air." She could still breathe.

"The mine didn't explode. It's starboard. See what you can do with it while I get us through this in one piece."

She scrambled but didn't understand. The Clockwork minefields had been destroyed years ago. There shouldn't be any left near the shipping lanes.

When she reached the catwalk opposite the crew cabins, Mission-7 was already there. A piece of twisted metal pierced the outer and inner hull, wedged so tightly no atmosphere could escape. The black torpedo whirred and emitted an occasional burst of gas. The cyborg used an emergency sealant canister to spray foam around the torpedo.

"I've sealed the breach," he said. "The mine hasn't exploded. It's analyzing its surroundings for some reason. They create the amount of explosive they need to destroy their target. It should take milliseconds, but this one is stuck in a loop."

Elso came out of his cabin, rubbed his eyes, and stretched. "What's going on? I can't sleep with the alarms."

"We've hit a minefield," Dorothy said. "This mine could go off at any minute. We thought you might want to be awake for that."

He stared at the blinking mine and took the stairs to join Syn in the cockpit.

Mission-7 watched him go. "The cockpit won't be any safer if this thing goes. I hope your mail is insured."

"That's the least of my worries," she said. "Could this stay in a loop until we reach Bennok? The authorities can disarm it."

Mission-7 studied it. "I wouldn't take the chance the loop will hold. I can stop it. It's what I did in the army."

She wondered how successful he'd been at disarming bombs since only his brain remained. The torpedo ticked faster. "Okay. Go ahead."

She grabbed the railing as the ship shook. Syn cursed from the cockpit as he tried to evade the mines.

Mission-7 sat his foam canister on the deck and removed a panel from the side of the torpedo. He handed it to Dorothy. "Please don't talk or make distracting moves. You might want to close your robe."

He disconnected wires and handed more components to Dorothy. He didn't need tools; his long thin fingers sliced their way inside. The mine's lights blinked faster as he worked. He was a blur, extracting more and more parts and handing them to her. After cinching her robe, she stacked them on the panel she held in her arms.

The mine stopped making sounds, then sputtered and growled. A high-pitch whine filled the air. She couldn't believe she'd be killed by a war that had been over for decades. On a stinking mail run her father had forced her into.

Mission-7 removed larger pieces, and the mine shrieked as if its guts were being ripped out.

Dorothy's arms ached as the load increased, and her ears throbbed from the mine's warbling, now sporadic and frantic. It hadn't detonated, and Mission-7 slowed. She'd never seen anyone move that fast, organic brain or not.

With a last jet of gas, the torpedo's lights died.

"You did it!" Dorothy exclaimed. Maybe it wasn't her day to die.

He reached for her loaded panel. "I'll take those. The explosives will need to be removed when we reach Bennok, but without the trigger, we're safe as long as the ship—"

The *Way* shuddered as if it had slammed into something.

"—doesn't get shaken too hard," Mission-7 finished.

She handed him the panel and took the ladder. The ship steadied before she reached Syn. Through the window, only empty space showed; Syn had gotten them through in one piece.

"How did we stumble into that?" Dorothy asked. "Why hasn't someone reported them being in the shipping lanes?"

Syn wiped his variegated brow. "They drift. The first ship to encounter them reports them, and the army deals with them. The mines are heavily shielded and undetectable until you stumble across them. Did you disarm the mine?"

"Mission-7 did. He has experience with Clockwork explosives."

Elso, sitting in the pilot's chair, grinned. "Since my robot saved your ship, I'll be expecting a passenger discount."

"He's not a robot. Get out of my seat."

"I've sent a warning to passing ships," Syn said. "The bomb squad will meet us when we dock."

"Good piloting, Mr. Syn," Dorothy said.

The cyborg climbed the ladder to join them.

"Thank you for saving us, Mission-7," Dorothy said. "Elso, get out of my seat."

He did, and she took his place to check for any further damage to the ship. There might be more leaks that needed sealed before she went back to bed.

"How long until we reach Bennok?" she asked.

Syn checked his console. "We've one more gate. Then, it's a half-day to Bennok orbit."

"How much time before the next gate?" If they were close, she wouldn't go back to bed.

"Three hours. You want to take the wheel for a while?"

"Let me change and chase our passengers back to bed." She wasn't sure Mission-7 slept. She'd given him a cabin, but he didn't need to rest to recharge his brain.

She stood to lead the passengers away. "You can set those pieces down, Mission-7."

"I'll store them in a maintenance locker and check for additional leaks. I'll keep an eye on the mine in case it reactivates."

"What if I need you?" Elso asked.

"All you have to do is call."

The merchant prince returned to his room.

As he passed Dorothy, Mission-7 said, "It's Murphy. My name is Alex Murphy."

Earthlike planets looked similar from space, all oceans and continents. Dorothy couldn't have identified the green and blue world of Bennok by sight.

"Looks like the mail will arrive on time," Syn said from the co-pilot's seat. "We've been assigned a docking port. Explosives guys are standing by."

The comms sputtered. *"Golden Way,* your landing site has been changed from the public docks to a private one. Please stand by for new coordinates."

"Understood." Dorothy closed the comm channel. "What's that all about, Syn?"

Elso entered the cockpit and leaned over her seat. "It's the Scholar. He's helping me."

Dorothy didn't like the sound of that. "When did you contact him?"

"TOTO sent a message for me before we encountered the mines. The Scholar says he has a plan."

Dorothy rubbed her temples and wished she'd gone back to bed. "When you contacted your family, they tried to blow you up. When you spoke to a gangster on Bennok, we ran into a Clockwork minefield. Do you think that's a coincidence?"

Mission-7 stepped behind Syn. "The minefields can only be directed by Clockworks."

Dorothy wouldn't put it past the Scholar to be working with Clockworks. Now she and her ship were landing on his private estate.

"Grab personal blasters," she told Syn. "We'll drop off the passengers and the mail and get the hell out of here."

They settled on the Scholar's pad, and an explosives' team entered the hold. Unloaders stood back, waiting to remove the mail.

Armed guards awaited them at the hatch and escorted Dorothy and her crew to the Scholar. The guards took their blasters and verified Mission-7's heart-lock remained secure.

Dorothy could have told the authorities, but who knew what control the Scholar had over local government? At least the mail had gotten through.

The guards remained outside after opening the doors of the Scholar's fancy office.

A tall man with graying hair and a plastic smile, he stood when Dorothy and the others entered. "Elso! Ms. Gale! How nice to see you."

Dorothy, Syn, and Mission held back as Elso rushed forward.

"Thank you, Scholar. I really appreciate it," he said.

"I'm here to help. I look forward to working with both you and Ms. Gale."

"Captain Gale," Dorothy said. "And I don't work for anyone."

The smile dropped from the Scholar's face. "So like your father. I was sorry to hear of your loss. It's good to see the *Golden Way* still in service."

Dorothy looked for exits. "It won't be for long. I intend to sell it as soon as I get home."

"That would be unfortunate," the Scholar said. "I need small smuggling vessels for delicate jobs."

"You can buy the *Golden Way* from me and have all the delicacies you want," Dorothy said.

"What about me?" Elso asked. "We had a deal."

"I'm sorry. Someone made me a better offer."

Who could influence a criminal kingpin? "Clockworks?" Dorothy asked.

The Scholar laughed. "You're smarter than your father. The Jolan family asked me to clean up the mess."

"They're collaborators like you?" Dorothy asked.

"Those who are not with me are against me, Ms. Gale." The Scholar pressed a button on his desk and the guards entered the room. "Take them to a cell in the basement and remove the robot's lock. He'll ensure they're bloody pulp before the authorities arrive. A tragic accident."

"No," Mission-7 said. "You mustn't."

Using their blasters, the guards herded them out the door and down to the basement several floors below.

A ten-by-ten-foot cage of iron bars awaited them. The guards detached the lock from Mission-7's chest, and he stood motionless as the Scholar's men locked the door and departed.

"Why did they remove Mission-7's lock?" Syn asked. "They're just for show, right?

Mission-7 stepped forward, each movement a struggle.

"They're just for show on a cyborg," Dorothy said. "But he's a Clockwork. That's why the Jolans blew up the *Spearhead*. Not because of contraband but because of Mission-7.

Mission-7's servos squealed as he stomped forward. "The captain is correct. Without a lock, a Clockwork must kill humans. I cannot stop myself."

Dorothy backed up with the others. "The mine looped because it recognized you as one of its own."

"If he's a Clockwork," Syn said, "why are the Jolans trying to destroy it and Elso?"

Dorothy's back bumped the bars. "To prevent anyone from discovering there are Clockworks masquerading as cyborgs. Elso would have been collateral damage."

"Run." Mission-7 reached for Syn.

He ducked.

"Stop!" Elso shouted, but Mission-7 knocked him against the wall."

The Clockwork caught Dorothy and placed his metal fingers around her throat. He lifted her off the floor.

"They lied to you," she wheezed, through a constricted airway. "You aren't Clockwork."

He stopped squeezing. "What?"

"You could have let Elso die on his ship. You could have let the mine destroy the *Golden Way*. You saved us. Even now, you're fighting to help your friends."

"Friends?"

"Yes, Alex. Friends. When they programmed you to be a cyborg, they did the job too well. Your human mannerisms. You liking a stiff drink. Telling me to close my robe. Whatever a human-hating Clockwork is supposed to be, you aren't it."

He dropped her, and she rubbed her throat. "Thank you."

Shaking his head in a very human manner, he said, "Alex. I'm Alex Murphy."

Dorothy smiled. "Yes, you are. Now, get us out of here. Somebody must need something delivered somewhere." She'd show the old man how to run a cargo vessel. She had new friends and a new career.

Elso and Syn joined her.

"But my lock has been removed," Mission-7 said. "I could harm someone."

Recalling her father's murder, Dorothy pointed at the cell door. "Mr. Murphy, I'm counting on it."

CRITICAL BLAST PUBLISHING
20¢
CRITICAL BLAST
THE NICK VICTORY CHRONICLES
PART FOUR: Half Baked
Paul Barile
THE NICK VICTORY CHRONICLES Part Four: Half Baked
NICK VICTORY CHRONICLES Part One: Nick's New Neighbor
LOVE AIN'T SWEE
WHEN NICK GOES U
AGAINST ONE TOUGH COO

YOU ARE THE ONLY THING!

PAUL BARILE is a writer whose main focus is Lucha Libre books for young adults through lexographicpress.com.
He also writes poetry and essays, and plays bass and write lyrics for the folk/rock duo The Grudge Brothers.

When I met Althea Price, I went ass-over-teacups. Dames like her don't give a gumshoe a second look every day and here she was talking to me like I was some regular Joe. She even held my hand at the Friday night fish fry over at the V. F.W. I never in a million years thought I'd find someone like Althea Price. Here she was and all I had to do was not blow it.

"You're something *else*, Nicky," she said. "I never met anyone like you. You're the *ginchiest*."

Knock me down with a feather – this dream walking thought I was ginchy. That just doesn't happen every day. Not in this town. Not in this life. But here it was, and I wasn't about to let her go.

"I'm going to ask her to marry me, Sabre," I said one morning over coffee and toast.

Sabre could take two slices of Wonder bread and make a meal fit for a king. I chewed slowly – relishing every bite. As a kid – my mother couldn't cook if the house was on fire so having someone like Sabre around was more than I deserved.

Sabre kept everything together for me all the time. A fella couldn't have a better friend than Sabre Bratcher. We shared meals and we shared work. I couldn't imagine my life without Sabre.

"Aren't you rushing things, Nicky?" Sabre asked spreading the good Irish butter on a piece of toast like we were the Kennedys or something.

"Could be," I said. "I just haven't felt this way in a long time. She makes me feel like I can do anything. A good woman can do that."

"A good breakfast can do that, Nicky."

"Yeah, but..."

"I'm not saying don't marry her. I'm saying long engagements make for longer marriages."

"I get your point."

We finished breakfast without talking. I was lost in thoughts of Althea Price and our little shack with the white picket fence. Sabre was probably thinking about ways to make the world – or a meatloaf – just a little bit better.

Our moment was dashed by the ring of the telephone. I jumped like a cat with my claws stuck in the ceiling. Sabre stood and stretched and answered the phone.

"Nick Victory Investigations, how can I help you?"

I tried to figure out the caller by the look on Sabre's mug – but he was a poker player who never gave an inch. He talked – mostly in short bursts and listened in longer ones. This wasn't some flim-flam trying to sell me an extended warranty for my car.

"We'll be right there," he said.

Sabre set the phone back down in the cradle. He began to put the groceries back into the ice box while he gave me the run down.

"Two children went missing from the school playground today," he started. "The recess bell rang and when the teacher did a head count, she was short two heads."

"This sounds like a job for the cops."

"The cops aren't making it a priority. They're calling the kids runaways."

"How old are the kids?"

"They're about to turn 11 years old. They're twins."

"You said they got a birthday coming up?

I scratched my head before I took my last gulp of joe. I wiped toast crumbs on the sleeve of my shirt as I stood up and walked out of the kitchen. I grabbed my gat and my fedora and my coat. I came back into the kitchen.

"What's the holdup; Sabre? We gotta go."

"Sure, but what made you change your mind?"

"Kids that age don't run away, and they especially don't run away right before their birthday. There's something sideways about this. Let's get down to that school."

"I think we should head back to school, Hank," Gertie said. "Mom's gonna be awful sore if we miss dinner."

"Don't you think I want to get home, Gert?" Hank said. "I don't know where we are. I mean I have an idea, but I'm not sure."

"Oh, great," Gertie said. "I should have known better than to listen to you."

"Wait – there's a house there – see it? Just beyond those trees. Let's see if they got a phone. Adults always help kids. We can call mom and she can come get us."

"She's not going to like that, but I'm starting to get scared."

They walked the crooked path and knocked on the door. A very old woman opened it and smiled widely at the kids.

"We're sorry to bother you," Hank said. "Can we use your phone to call our mom?"

"Are you lost?" the old woman asked.

"A little," Hank said.

"A lot," Gertie answered.

"Come on in, children," she said.

She closed the door behind them.

When we got to the school, most of the kids were gone. There's always a couple that hang around after to bang out the old erasers. Some even do it by choice. We were brought to the principal's office. Miss Lohan—the old battle-axe who gave me *what for* when I was a kid at that school—was still there giving kids nightmares.

I could tell she remembered me by the hairy eyeball I got while we were waiting for Mr. Dinkle to get off the phone.

"Nicholas Vittorio," she said. "To what do we owe the pleasure?"

"Mr. Dinkle called me."

"I'm sure you thought your days of getting called to the principal's office were behind you."

"I hadn't thought about it that way."

I didn't say nothing else. The thought of Miss Lohan and her rulers and wooden pointer sticks could put any kid into fits; and even though I was hardly a kid anymore, I have a great memory.

The door to Mr. Dinkle's office opened with a whiff like he was in a hurry. He caught my eye and gave me the come along wave. I caught up with him. Sabre was right behind us. We trotted toward the back of the building.

We got to the door that led down to the boiler room. Mr. Dinkle opened it and then stepped back. He motioned for me to lead the way. I did.

At the bottom of the stairs, we turned to the left and there was some sap's cot and a small stack of books. It was clear someone was squatting here, but I had no idea who.

"That's Mr. Garland's bed," Mr. Dinkle said. "Irv Garland is our handyman. He lives down here during the week. He worked here when you were here."

Funny we don't notice people – full-sized people when we see them every day. I wonder if it's because they don't want to be noticed. I can't believe this guy lived in this building for all the years I was here, and I never saw him.

"I think he knows about the missing kids," Mr. Dinkle said.

"What do you mean?"

"I think he knows more than he's admitting about the kids."

Just then old Mr. Garland came around from behind the boiler. It was clear from jump street he didn't know anything about the kids. I'd have been surprised if he knew where he was. He was as frail as a rice paper Easter bonnet. He shuffled to us and – after a quick nod – he took his chair.

"Irv," Mr. Dinkle started. "Have you seen Hank and Gertie Grimm? They disappeared today at recess."

"No, sir." Irv said. "I've been down here most of the day."

I just stood and watched. This guy was no miscreant. He was older than the laws on the books – and he was as tired as a one-legged man in a jitterbug contest. There was no way old Irv Garland did anything to those kids.

"We need to go up to my office, Irv," Mr. Dinkle said. "We need to look into this. We can't have children disappearing from the playground."

When Irv stood up, he put his hand into the pocket of his trousers. He pulled out his handkerchief.

"It sure is hot down here," he said as he wiped his forehead with the hanky. I could see the GG embroidered in bright red on the clean white hanky.

As we walked to the stairs – I drew Dinkle's attention to the piece of material that was cleaner than anything down there in that boiler room. Dinkle caught it and I knew it was curtains for the old guy. I still didn't like it. It was too easy.

When we got to the office, he called the cops. We could hear the sirens faster than you could say *innocent until proven guilty*. They busted in flashing badges and surrounded old Mr. Garland. One of the uniforms grabbed the hanky out of his hand.

"G.G." he said reading the embroidery.

"We believe that belongs to Gertie Grimm," Mr. Dinkle said.

"You're coming with us," the cops said as they dragged the old guy out of the building and down the stairs.

I just didn't like it. It was hinky. Nothing made sense. In the first place – if the old codger nabbed the kids – where were they? He didn't hide them in the boiler room. Then there's the fact that this guy was ancient. He didn't have the physical strength to nab two kids.

"Thanks for your help, Nick."

"*Natch*," I said.

As we walked out of the school – I couldn't shake the idea that something was wrong with this whole thing.

That night I took Althea Price to this chophouse for a little bite before heading down to Bogat's where we could cut the rug until the stars went out. Over dinner – I popped the question. I'm not much of a romantical guy, but I did get down on one knee between the French onion soup and the poached salmon and asked Althea Price for her hand in marriage.

"I would be honored to be Mrs. Victory," she said. "There's just one thing."

"Name it," I said. My voice was thick in my throat.

"You have to buy a house. Classy wives don't live in apartments. They live in houses, and I would really prefer we start our life together in a house."

"You got it," I said. "Now let's eat."

I found a sweet little joint at a price I couldn't beat. We had the city out the front door and the woods out the back door. I could see Mustangs out the front window and Althea could see deer out the back door. The best of both worlds.

Our neighbor to the east was a little old lady. She was more bent than a St, Louis judge. She came by with a tray of cookies as they were unloading the trucks. She handed the tray to the new Althea *Victory*.

"If you need anything, I'm just there."

Then she went back to her little house. We watched the smoke coming out of her chimney and it made me want to carry my new wife over the threshold and cuddle up next to a fire of our own.

Once the movers were gone and everything was in the house – I torched up the fireplace and popped a bottle of sweet red. She put the cookies on the table. I never woulda thought cookies would go with vino – but it wasn't bad.

As the fire died, we dozed like drunken alley cats.

In the morning – the kid threw the paper at the front door. The headline said two more kids gone. I read the article, and it said over the past month six kids had disappeared. They apparently had no clues and no leads. The article also said Old Irv Garland – the initial suspect - passed away in jail. He was survived by his wife, Grace Garland.

The knock at the door made me jump. I was expecting Sabre, but it was the new neighbor. She had a tray of little meat pies. They smelled like someone put heaven into a pie crust.

"My name is Margaret," she said. "I hope you liked the cookies."

"They were delicious. Me and the missus loved 'em."

"That's good to hear. Remember, if you need anything, I'm just there."

I closed the door and turned to see my new bride standing there decked out like Old McDonald. She had the overalls and the straw hat with a red ribbon. Her gloves had little flowers. She was an angel – she was *my* angel.

"I'm going to work in the garden," she said.

"We don't have a garden," I laughed.

"We should. Every house should have a garden. I'll call it our *Victory Garden*."

She was the end of the world for a bum like me, but I was okay with every inch of that. There was another knock at the door.

"Boss," it was Sabre. "We got more missing kids."

"I saw the newspaper."

"Two more. They were last seen heading into the woods."

"What are kids doing in the woods these days. Don't they have books or erector sets or anything to keep them in the house?"

"They're kids. They're curious."

"Go save the world, Nicky. I'll be here when you get back."

"Let me get my coat," I said.

We left the house and hustled down to the woods. There was no telling where the youths would be, but it seemed me and Sabre might be their best bet. I didn't know the woods, but Sabre could find his way out of a fun house in a blind fold.

He led the way like some scout who could tell the time with a rock and a stick. It seemed like we'd been walking for hours when we got to a clearing and realized we were at the cobblestone path that led to my new neighbor's kitchen door.

"Let's go talk to Margaret," I said. "Maybe she saw something."

Margaret opened the door like she was the doorman at the Waldorf. She was all smiles and glad hands. We stepped in. I introduced her to Sabre.

"Would you boys like to try my new cookies? They are fresh out of the oven."

I had to admit I was ready for a bite. Sabre came knocking and foiled my scrambled eggs before I could scramble them. I knew her cookies were the cat's meow — so I didn't see any harm.

She laid out a big glass tray stacked with cookies, and me and Sabre jumped in like schoolboys at a taffy pull. I had to stop from time to time to count my fingers.

"They're so fresh," Sabre said.

"Thank you," she said. "Eat up."

We did. We fairly cleared the plate. Sabre wrapped one in a napkin and stuck it in his pocket. On the way out – I spotted a ball cap and a pair of boy's shoes under the stairs. I looked back at Margaret. She never mentioned grandkids. I never met a grandmother who doesn't start every conversation with some boring story about the grandkids.

Back outside, I told Sabre that I was a little concerned about the old broad. I'm not one to look a gift horse in the yap, but something wasn't quite right with her. Sabre agreed, but neither of us could pin it down.

We stood on the stoop – Sabre nibbling the cookie he'd pinched and me scanning the woods to see if there was any clue about the kids. The thick, black, sweet smoke poured out of the chimney.

"I hope she's okay," I said. "I really loved those cookies."

As the words were coming out of my maw – we saw two kids – probably brother and sister coming out of the woods. I looked at Sabre. He looked at me. What is it with kids and woods these days?

"Hey kids," I yelled.

"Hey, Mister," the girl answered. The girls are always braver than the boys.

"What're you doing out here?" I asked.

"We were just wandering in the woods and became famished," she said.

Famished. I love a kid with a good education. Things ain't like when I was a kid, and they were teaching us really good.

"We saw the smoke and followed it here," the boy said.

"She's a nice lady," I said. "She'll give you cookies."

"I love cookies," the boy said, and they ran toward the house.

We didn't even give it a second thought. We let the kids go. They didn't seem lost. They just seemed hungry. Margaret welcomed the kids into her house.

Me and Sabre headed back out into the woods to look for kids who might *actually* be lost. Before long we saw more smoke coming from the old woman's chimney. It was sweeter than the other smoke. There was a lot of it.

"I don't like the looks of *that*," Sabre said pointing at the chimney.

"I agree, but what are we looking at?"

"Kids go inside and the smoke changes like that? I don't know – it's curious."

"That *is* a lot of smoke," I said.

We walked back to the house and knocked on the door. Margaret answered, but she wasn't happy to see us this time. She was as nervous as a cat in a rocking chair factory. I looked past her shoulder and saw two piles of kids' clothes and a large bloody knife.

"What the...?"

Margaret slammed the door. Sabre kicked the door right back in. Soon enough we were back in the kitchen chasing Margaret around like a greyhound and a mechanical rabbit. She was quick, but I was quicker. I tackled her and held her while Sabre called Johnny Law.

While we were waiting, we found two bins under the stairs that contained the clothes of about a dozen kids. There were school uniforms and Halloween costumes. This old broad had quite a collection.

The cops came and got her and hauled her away in their paddy wagon. A couple of the flatfoots stuck around to protect the crime scene and start their investigation. Me and

Sabre headed out the front door. I stopped when I saw the straw hat hanging on the coat rack. The red ribbon caught my eye.

"That looks familiar," I said.

"You know women and their hats. Let's go home," Sabre said.

We walked down her cobblestones and up mine and into the house. I called out for Althea, but there was no answer.

"Isn't she outside working on a garden?" Sabre asked.

I gotta say, I was relieved. Why didn't I think of that? I headed through the kitchen. Before I got to the door, I saw the note she left.

"Honey, I went to see Margaret to get her recipe for the cookies. I wanted to be able to feed you like a good wife would."

I fell into the chair. I knew then where my Althea was. She wouldn't be coming home with any recipe any time soon. She was gone.

Sabre came into the kitchen and took one look at me. He immediately knew something – but he didn't say anything. That was why I loved Sabre. He always knew everything – but he rarely said anything.

I put the house on the market the next day and took my old apartment back. It was where I belonged anyway. It was quiet and just enough room for one person. My neighbors were working class stiffs. That old trap was my home.

Nick Victory Chronicles Part Four: Half Baked

ALAN DEAN FOSTER
We Three Kings

ALAN DEAN FOSTER is an American writer of fantasy and science fiction. He has written several book series, more than 20 standalone novels, and many novelizations of film scripts.

It was overcast and blustery and the snow was coming down as hard as a year's accumulation of overdue bills. Within the laboratory, Stein made the final adjustments, checked the readouts, and inspected the critical circuit breakers one last, final time. There was no going back now. The success or failure of his life's work hinged on what happened in the next few moments.

He knew there were those who if given the chance would try to steal his success, but if everything worked he would take care of them first. Them with their primitive, futile notions and dead-end ideas! All subterfuge and smoke, behind which they doubtless intended to claim his triumph as their own. Let them scheme and plot while they could. Soon they would be out of the way, and he would be able to bask in his due glory without fear of theft or accusation.

He began throwing the switches, turning the dials. Fitful bursts of necrotic light threw the strange shapes that occupied the vast room in the old warehouse into stark relief. Outside, the snow filled up the streets, sifting into dirty gutters, softening the outlines of the city. Not many citizens out walking in his section of town, he reflected. It was as well. Though the laboratory was shuttered and soundproofed, there was no telling what unforeseen sights and sounds might result when he finally pushed his efforts of many years to a final conclusion.

The dials swung while the readings on the gauges mounted steadily higher. Nearing the threshold now. The two huge Van de Graff generators throbbed with power. Errant orbs of ball lightning burst free, to spend themselves against the insulated ceiling in showers of coruscating sparks. It was almost time.

He threw the final, critical switch.

Gradually the crackling faded and the light in the laboratory returned to normal. With the smell of ozone sharp in his nostrils, Stein approached the table. For an instant, there was nothing more than disappointment brokered by uncertainty. And then—a twitch. Slight, but unmistakable. Stein stepped back, eyes wide and alert. A second twitch, this time in the arms. Then the legs, and finally the torso itself.

With a profound grinding sound, the creature sat up, snapping the two-inch wide leather restraining straps as if they were so much cotton thread.

"It's alive!" Stein heard himself shouting. "It's alive, it's alive, it's alive!"

He advanced cautiously until he was standing next to the now seated Monster. The bolts in its neck had been singed black from the force of the charge which had raced through it, but there were no signs of serious damage. Tentatively, Stein reached out and put a hand on the creature's arm. The massive, blocky skull swiveled slowly to look down at him.

"Nnrrrrrrrrrgh!"

Stein was delighted. "You and I, we are destined to conquer the world. At last, the work of my great-grandfather is brought to completion." His voice dropped to a conspiratorial whisper. "But there are those who would thwart us, who would stand in our way. I know who they are, and they must be—dealt with. Listen closely, and obey...."

Outside, the snow continued to fall.

In the dark cellar Rheinberg carefully enunciated the ancient words. Only a little light seeped through the street-level window, between the heavy bars. Seated in the center of the room, in middle of the pentagram, was the sculpture. Rheinberg was as talented as he was resourceful, and the details of his creation were remarkable for their depth and precision.

An eerie green glow began to suffuse the carefully crafted clay figure as the ancient words echoed through the studio. Rheinberg read carefully from the from the copy of the ancient manuscript in a steady, unvarying monotone. With each word, each sentence, the glow intensified, until softly pulsing green shadows filled every corner of the basement studio.

Almost, but not quite, he halted in the middle of the final sentence, at the point when the eyes of the figure began to open. That would have been dangerous, he knew. And so, fully committed now, he read on. Only when he'd finished did he dare allow himself to step forward for a closer look.

The eyes of the Golem were fully open now, unblinking, staring straight ahead. Then they shifted slowly to their left, taking notice of the slight, anxious man who was approaching.

"It works. It worked! The old legends were true." Unbeknownst to Rheinberg, the parchment sheet containing the words had crumpled beneath his clenching fingers. "The world is ours, my animate friend! Ours, as soon as certain others are stopped. You'll take care of that little matter for me, won't you? You'll do anything I ask. You must. That's what the legend says."

"Ooooyyyyyyyy!" Moaning darkly, the massive figure rose. Its gray head nearly scraped the ceiling.

Within the charmed circle something was rising. A pillar of smoke, black shot through with flashes of bright yellow, coiling and twisting like some giant serpent awakened from an ancient sleep. Al-Nomani recited the litany and watched, determined to maintain the steady sing-song of the nefarious quatrain no matter what happened.

The fumes began to thicken, to coalesce. Limbs appeared, emerging from the roiling hell of the tornadic spiral. The whirlwind itself began to change shape and color, growing more man-like with each verse, until a horrid humanoid figure stood where smoke had once swirled. It had two rings in its oversized left ear, a huge nose, and well-developed fangs growing upward from its lower jaw. For all that, the fiery yellow eyes that glared out at the historian from beneath the massive, low-slung brow reeked of otherworldly intelligence.

"By the beard of the Prophet!" al-Nomani breathed tensely, "it worked!" He put down the battered, weathered tome from which he had been reading. The giant regarded him silently, awaiting. As it was supposed to do.

Al-Nomani took a step forward. "You will do my bidding. There is much that needs be done. First and foremost there is the matter of those who would challenge my knowledge, and my supremacy. They must be shown the error of their ways. I commit you to deal with them."

"Eeeehhhhzzzzz!" Within the circle the Afreet bowed solemnly. Its arms were as big around as tree trunks.

Stillman was cruising the run-down commercial area just outside the industrial park when he noticed movement up the side street. At this hour everything was closed up tight, and the weather had reduced traffic even further. He picked up the cruiser's mike, then set it back in its holder. Might be nothing more than some poor old rhummy looking for a warm place to sleep.

Still, the vagrants and the homeless tended to congregate downtown. It was rare to encounter one this far out. Which meant that the figure might be looking to help itself to something more readily convertible than an empty park bench. Stillman flicked on the heavy flashlight and slid out of the car, drawing his service revolver as he did so. The red and yellows atop the cruiser revolved steadily, lighting up the otherwise dark street.

Cautiously, he advanced on the narrow roadway. He had no intention of entering, of course. If the figure ran, that would be indication enough something was wrong, and that's when he'd call for backup.

"Hey! Hey, you in there! Kinda late for a stroll, especially in this weather, ain't it?" The only reply was a strange shuffling. The officer blinked away falling snow as something shifted in the shadows. He probed with his flashlight.

"Come on out, man. I know you're back there. I don't want any trouble from you and you really don't want any from me. Don't make me come in there after you." He took a challenging step forward.

Something vast and monstrous loomed up with shocking suddenness, so big his light could not illuminate it all. Officer Corey Stillman gaped at the apparition. His finger contracted reflexively on the trigger of his service revolver, and a sharp crack echoed down the alley. The creature flinched, then reached for him with astounding speed.

"Nnrrrrrrrrr!"

Stillman never said a word.

His head was throbbing like his brother's Evenrude when he finally came around. Groaning, he reached for the back of his skull as he straightened up in the snow. Memories came flooding back and he looked around wildly, but the Monster was gone, having shambled off down the street.

Eleven years on the force and that was without question the ugliest dude he'd ever encountered. Quick for his size, too. Too damn quick. He was sure his single shot had hit home, but it hadn't even slowed the big guy down. Wincing, he climbed to his feet and surveyed his surroundings. His cruiser sat where he'd left it in the street, lights still revolving patiently.

His gun lay in the snow nearby. Slowly he picked up the .38, marveling at the power which had crushed it to a metal pulp. What had he encountered, and how could he report it? Nobody'd believe him.

A figure stepped into view from behind the building. He tensed, but big as the pedestrian was, he was utterly different in outline from Stillman's departed assailant. Seeking help, the officer took a couple of steps toward it—and pulled up short.

The enormous stranger was the color of damp

clay, save for vacant black eyes that stared straight through him.

"Good God!"

Startled by the exclamation, the creature whirled and struck.

"Ooyyyyyyyyyy!"

This time when Stillman regained consciousness he didn't move, just lay in the snow and considered his situation. His second attacker had been nothing like the first, yet no less terrifying in appearance. He no longer cared if everyone back at the station thought him crazy; he needed back-up.

Too much overtime, he told himself. That had to be it. Too many hours rounding up too many hookers and junkies and sneak thieves. Mary was right. He needed to use some of that vacation time he'd been accumulating.

Body aching, head still throbbing, he struggled to his feet. The cruiser beckoned, its heater pounding away persistently despite the open door on the driver's side. Recovering his hat and clutching the flashlight, he staggered around the front, pausing at the door to lean on it for support. The heat from the interior refreshed him, made him feel better. He started to slide in behind the wheel. The seat was already occupied by something with burning yellow eyes and a bloated, distorted face straight out of the worst nightmares of childhood. It was playing with the police radio scanner, mouthing it like a big rectangular cookie.

He'd surprised it, and of course it reacted accordingly.

"Oh no!" Stillman moaned as he staggered backwards and an unnaturally long arm reached for him, "not again!"

"Eehhhzzzzzzz!"

The wonderful profusion of brightly colored street and store lights slowed the Monster's progress, mysteriously diluted its intent. The lights were festive and cheerful. Even as it kept to the shadows, it could see the faces of smiling adults and laughing children. There were the decorations, too: in the stores, above the streets, on the houses. Laughter reached him through the falling snow; childish giggles, booming affirmations of good humor, deep chuckles of pleasure. Invariably, it all had a cumulative effect.

Memories stirred: memories buried deep within the brain he'd been given. The lights, the snow, the laughter and ebullient chatter of toys and candy: it all meant something. He just wasn't sure what. Confused, he turned and lurched off down the dark alley between two tall buildings, trying to reconcile his orders with these disturbing new thoughts.

He paused suddenly, senses alert. Someone else was coming up the alley. The figure was big, much bigger than any human he'd observed so far that night. Not that he was afraid of any human, or for that matter, any thing. Teeth and joints grinding, arms extended, he started deliberately forward.

There was just enough light for the two figures to make each other out. When they could do so with confidence, they hesitated in mutual confusion. Something strange was abroad this night, and both figures thought it most peculiar.

"Who—what—you?" the Monster declaimed in a voice like a rusty mine cart rolling down long-neglected track. Speech was still painful.

"I vaz going ask you the same qvestion." The other figure's black eyes scrutinized the slow-speaking shape standing opposite. "You one revolting looking schlemiel, I can tell you."

"You not—no raving beauty yourself."

"So tell me zumthing I don't know." The Golem's massive shoulders heaved, a muscular gesture of tectonic proportions.

"What be this, pbuh?" Both massive shapes turned sharply, to espy a third figure hovering close behind them. Despite its size it had made not a sound during its approach.

"Und I thought you vaz ugly," the Golem murmured to the Monster as it contemplated the newcomer.

"Speak not ill of others lest the wrath of Allah befall thee." The Afreet approached, its baleful yellow eyes flicking from one shape to the next. "What manner of mischief is afoot this night?"

"Ask you—the same," the Monster rumbled.

The Afreet bowed slightly. "I am but recently brought fresh into the world, and am abroad on a mission for my mortal master of the moment." It glanced back toward the main street, with its twinkling lights and window-shopping pedestrians blissfully unaware of the astonishing conclave that was taking place just down the alley. "Yet I fear the atmosphere not conducive to my command, for what I see and hear troubles my mind like a prattling harim."

"You too?" The Golem rubbed its chin. Clay flakes fell to the pavement. "I vaz thinking the same."

"I think I know—what is wrong." The other two eyed the Monster.

"Nu? So don't keep it to yourself," said the Golem.

"I have been pondering." Eyes squinted tight with the stress of the activity. "Pondering hard. What I think is that the season," the creature declared slowly, "is the reason."

"Pray tell, explain thyself." The Afreet was demanding, but polite.

The Monster's squarish forehead turned slowly. "The brain I was given—remembers. This time of year—the sights I see—make me remember. The time is wrong—for the command I was given. All—wrong. Wrong to kill—at the time of Christmas."

"Kill," echoed the Afreet. "Strange are the ways of the Prophet, for such was the order I was given. To kill this night two men; one of art and one of learning. Felix Stein and Joseph Rheinberg."

The Monster and the Golem started and exchanged a look. "I vaz to stamp out Stein alzo," muttered the Golem, "as vell as a historian name of al-Nomani. Rheinberg is my master."

"And Stein—mine," added the Monster.

"Fascinating it be," confessed the Afreet. "For al-Nomani is the one who called me forth."

"He is one whom I was to—slay," announced the Monster. "And this Rheinberg—too."

The formidable, and formidably bemused, trio pondered this arresting coincidence in silence, while cheerful music and the sound of caroling drifted back to them from the street beyond. Though least verbal of the three, it was again the Monster who articulated first.

"Something—wrong—here. Wrong notion. Wrong time of—the year. Everything—wrong."

"Go on, say it again," growled the Golem. "Not just Christmas it is, but Chanukah also. Not a time for inimical spirits to be stirring. Not even a mouse."

"The spirit of Ramadan moves within me," declared the Afreet. "I know not what manner of life or believers you be, but I sense that in this I am of similar mind with you."

"Then what—we—do?" the Monster wondered aloud.

They considered.

Stillman blinked snow from his eyes. By now there wasn't much left of his cap, or his winter coat. He fumbled for the flashlight, somehow wasn't surprised to find that the supposedly impregnable cylinder of aircraft grade aluminum had been twisted into a neat pretzel shape.

He saw the cruiser in front of him and began crawling slowly towards it. Nothing inside him seemed to be broken, but every muscle in his bruised body protested at the forced movement. The rotating lights atop the car were beginning to weaken as the battery ran down.

He was a foot from the door when he sensed a presence and looked to his right.

Three immense forms stood staring down at him, each all too familiar from a previous recent encounter. It was impossible to say which of the trio was the most terrifying. A clawed hand reached for him.

"Please," he whispered through snow-benumbed lips, "no more. Just kill me and get it over with."

The powerful fingers clutched his jacket front and lifted him as easily as if he were a blank arrest report, setting him gently on his feet. Another huge hand, dark and even-toned as the play clay his little girl made mudpies with, helped keep him upright. Trembling in spite of himself, he looked from one fearsome face to the next.

"I don't get it. What is this? What are you setting me up for?"

"We need—your help," the Monster mumbled, like a reluctant clog in a main city sewer line.

Stillman hesitated. "You need my help? That's a switch." He brushed dirty snow from his waist and thighs. "What kind of help? To be your punching bag?" He blinked at the Monster. "Uh, sorry about shooting you. You startled me. Heck, you still startle me."

"I—forgive," the Monster declaimed, sounding exactly like Arnold Schwarzenegger on a bad shooting day.

"Yeah—okay then. Well—what did you—boys—have in mind?"

The Afreet's eyes burned brightly. "In this Time, praise be, is it still among men a crime to set another to commit murder?"

Stillman stiffened slightly. "Damn straight it is. Why do you ask?"

The Afreet glanced at its companions. "We know of several who have done this thing. Should they not, by your mortal laws, be punished for this?"

"You bet they should. You know where these guys are?" All three creatures nodded. Stillman hesitated. "You have proof?"

The Golem dug a fist the size and consistency of a small boulder into its open palm. "You shouldn't vorry, policeman. I promise each one a full confession vill sign."

"If you're sure...." Stillman eyed the stony figure warily. "You're not talking about obtaining a confession under duress, are you?"

"Vhat, me?" The Golem spread tree-like arms wide. "My friends and I vill chust a little friendly visit pay them. Each of them."

Stillman delivered the three badly shaken men to the station by himself. There was no need to call for backup. Not after his hefty acquaintances warned the three outraged but nonetheless compliant tamperers-with-the-laws-of-nature that if any of them so much as ventured an indecent suggestion in the officer's direction, the improvident speaker would sooner or later find himself on the receiving end of a midnight visit from all three of the—visitants. In the face of that monumentally understated threat, the would-be masters of the world proved themselves only too eager to cooperate with the police.

Stillman presented the thoroughly disgruntled experimenters to the duty officer, together with their signed confessions attesting to their respective intentions to murder one another, a collar which was sure to gain him a commendation at the least, and possibly even a promotion. It was worth the aches and pains to see the look on the lieutenant's face when each prisoner meekly handed over his confession. It further developed that all three men were additionally wanted on various minor charges, from theft of scientific equipment and art supplies to failing to return a six-year old overdue book from the University's Special Collections library.

The members of the unnatural trio who had propitiated this notable sequence of events were waiting behind the station to congratulate Stillman when he clocked off duty. He winced as he stretched, studying each of them in turn.

"So—what're you guys gonna do now?" he asked curiously. "If you'd like to hang around the city, I know for a fact you could probably each get a tryout with the Bears."

"Bears?" the Monster rumbled. "I like to eat bear."

"No, no. It's a professional sports team. You know? Pro football? No," he reflected quietly, "maybe you don't know."

"If it be His will, we shall each of us make our way to a place of solitude and contentment. For such as we be, there is a special path for doing so. But we must wait for the coming of day to find the true passageways."

Stillman nodded. "Seems a shame after what you've done tonight to have to hang out here, by yourselves, in this crappy weather."

Mary Stillman came out of the kitchen to greet her returning husband. She was drying a large serving dish with a beige towel spotted with orange flowers.

"Mary," Stillman called out, "I'm home! And I've brought some friends over for a little late supper. Do we have any of that Christmas turkey left?"

"Urrrrr—Christmas!" the Monster growled like a runaway eighteen-wheeler locking up its brakes at seventy per, and his sentiment if not his words were echoed by his companions.

While the Golem skillfully caught the dish before it struck the floor, the well-mannered Afreet performed the same service for a falling Mary Stillman. When she recovered consciousness and her husband hastily explained matters to her, she nodded slowly and went to see what she could find in the kitchen, whereupon they all shared a very nice late-night snack indeed, wholly in keeping with the spirit of the Seasons.

THE MAFIA IN HOLLYWOOD STORIES FROM PRE-CODE FILM TO DEEP THROAT
THE BUFFALO MOB THE RETURN OF ORGANIZED CRIME TO THE QUEEN CITY
THE MONSTERS NEXT DOOR EDITED BY R.J. CARTER
THE BROTHERS GRIMM The Complete Illustrated Fairy Tales
THE DEVIL YOU KNOW Edited by R.J. Carter
THE DEVIL YOU KNOW BETTER Edited by R.J. Carter
THE DEVIL YOU KNOW BEST Edited by R.J. Carter
GODS & SERVICES Carter
BULLETPROOF Mitchell
BULLETPROOF
THE BLACK DIAMOND EFFECT by GEORGE PETER GATSIS
INCANTESI BOOK 1 & 2 COLLECTED EDITION by Rich Perrotta
THE BLACK DIAMOND EFFECT
THE BROTHERS GRIMM The Complete Illustrated Fairy Tales
THE BUFFALO MOB THE RETURN OF ORGANIZED CRIME TO THE QUEEN CITY
CRITICAL BLAST PUBLISHING COLORS NOT INCLUDED! 02
CRITICAL BLAST PUBLISHING COLORS NOT INCLUDED! 01
GENUINE COMICS — PERFECT TO ARTIST EDITION — 1
CRITICAL BLAST PUBLISHING
GIBSON
ASAGI
QUIROGA
POWERS
GIBSON
ASAGI
QUIROGA
POWERS
BIG TROUBLE IN NEO DETROIT

MORE GREAT BOOKS AVAILABLE AT CRITICAL BLAST PUBLISHING...
GO TO : CRITICALBLAST•COM NOW!
MICHAEL DERRICK • PRAMIT SANTRA • EUGENIU KOTEI • JAYMES REED
GRAY SKALE
WELCOME TO GLITTER CITY

CRITICAL BLAST PUBLISHING
THE DEVIL YOU KNOW
THE DEVIL YOU KNOW BETTER
THE DEVIL YOU KNOW BEST
Edited by R.J. Carter
THE MAFIA IN HOLLYWOOD
GODS & SERVICES
THE BUFFALO MOB
GHOST STORY
gavelockstudio.com
BLACK DIAMOND EFFECT
COLLECTED EDITION by Rich Perrotta
by GEORGE PETER GATSIS
JOE KING JOB ADS
PERFECT 10 ARTIST EDITION
THE MONSTERS NEXT DOOR
EDITED BY R.J. CARTER
SOUTHERN KNIGHTS
THE MORRIGAN WARS
FLARE LEAGUE OF CHAMPIONS
FLARE
ARCHIVES VOLUME 1
HEROIC
SOUTHERN KNIGHTS
COMPLETE COLLECTION
CAPTAIN THUNDER AND BLUE BOLT
ARCHIVES VOLUME 1
HEROIC
ARISTOCRATIC XTRATERRESTRIAL TIME-TRAVELING THIEVES
COMPLETE COLLECTION
LEAGUE OF CHAMPIONS
VOL 6: THE MORRIGAN WARS
FLARE SOUTHERN KNIGHTS
CriticalBlast•com

CRITICAL
BLAST
PUBLISHING

9 798900 200071